To Peg
Keep writing
Thanks !

Student Body

By

Neil Howard

Lighthouse Press, Inc.
Deerfield Beach, FL

Lighthouse Press, Inc.
P.O. Box 910
Deerfield Beach, FL 33443
www.LighthouseEditions.com

ISBN: 0-9714827-2-1

To my family with love.
Special thanks to Terrie for her proofreading skill.

CHAPTER 1

The Shenandoah Valley opened like an invitation to the Promised Land. Tyler Richmond had just passed through Winchester, Virginia, and was heading south on Interstate 81. The three-year-old Toyota Corolla strained from the effort of pulling a U-Haul trailer containing all his worldly goods. He was not a man of many possessions and had packed everything he owned in the trailer.

He smiled at the memory of receiving the letter that had launched this journey. It had been formally addressed to Mr. Tyler Richmond, New York City, from Carter Henderson, Dean, Stonewater College.

Dear Mr. Richmond:
It is with great pleasure that I offer you the position of Instructor in the Department of Performing Arts. Your qualifications clearly placed you at the top of the candidate list. Based on the recommendation of the selecting committee, I am authorized to tender you a one-year contract.

The letter evoked conflicting sensations of exhilaration and trepidation in the new drama instructor. Virginia existed in another universe apart from New York City. He welcomed his escape from the nether world of struggling actors, but felt a sense of foreboding about his new responsibilities. The twenty-eight year old had never taught college courses, even though his Masters Degree from Cornell University qualified him for the job. In the end, he convinced himself to take on the challenge without any regrets.

Road signs along Interstate 81 advertised the ENDLESS CAVERNS and the NEW MARKET BATTLEFIELD. He followed one sign to the NEW MARKET DINER. The sign on the diner promised *Genuine Home Cooking!* He eagerly got out of his car.

The diner was filled with cigarette smoke and men in work clothes. He could not help noticing their rough, callused hands. These were hands that knew the meaning of real work and hardship. These were hands that worked in soil and muscled 100-pound bags of grain. Tyler admired the honesty of their existence. He kept his soft, academic hands stuffed in his pants' pockets. The amused glances of the diner patrons indicated they considered him a harmless outsider. Also, the mustache and the U-Haul trailer must have marked him as a transient. He settled his six-foot frame into a booth at the far end of the diner.

"Do you want a men-u?" the waitress inquired.

Her nametag identified her as BETTY. The weary woman had dark circles under her eyes, and shifted her weight from side to side to take the pressure off her aching feet. The movement had a strange rhythmic quality to it, and Tyler felt a mischievous impulse to ask the plump plain waitress to dance.

"Please," he replied, stifling a grin.

She regarded him curiously and grabbed a menu from the next table. "The special today is Virginia ham and black-eyed peas. The ham is right good."

He smiled up at Betty and decided to simplify her life by ordering the ham.

She wrote down the order and ambled away.

His neighbor in the next booth turned and smiled, revealing yellow-stained teeth. He wore a baseball hat advertising *Red Man* chewing tobacco. A boy, who appeared to be a smaller clone of the farmer, sat across the table wearing a *Farm Bureau* hat.

"Looks like you've been on the road a good while," the farmer observed.

"Yes, I have," Tyler replied. "I left New York yesterday."

2

"I've never been way up north – was always too busy to leave the farm. Never had enough time to travel. Where you headin'?"

"Stonewater. I was offered a job at the college."

"Stonewater's a nice town. I've been down there a few times. They've got a big plant that processes chickens and turkeys. This is the turkey capital of the world. Bet you didn't know that." The farmer puffed out his chest.

Tyler suppressed a smile. "No, I didn't."

"Lots of history and tradition in this part of the country. Battle of New Market was fought just down the road. Bunch of VMI boys got themselves killed in that one. You picked a fine place to make a new home."

"I didn't exactly pick it," Tyler confessed. "It was the only college that offered me a job."

"Well then, you got lucky. Good people live in the valley. People down here are real friendly and God fearin' folks. They'll make you feel right at home."

"I feel welcome already," he smiled. "How much farther is Stonewater from here?"

" 'Bout eighty miles. You're almost home, boy. Have a real safe trip, you hear?"

"Thanks," Tyler replied.

Betty arrived with his meal, and he viewed the food hungrily. A huge slab of ham, surrounded by peas, filled the plate. The first bite of the smoke-cured meat tasted delicious, and he attacked it with relish. After finishing the meal, he left Betty a generous tip, and thanked her on the way out.

"That ham was delicious, thanks." He put his arm around her. "But, Betty, you really look exhausted. You need to get some rest."

"Why, thank you, honey. I am right tired, but I don't have the time. Come back again soon."

Tyler promised to stop on a return trip and headed back to the interstate.

'Stonewater, 10 Miles', proclaimed the road sign. He

felt a surge of excitement as he traveled the last few miles to his final destination. The journey ended when he exited at *Stonewater, Home of Stonewater College.*

The rural location amazed him. He expected the college to exist in a more cosmopolitan setting. The landscape looked like something out of a CURRIER AND IVES print. His astonishment increased as he passed a black horse and buggy, with an orange caution triangle attached to the bumper. The driver, dressed in a black coat and hat, waved as Tyler drove by him slowly.

"Where am I?" he shouted, and laughed out loud.

The large sign at the gates of the town answered his question.

WELCOME TO STONEWATER, VIRGINIA
"We take pride in the past and
Pray for the future"

He encountered a large Farm Bureau complex on the outskirts of Stonewater. Farmers busily loaded their trucks with bags of grain and supplies. Farther down the road was an open market selling fresh produce. He parked and observed the scene. Several horse-drawn buggies filled spaces in a reserved lot. The horses twitched in the heat while their owners tended to the market stalls. The men arranged melons and vegetables for display. The women, in long, gray dresses and white lace bonnets, set out loaves of bread, jars of honey, crocks of fresh butter, and mason jars filled with fruits and vegetables. The children played tag at a safe distance from their parents. He watched in awe as these simple people went about their work.

Tyler chatted with the Mennonites about their goods as he purchased a small bag of tomatoes. They cheerfully explained how they mixed animal fertilizer with the native soil to grow high-quality produce. They never used anything artificial. He thanked them for the chemical-free tomatoes and returned to his car.

He left the Farmers' Market and followed the signs to

Stonewater College. He felt compelled to take a quick look at the institution that had claimed his services. What type of college could possibly exist in this land of no artificial ingredients? His first glimpse of the campus provided him with an unexpected surprise.

Stonewater College was a stately and well-manicured center of higher learning. The traditional buildings had all been built of gray stone, and were systematically erected on and around rolling hills. A rushing brook guarded the main entrance. Faculty members and students crossed over a stone bridge before passing through the college portals. Each building had a bronze plaque at the main entry to advertise its function, and white directional signs pointed the way to all sites of interest. He followed one of the signs to the campus center. After parking his Toyota, he walked to a marble marker. The inscription read:

STONEWATER BIBLE COLLEGE
Founded 1848
Dedicated to young men who seek knowledge and pledge
service to the Lord

Nearby, stood a statue of a Civil War soldier. It honored the men of the college who had given their lives to the Confederate cause. He smiled while observing these testimonials to southern tradition. Nothing in his past experience compared with these regional monuments. He braced himself to make the cultural leap.

CHAPTER 2

Heather Andrews showered with absolute contentment in her dormitory bathroom. The warm water pelted against her skin, and helped relieve the tension in her body. She had been on her feet all afternoon running between classes. It was late Friday afternoon. She had just completed her first week on campus after returning from summer vacation. The young student had officially embarked on her sophomore year at Stonewater College.

Heather attempted to focus on courses that would prepare her for a career. Time was running out and it would soon be necessary to make critical life decisions. What do I want to be when I grow up? There were so many options, and she had so many interests. She had narrowed the choices to science and advertising. Biology had captured her attention, and she also exhibited a talent for journalism. It was exhilarating to capture real events on paper and write short fiction. Teachers praised her for having a fertile imagination.

Heather rinsed the conditioner from her hair, and let the spray wash away the soapsuds from her body. She stepped from the shower and briskly rubbed herself dry with a towel. After applying peach body lotion, she smiled at herself in the mirror. The mirror paid tribute to her image. She accepted her natural beauty without vanity, but tonight she wanted to look her best.

Her roommate, Molly Cross, was waiting outside the bathroom. "Looks like you've got a big date tonight."

Molly had red hair and freckles, and was not attractive in a traditional sense. However, she possessed a unique sparkle and a storehouse of energy. She and Heather had been friends since freshman year.

"No date, babe. I've been invited to an important college dinner function. Only a few select students have been invited to attend."

"Sounds boring as hell," Molly yawned. "This is Friday night. You should be going out with some really neat guy who'll sweep you off your feet and profess his undying love to you."

"You're so dramatic. It's really not like that. Some guy did ask me out, but I brushed him off. We've got all year to fall in love. Tonight, I'm about to enter a more important social circle."

"All right, so 'fess up. What's this all about? Where are you going?"

Heather put her arm around her friend. "I wish I could tell you. The truth is, I've been sworn to secrecy. It's no big deal, but the idea is to keep the dinner low-key. Maybe I can tell you more about it later." She patted her on the head.

"Great. Treat me like a peasant. I hope you have a terrible time," Molly snorted.

"We get so red in the face when we're angry," she teased.

"I don't like it," Molly snapped back. "We're roommates. We're not supposed to keep secrets from each other."

"I'm sorry. I really am. Trust me on this one, okay? It's very important to me."

"Sure, you're a great one to talk about trust. What am I supposed to tell the media?"

"Tell them I'm on a secret mission to save Stonewater College from crime and exploitation."

"Right. You're such an expert."

"Of course. Now, let me finish getting ready."

Heather selected a conservative blue dress and white blouse. She wanted to look mature and professional. "How do I look?" She turned slowly to give Molly a look at all the angles.

"Okay, I guess," Molly sniffed.

"C'mon, don't be mad at me. This is important." She put her arms around her roommate.

Molly was not convinced. "Sure it is. But if you get in trouble, you do know how to dial 9-1-1?"

"Stop worrying. I won't be late. I promise." She blew Molly a kiss and breezed out the door.

Heather was aware of her destination. The directions had been specific, and she knew to arrive by seven o'clock. She steered her Geo Prizm away from the campus. The automobile had been a high school graduation gift from her parents. Her dad insisted she needed transportation to the college, and a way to travel back home on the weekends. It was his way of maintaining a paternal connection.

The residence was only a short drive from the college. The young sophomore found an empty parking space and checked her watch. Six-fifty-eight – right on time. After carefully locking the car doors, she slipped the keys into her purse. She walked to the front door and nervously rang the bell.

A smiling man opened the door. "Come on in, Miss Andrews. I'm very pleased you accepted my invitation. Here, let me take your purse." He placed her purse on a side table, and ushered her into the living room. "You're the first one to arrive this evening. I expect the others at any moment."

"Thank you," she replied.

She looked around the room. It was tastefully decorated with leather furniture, French impressionist art, and potted plants. Bowls of chips and finger foods were arranged on the center table.

"Can I get you a drink while we're waiting for the others?" he offered. "I have beer, soda, and wine."

Her first impulse was to request soda, but then remembered this was an adult gathering. "I'll have some white wine, please."

"Great choice. Please sit down, and I'll be back in a moment." He left for the kitchen.

Heather took a seat on the sofa. She reached for the bowl of nuts and picked up several cashews. Music played softly in the background. It was difficult to identify the style, but it sounded like a form of New Age jazz. The decor and music were pleasant, but a chill ran up her spine. Something about the atmosphere caused her discomfort. The cheerful man returned with a glass of wine and a bottle of beer.

"There, now we can relax." He handed her the wine and settled into a chair across from her.

"Thank you," she replied.

He leaned forward. "I know you're curious about the dinner party and why you were invited."

"A little," Heather admitted. She sipped her wine. It tasted light and dry.

"It's really quite simple," the man smiled. "Each new school year, I invite a few students and some faculty friends to dinner. It helps break the ice. I've found it makes the learning experience much more relaxed and productive."

"That makes sense," she reasoned. "I'm usually scared to death of my new professors." The wine tasted delicious and she took a big gulp.

"I'm glad you agree. The thing is, I have to keep these gatherings low-key. The dean and some of the professors don't approve of social contact with students. There's no sense in creating controversy. You didn't mention to anyone you were coming here tonight, did you?"

"No, I swear I didn't. My roommate was curious, but I didn't tell her anything." She began to notice a warm glow behind her eyes, and her lips started to feel numb.

"Good. I have no idea where the other guests are. At least, you were punctual. Let me freshen your glass."

She handed it to him, and he left for the kitchen. Heather began to feel unsteady. She stood up to stretch and experienced a wave of dizziness. She sat back down on the sofa. White wine had never affected her like this. She decided not to drink much more. The professor returned with a fresh glass.

"Let's drink a toast to new friendships and a new school year." He raised his beer bottle and lightly touched it to Heather's glass.

She set the glass down unsteadily. A knot of nausea formed in her stomach. "I'm sorry." Her tongue felt thick. "I'm not feeling well. I think I need to go home."

"That's too bad. Can I get you something?"

"No. I just need to go home." The words seemed distant and unreal.

"Why don't you just rest for a minute," he suggested. "Maybe, you'll feel better."

He placed a pillow behind her head and slipped the shoes off her feet. She attempted to protest, but her strength had disappeared. It felt good to close her eyes. In a few minutes, time and place ceased to exist. Voices. Whispering. Someone else was in the room. Heather tried to focus, but the words were in another dimension. Someone was touching her…moving her.

"Help me take her into the bedroom."

Someone carried her through space. There could be no argument or complaint. Her will had disappeared and the only thing left was submission. Molly had said call 9-1-1, but the numbers had no meaning. Nothing made sense and reality became a blur of dizziness and confusion.

"Quick, get her clothes off."

They removed her dark blue dress and white blouse. They peeled the bra and panties from her body. They left her exposed. She was helpless to resist.

"God, she's beautiful."

"Get it done quickly. I want her out of here."

Hands moved roughly over her body. Someone pulled at her legs. She tried to yell 'Stop', but no words came out of her mouth. She heard grunts and groans in the distance. Jolts of pain shot through her body. Lights flashed in the bedroom, and in her mind. She was pushed and twisted into different positions. More lights flashed. More groans. More pain. More hands. More twisting, and then – the ordeal ended.

Later, someone returned and cleaned her with a wet cloth. He dried her with a towel and dressed her. Hands carried her back to the sofa. The hands felt gentle and soothing. The fog in her head began to recede, but pain filled the void. The man with the comforting voice returned, and helped her into a sitting position.

"Here, take these. They'll help you feel better."

He handed her two pills and a small glass of water. It was difficult to swallow.

"You've had a rough time. Rest now. I'll be back."

He lowered her head onto the pillow and left. Time had no meaning. The only things remaining were the dizziness, nausea, and nightmare memories. Something terrible had happened to her. Why? Men had hurt her. Why? What had she done? The professor should have protected her. How could he let this happen? The pain moved from her head into the rest of her body. Consciousness was returning.

"Wake up. Can you hear me?"

Heather struggled to focus on the face above her. "Yes," she replied.

"Good. You've been a very naughty girl. I've never seen a girl do so many nasty things in bed."

"I didn't do anything," she replied, hoarsely.

"Oh, but you did. I have photographs to prove it. I've got some great shots of you in action."

"It's not true!" She held her hands over her face.

"My dear, Heather, it is true." The professor gently removed her hands from her face.

"Oh, God!"

"There is some good news. I have a short memory. If you forget all this, I will too. If you try to make trouble, I'll send copies of the photos to the dean, your parents, and your friends. What do you think will happen then? Answer me, Heather."

"I don't know," she moaned.

"Yes, you do. Your reputation will be destroyed. Your friends will call you a slut. Your life will be over. You believe me, don't you?"

She nodded her head in agony.

"There's also the matter of your father's reputation. I understand he's the mayor of Bellville, Maryland. How do you think the voters will react to a scandal involving the mayor's daughter? He'll resign from office in disgrace. Do you want that to happen?"

"No," Heather sobbed. "How did you know?"

"I'm very thorough. I did a complete check on your background. No one knows you came here tonight. You have no proof anything happened. Once you get back to your room, you can never say a word to anyone. If you do...well, you already know that part. Do you understand?"

She nodded again.

"Great. I'm delighted we understand one another. All right, let's get you home. It was great having you at my party."

Heather pounded her fists against his chest. "You bastard! I hate you!"

He grabbed her wrists and squeezed hard. "Easy now. You probably hate me right now, but who knows...after a period of time we might become good friends."

"Never," she hissed.

"We'll see. Come on, I'll drive you home in your car. We'll talk again."

He took the car keys from her purse and followed her into the parking lot. The drive back to the dorm took place in uneasy silence. Heather stared at her hands in her lap. She felt dirty and humiliated. She could do nothing for the time being. The professor held the advantage. No one would believe a member of the faculty had drugged and abused her. She imagined her father looking at the photographs. He would feel devastated and betrayed.

"Here we are. Remember what I said." The professor locked her car and placed the keys back in her purse. "Good night."

He left her standing alone in the lot, and walked to another car waiting for him in the darkness. He slipped quietly into the passenger side of the vehicle, and drove away with his accomplice.

Heather stumbled up the stairs to her room. She had no idea of the time, and undressed silently in the darkness. She tried not to wake her roommate.

Molly called out from her bed. "Well, did you have a good time, your highness?"

Heather pulled back the sheets and climbed into bed without responding. She glanced at her digital clock. One-twenty a.m.

"Are you okay?" Molly called out, softly.

"Yeah. I'm fine. Go to sleep."

Heather turned away from Molly and sobbed silently into her pillow.

CHAPTER 3

Tyler drove to Dogwood Apartments, and checked into his new digs on the second floor. The apartment fit his needs perfectly. It had a bedroom, living area, kitchen, and bathroom. The apartment still had that fresh-coat-of-paint smell. He groaned at the thought of arranging all the stuff from the U-Haul into the empty space. Eventually, he dragged everything up the stairs and plopped his mattress down on the bedroom floor. After completing the chore, he walked out onto the balcony and listened to the laughter rising up from the swimming pool. The new resident of Dogwood Apartments felt a sense of contentment as he listened to his neighbors frolicking in the water below. Someone knocked on the door.

"Hello, I'm the welcoming committee."

A short thirty-ish man, with dark curly hair, stood smiling in the doorway. He was holding two bottles of imported beer.

"I make it a habit to harass my new neighbors. Welcome to Dogwood Apartments. I'm Barry Zucker." He held out one of the beers.

Tyler accepted it and shook Barry's hand. "Thanks, I really need this. I'm Tyler Richmond."

"You wouldn't be a new member of our faculty, would you?"

"Right you are. Department of Performing Arts," he replied. "I used to be a struggling actor in New York. Now, I'm on a quest to shape young minds and groom new actors for the Broadway jungle."

"Sounds like a great ambition," Barry laughed. "I'm Zucker, Psychology Department. I train young minds to peer into the dark recesses of the human psyche. Basically, I confuse the hell out of them."

"Have a seat, Barry."

Zucker settled down on one of Tyler's packing boxes. "I don't envy you. The chairman of your department retired last year. The college decided to cut expenses by dumping on the arts. They hired you to run things without having to pay a big salary for a department chairman. The bad news is, you'll be working directly for ol' Dean Henderson. He'll pat you on the back with one hand, and cut off your balls with the other."

"Sounds like my kind of guy. I knew lots of theatre producers in New York like that."

"Well, then, you'll feel right at home," Barry chuckled. "Henderson delights in terrorizing young instructors. After a complete psychological analysis, I've determined he must have been an abused child. He hasn't accepted the fact Stonewater is a liberal arts college. He hates the word 'liberal' and has no use for the arts."

"I'm beginning to like him more all the time," Tyler groaned.

Barry took a long drink of beer. "That's not all. You're being saddled with two of the strangest characters on the faculty – Dr. Hugh Newsome and Ms. Edna Plum. Old Hugh teaches speech in your department. He went around the bend years ago, and has to take a steady diet of Valium just to face his students. Hugh should have been promoted to department chairman, but regular meetings with Dean Henderson would have devastated the old boy. That's why they put you in charge."

Tyler collapsed onto his one good chair. "Great. What's the story on the other one?"

"Ah, Ms. Edna Plum. She's the part-time dance instructor. No one knows how many husbands she's buried – a real black widow. Her taste in dance styles borders on the bizarre. She talks a lot about Isadora Duncan and favors eclectic forms of movement. Her dance recitals are a disaster. Only a few disgruntled parents and faculty members attend. I got dragged to one against my will. The dancers flapped around like vultures during one sequence. Later, one of them seemed to portray the pain of giving birth to an elephant. That was my last experience with your dance department."

Tyler finished the last of his beer. "I can't say I blame you."

"But, cheer up – that's all the bad news. I am also the harbinger of good news."

"Great. I need some."

"This is the land of opportunity," Barry declared. "The social life is great. We live to party at the old Bible College. In my own small way, I've hosted numerous social events. My guests willingly engage in bacchanalian delights. The result is either the discovery of true love or lust – whichever suits their fancy. In fact, you're invited to my 'Welcome Back' bash next weekend. It'll be a chance for you to meet the natives."

"Thanks. I accept," Tyler grinned.

"Great." Barry got up. "Let me get out of your way. Looks like you've got lots of work to do."

"I guess I do. Thanks for the welcome, and the invitation."

"No problem. I'll see you around the campus." Barry left him to deal with the disorder in the apartment.

It took all weekend for Tyler to install his meager belongings in the apartment. The result was not wholly satisfactory. He could only do so much with theatre posters and several assorted sticks of furniture. The only things he owned in abundance were books. New bookshelves would be a top priority. He also decided to invest in some more furnishings once the cash began to flow.

He dressed in his best suit for the Monday morning meeting with Dean Henderson. He trimmed his mustache and attempted to adopt a professional demeanor. The dean kept him waiting in the outer office for over fifteen minutes.

"You may go in now, Mr. Richmond," the tight-lipped secretary announced. A multitude of tormented souls must have passed by her desk during her many years on guard duty.

"Welcome to Stonewater College, Mr. Richmond."
Dean Henderson got out from behind his desk with some
effort, and moved to shake hands. He was slight of build and
appeared to be over sixty. He had piercing blue eyes and a
receding hairline.

"Thank you, sir," Tyler replied.

"Please take a seat," Henderson requested. "Well, have
you settled in yet?"

"Yes, I have an apartment close by."

"Good. I expect you to have a challenging year. Our
Performing Arts Department is a little disorganized right now.
It will take a firm hand to straighten things out."

"I'll do my best."

"Good. You certainly appear qualified...on paper. It takes
more than impressive credentials to succeed in this business.
I expect we'll find out about you soon enough."

"I'm sure we will."

"We've already discussed the terms of your contract over
the phone. Your salary will be $22,000. The contract runs
for one year, and will be renewed if you successfully complete the probationary period. I will determine if your performance is successful or not. You will teach four classes each
semester and direct two plays during the year. You will be
required to make time on your schedule to advise your students. You will also be expected to sit on at least one faculty
committee. Do you have any questions?"

"No, sir. I think you just about covered everything."

"Good. Student registration begins after lunch. I would
like you to assist our students in registering for your classes.
Class rosters will be provided at the table. Here is the key to
your building. Please, don't lose it. Is there anything else?"

"No, I'd just like to say how pleased I am to be part of
this college."

"Good. We'll talk again soon." The dean rose stiffly
from his chair and offered his hand.

Tyler shook it and abruptly left the office. He let out his

breath once he made it to the hallway. He had embarked on a venture laden with obstacles. Dean Henderson displayed no hesitation about communicating veiled threats. The promise of swift retribution for unsatisfactory performance clung to his memory. The old man seemed to take satisfaction in his powers of intimidation. Tyler considered fleeing back to New York, but there was no way he could return to his former life. He had made a commitment to Stonewater College and would make the most of this uncertain opportunity.

CHAPTER 4

Molly Cross was worried about her roommate. Three weeks had passed since Heather's return from the mysterious dinner party. Heather refused to discuss what had happened, and her mood began to deteriorate. Molly noticed her friend was beginning to withdraw from college activities and only attended mandatory classes. There seemed to be no joy in her life. She moved through each day in a trance. The gulf between the two roommates widened.

One day, after classes, Molly exploded. "You know, as a roommate and a friend, you really suck!"

Heather reacted with a cold stare. "If you really feel that way, maybe you need to find a new roommate...and friend."

"Great! Blow me off! What's happened to you?"

Her eyes darted around the room as if looking for a way to escape. "Nothing. Seriously, Molly, maybe one of us needs to move out."

"Molly? Molly? What happened to 'babe'? You used to call me 'babe', remember?"

"Sure. Listen, I'm really not in the mood for this."

"Tough shit! We're going to talk. You can kick me out if you want, but I'm not going without a fight!"

Heather looked trapped. "Please, I can't do this now."

Molly grabbed her by the shoulders. "If not now, when? Something's really wrong. I'm your friend. I care about you. What's going on?" She shook her.

Heather broke free and collapsed on the bed. "I can't tell you."

"Great. We're making progress. At least, you admit there's a problem."

"Look, if you want to be my friend don't ask any more questions. I've got to do this on my own."

"Miss Independent, friends are supposed to help. It's obvious that you need a friend."

"I can handle this. Too many people will get hurt." Heather began to sob.

Molly put her arm around her. "I can help. What is it? Tell me."

"I can't. I can't," Heather moaned.

Molly hesitated for a moment. She was close to a break-through. "You've got to. I can't help, unless you tell me everything."

Heather jumped up, and turned away. "Stop it – no more! Don't you see they...they hurt me. They'll hurt you too. Please, stay out of it."

Molly sat stunned for a moment. "Okay, I won't ask anything else – not right now. Just remember, you have a friend who wants to help."

"Thanks. It won't be much longer. I'm sure I can handle it," Heather smiled bravely.

"I hope so. Keep me posted. If anyone hurts you again, I'll rip his guts out."

"Thanks, babe." Heather gave her a hug. "I believe you would."

"Sure. What are friends for?"

At least Heather had left the door open on their friend-ship.

******

Heather forced herself to go through the motions of being a student. She attended classes, but without enthusiasm. She rarely contributed to group discussions. Her professors noticed her gloomy demeanor, and her class standing began to erode. One professor, in particular, took special note of her condition. A typewritten note addressed simply to HEATHER appeared in her mailbox the next day. The message was clear and frightening.

I need you to come see me tonight at 7 p.m. We have important things to discuss. Don't be late.

The note was unsigned. It did not need a signature. She cringed at the thought of returning to the scene of her nightmares. For a moment, she considered ignoring the message, but feared the consequences of defying the order. She would meet the professor at the appointed time.

Heather took pains to dress unattractively. Unlike the last meeting, she wanted to appear dowdy and unappealing. She searched for any means to enhance her personal protection. She wore old blue jeans, calf-high leather boots, and a heavy sweater. She arranged her hair in a tangled mess, and removed any traces of make-up.

As she drove to the confrontation with the professor, she considered a number of options in dealing with him. Murder topped the list, but she had never explored that dark side of her nature. She was traveling in uncharted territory. In the end, she decided to wait for an opportunity to strike back at her tormentor. She parked and moved heavily toward the front door. It was 7 p.m.

"Good girl. Right on time. Come in." The professor scrutinized her with distaste. "God, you look like shit! What have you done to yourself?"

"Nothing," she snapped. "I was fine until my last visit here."

"Now, now. Don't be bitter. We have some important things to discuss. Come over here and sit down." He took her elbow.

She pulled away. "Don't touch me."

The professor smiled. "It's not like that. No tricks this time. I promise. I just want to talk. Please, sit down."

She stared at him defiantly, but took a seat on the couch.

"That's much better. Now, may I get you something to drink?"

Heather exploded. "How stupid do you think I am? You're not going to pull that shit on me again. I want nothing to drink or eat – ever!"

He appeared unruffled. "That's too bad. Do you mind if I get myself a drink?"

Heather ignored his request.

"I'll be right back." He got to his feet. "By the way, why don't you look inside the folder on the coffee table? It's yours to take with you. We'll discuss the contents when I get back. Please, don't leave before I return. I'd be very upset if you did."

He smiled, and left the room. Heather picked up the folder. Her hands trembled as she reached inside. She pulled out 8 X 10 color photographs of herself having sex with a man. Her features were unmistakable. The man's identity, however, was obscured, but it was not the professor. Heather gagged at the lurid details. The images showed her exposed, performing sex acts beyond her wildest imagination. The folder fell from her hands, and she began to sob.

The professor returned from the kitchen. He sat down across from her, and gave her a moment to regain her composure.

"I'm sorry I had to show you those. But if I hadn't, you might not have believed me."

"You're a pig!"

"Yes, you're upset," he replied. "Let's get beyond all this emotion, and talk about business. Are you ready to listen?"

She nodded, weakly.

"Good. First of all, those photographs are yours to keep. As you can imagine, I have more copies. Is that clear?"

She nodded with her eyes downcast.

"Heather, please look at me. The sooner we agree on certain matters, the sooner you can go back to the dorm."

She reluctantly met his eyes.

"Good girl. Next, you must change your appearance. I want you looking pretty again like your old self. Do you agree?"

She agreed.

"Third, you need to clean up your act in class. You must get involved and bring up your grades. Don't worry about my class, I can cover for you, but you need to do better in the others. I've talked to your teachers. They're worried about you. Tell them you've had some personal problems, and promise to do better. Do you understand?"

Heather nodded.

"Next. Get a social life. Go to parties. Date. Act normal. We don't want you attracting attention to yourself, do we?"

She shook her head.

"Hang in there. We're almost finished."

She slumped on the couch.

"Lastly, I'll send you notes from time to time. I expect you to respond to them without question. Nothing too difficult," he assured her, "but I will need you to comply. I may have a little task for you in a few weeks."

Tears flowed down Heather's cheeks. "Please make this all stop." She pressed her hands over her eyes.

"It will. It will," he promised. "A few months tops, and it'll be over. I'll destroy the evidence, and you can have your life back."

"Do you really expect me to believe that?"

"Yes, because the plan is always the same. Three or four months are all I need."

She considered the implications of his statement. "Okay, I'll do everything you ask, but please don't make me go through this again." She pointed in disgust at the folder.

"Don't worry; nothing like that. I just needed to get your cooperation. The rest will be easy. Are you with me?"

She nodded reluctantly.

"Good girl. Do everything I ask, and it will soon be over. Now, go home. See, no tricks."

"Sure. No tricks." She started to pick up the folder.

"Go ahead. It's yours." He gave her an evil smile.

"No thanks. I don't keep garbage."

"Suit yourself. I'll hold them for you, if you change your mind."

"I won't." She moved to the door.

The professor opened it for her. "Goodnight, I'll be in touch."

Heather drove back to the dorm in anger and disgust. The professor had outmaneuvered her at every turn. Viewing the graphic evidence from that horrible night had crushed her resistance. The photographs had sealed her fate. The nightmare would continue.

CHAPTER 5

Tyler climbed the steps of the Performing Arts building on the first day of registration. He reached into his pocket for the key given to him by the dean. The idea of losing the sacred object sent a chill down his spine. The good dean, in his condescending way, had made it clear failure to protect the key would constitute gross negligence. The new instructor expected to receive criticism for his academic shortcomings, but refused to take a reaming for losing a key. There were no casting directors or producers here, but this play had a stage, actors, and at least one critic. The first act was about to begin.

He found his office located next to Dr. Newsome's. The speech professor was bent over his desk writing furiously. Tyler decided to delay introductions. He entered his new office and dropped the briefcase on the desk. The room was small with one window overlooking the campus. It suited his needs just fine. The springs creaked as he settled into the ancient, metal office chair. The desk looked like a relic from the Depression. Faculty salaries and office furniture must have been a low budget priority. He opened the desk drawers and discovered a few office supplies and a note addressed to *MY ESTEEMED SUCCESSOR.*

Tyler hesitated before opening the envelope, but curiosity won out.

Sir or Madam:
I leave you the few assorted drama books and theatre scripts on the bookcase. There is little I can offer you in the way of

advice, except to defend our small piece of the college as much as you are able. There will be those who oppose you, but the Arts deserve a champion at Stonewater College. Someone with more resolve than I could muster. I wish you well in your endeavors.

Respectfully,
Joshua Kimball

Tyler attempted to visualize the confrontations that must have occurred between Dr. Kimball and Dean Henderson. It seemed obvious the Performing Arts Department had not benefited from Dr. Kimball's exertions. The new drama instructor felt unprepared for the challenge. There was still much to learn.

He checked his class rosters and found a number of vacancies in each of his four courses. There were at least five to ten empty slots in each class. He had hoped to make more of an impact during registration. A number of students seemed impressed with his salesmanship, but many opted to make other selections. This was not a good omen.

"Excuse me. May I come in?"

A female student stuck her head into his office. She had curly red hair and a wide smile.

"Sure. It's great to see a friendly face," he replied.

She extended her hand and Tyler shook it. "Hi. I'm Molly Cross."

"Tyler Richmond. Have a seat. You're my first visitor."

"Thanks. I just wanted to give you a welcome. I've signed up for two of your classes."

"Two? I was just going over the class rosters. Most students avoided me like the plague."

"Don't worry," she laughed. "You're new. Once the rest of the guys find out you're okay, they'll sign up. We've got two weeks to switch classes."

"But you were willing to take a chance on me."

"Hey, theatre is my life. You're stuck with me for the next three years."

"Great. I need all the support I can get. I'll try to teach you a few things along the way."

"I heard you were on TV for a while, and did some professional acting in New York."

"Just for two years. Small stuff Off-Broadway, and a few minor roles on Soaps."

She leaned forward with interest. "Which Soaps?"

The Old and the Toothless and *All My Heartburn*. It really doesn't matter." He shrugged. "The roles didn't last long."

"I'd love to be on TV, or in the movies," she gushed.

"There's lots of competition out there. You'll know after college if you're ready to take them on. Don't rush it."

"I can hardly wait." Molly jumped out of her chair. "Anyway, if you need help getting settled, let me know. I know where to find some muscle."

"Thanks. I might take you up on that. I'll see you in class."

"Right. I'm really excited."

Tyler smiled as she bounced out of the office. Her energy was infectious, and he felt better after her visit. He hoped there were more students with as much enthusiasm. He decided it was time to meet the neighbors. He knocked on Dr. Newsome's door.

"Dr. Newsome, may I come in?"

"Come in. Come in."

Hugh Newsome was short and plump, with wispy white hair. Tyler thought it odd for him to be wearing a sweater on such a warm day.

"Sorry to bother you, but I wanted to introduce myself. I'm Tyler Richmond."

"Ah, yes. I heard you were here – down from New York." Dr. Newsome leaned back in his chair.

"Yes, New York City. I couldn't pass up the opportunity to teach at Stonewater."

Dr. Newsome regarded him with amusement. "Teach here? You *wanted* to teach here. What prompted that impulse?"

Tyler felt irritated, but did not want to alienate his new colleague – yet. "I heard Stonewater was a good school with a fine tradition for learning."

"Ha! Well, I suppose we are responsible for imparting a small amount of knowledge to our students. But the truth is, students don't come here to learn, and the administration doesn't care if we teach. Stonewater College is all about keeping up appearances. Dissension and scandal are strictly prohibited here. If you maintain the façade and accept the farce – you should do well. Good teaching has nothing to do with it."

Tyler regarded Newsome with caution. "I hope you're wrong about that. I have plans to be a very good teacher."

"I suppose you're entitled to your illusions," Newsome sighed. "I came here over twenty years ago with the same dream. After you struggle to get recognized for your hard work and get knocked down, over and over, you change. At first, you're willing to accept small compromises to keep out of trouble. You avoid controversy and adjust your teaching style to meet acceptable standards. After time, you submit to their control. That's when they own you."

"Why do you stay?" Tyler inquired.

"I really don't know. Force of habit, I guess. I trained long and hard to be a professor. That's what I am. I don't think I could do anything else."

"But there are other colleges."

"Conditions are the same everywhere. I accepted my fate long ago."

Tyler forced himself not to overreact. "You make it sound like you're trapped in Dante's Inferno."

"I haven't given it much thought," Newsome chuckled. "I guess the worst aspects of hell can be found in familiar surroundings."

"I think we're responsible for our own conditions, and hell is not one of my choices," Tyler countered.

"Forgive me. I shouldn't burden you with my circumstances. I always get carried away this time of year."

"Sure. I feel the pressure, too. I hope everything works out for you."

"It always does. Good luck with your future. Let me know if you need anything."

Tyler got up to leave. "Thanks, I appreciate the offer."
He walked away without looking back.

Tyler experienced some jitters during initial meetings with his students, but became more confident as the week progressed. Molly Cross did her best to infuse energy into the proceedings and encouraged more students to fill vacant class slots. He sighed with relief as new recruits swelled the ranks. The new instructor used a variety of teaching methods. He encouraged his actors to get comfortable with their bodies and voices. He taught them how to breathe properly and use their sight and hearing. Good actors had to be aware of their surroundings. One exercise required them to go outdoors and lie in the grass. The objective was to get in touch with nature and stimulate their sensory awareness. Dean Henderson observed one of these proceedings while walking across campus. He did not seem to be amused.

Barry Zucker's party on Saturday night served as a welcome diversion.

" I want you to meet someone recently divorced, and gorgeous. Tyler Richmond, this is Sheila Lawson. Dr. Lawson is a prominent professor of biology. She specializes in exploring exotic body parts. You're in good hands." Barry kissed her cheek and faded away.

"How do you do, Mr. Richmond? Welcome to our little social group." She extended a long, graceful hand to him. She was blonde, sophisticated, and in her early thirties.

"Call me, Tyler. May I call you Sheila?"

"Please, do." She smiled, and leaned closer.

The guests were faculty members and a few of Barry's neighbors. Most arrived alone, but there were several couples thrown into the mix. No one appeared much over forty. They all seemed eager to meet the new drama instructor. They bombarded him with questions about New York and Broadway. He responded without any negative commentary on his former life. Following a break in the conversation, he slipped away from Sheila to meet the other guests. One professor insisted on sharing his insights on college opportunities. He introduced himself as Jack Lucas, professor of economics. He appeared long past sobriety. Jack took the newcomer by the arm and guided him to a neutral corner of the room.

"Stonewater College is a great repository for beauty. In the old days, the college used to be open to men only. Thank God, they changed all that. Now, more than half the students are women. Think of the possibilities."

Tyler pulled away from his grasp. "I'm not sure I know what you mean."

"Sure you do." Jack winked, and slapped him on the shoulder. "It's a carefully guarded secret. I tell you this in confidence. It happens all the time, but never in the open. The college couldn't stand the scandal. No one gets hurt, and no one is the wiser."

Tyler wanted to smack the leer off his face but checked the impulse. Nothing could be gained by hitting a drunk. He left Jack Lucas leaning against the wall.

Barry seemed disappointed when Tyler announced he had to leave the party. "At least, don't go home alone. There are several charming ladies here who'd love to go with you."

"Thanks, but I'm really beat. It was a good party, Barry. Thanks for inviting me."

"Sure. Sure, maybe next time. I just want you to enjoy our southern hospitality."

"I did. I'll see you tomorrow."

Tyler left the noise and cigarette smoke behind. He had met some interesting people at the party, but the whole experience had turned sour after the confrontation with Jack Lucas. The scheme of exploiting female students reminded him of his past life in New York where young actors and actresses fell prey to casting directors. Obviously, Stonewater College supported the same type of scum. As he climbed the stairs to his apartment, he made a promise to keep an eye on the extra-curricular activities of Dr. Lucas.

CHAPTER 6

Tyler's first four weeks at Stonewater College passed at a rapid pace. The Shenandoah Valley had begun to dress itself in vivid fall colors. The maple and oak trees displayed brilliant hues of red, yellow, and orange. The night air turned crisp and cool. Frost had not yet decorated the grass with crystalline splendor, but the cycle of seasons ensured its arrival. It would only be a matter of weeks before the colors began to fade, and the leaves surrendered their hold on life.

The instructor's days quickly filled with class preparation, teaching duties, student meetings, faculty meetings, and personal introductions. Tyler made it a point to meet each faculty member on his or her home ground. The process was time-consuming, but paid good dividends. It helped him establish a rapport with his peers, and provided valuable insights into the character and political climate of the college. Most members of the faculty seemed flattered by the overtures of their young associate. Normally, new college employees were too reserved to initiate introductions. On the whole, he received good notices for his efforts.

"So, how did you find things in the Biology Department?" Barry grinned wickedly.

"Very informative," Tyler replied.

The psychology professor threw up his hands in frustration. "What's wrong with you, boy? She's beautiful, over twenty-one, and available. In my book, the chemistry is perfect."

Tyler laughed. "I can't fault your logic, but I'm not ready

for any entanglements yet. I'm too busy getting my feet on the ground."

Barry slapped him on the back. "That's the problem, boy. You need to get your feet *off* the ground. Dr. Lawson has the right prescription."

"One challenge at a time, Barry. That's all I can handle."

"Challenge? Who's talking challenge? This is a sure thing."

"Okay. Okay. Who else do I need to meet?"

Barry, reluctantly, dropped his endorsement of Dr. Lawson to provide more advice about his colleagues. Tyler's mental catalog soon became filled with faculty trivia.

He enjoyed his first meeting with the dance instructor, Ms. Edna Plum. Thick layers of make-up covered her face and she had painted her cheeks bright pink. An artificial mole marked the corner of her mouth and she wore a smear of cherry red lipstick. A wig served to disguise her natural hair. She appeared to be on the upper end of sixty, but possessed a perfectly proportioned body. Tyler had no doubt she still maintained a rigorous dance regimen. Ms. Edna asked him about his experiences with the New York dance scene. Fortunately, he had attended some ballet performances, and a few productions by the Alvin Ailey Dance Company. Ms. Edna grilled him about every detail. The college met her physical needs, but her heart lived elsewhere. She despised all college bureaucrats and harbored no love for Dean Henderson.

"The man's an old goat," she sputtered. "He never attends any of our dance recitals, and has no artistic appreciation in his body. All he ever talks about is money."

"The Arts always suffer when the budget is tight," Tyler replied.

"Can you imagine," Ms. Edna sniffed. "Isadora believed the Arts are a mirror of the soul. Everyone has a soul, except the old goat."

"I believe you're right," he said, with a smile.

"Of course, I'm right. Now look here, young man. Go get us some money. You look like you can put up a fight. I need more music tapes, and books on modern dance."

"I'll do my best, but I'm pretty new at this."

"Nonsense. If you wait too long, you'll end up a muttering idiot like Hugh Newsome." Ms. Edna poked him in the ribs.

"A fate worse than death," he agreed, laughing.

"That's right. Now, get to it!"

Tyler promised to give it a shot, and made a hasty retreat. Ms. Edna would probably nag him until she got her funding.

His meeting with Dr. Jack Lucas was not as pleasant. Jack appeared distracted during the entire session.

"I'm sorry about the party at Barry's place. I was pretty blasted," he apologized.

"No problem," Tyler noticed a photo behind Jack's desk of a smiling woman and two small boys. "Nice family you have."

"Thank you," Jack replied. "We, ah...we're not together any more. I moved into an apartment near Barry's. I still spend time with the boys. We go to ball games and other stuff."

"That's good."

A moment of uneasy silence passed between them.

"Well, what do you think of our college?"

"It's great. Most of the people I've met have been a great help."

"Glad to hear it. I think you'll like it more once you learn your way around." Lucas shuffled his feet. "By the way, I really didn't mean what I said about female students the other night. That was the booze talking. I've got enough trouble without that."

Tyler regarded him skeptically. "Sure. No problem."

Jack looked up at the ceiling. "I mean, I've been tempted. You'll be tempted, too, but it's not worth the risk."

"I'm sure you're right about that."

"Stick to business and you'll do fine."

"Thanks, I intend to."

"If you ever need anything give me a call. After all, we're neighbors."

"Thanks, and I appreciate the advice."

34

Tyler shook Jack's hand and walked out of the office. He did not expect to form a lasting relationship with Jack Lucas. The economics professor hid too much beneath the surface. It was hard to trust anyone who had a difficulty looking you in the eye.

The meetings ended on a positive note. Most of the professors responded well. They seemed to appreciate his outgoing style and sincerity. Tyler felt confident he had made some new friends.

True to his word, Dean Henderson assigned him to sit on a faculty committee – the Cultural Affairs Committee. Its primary responsibility was to promote artistic endeavors on campus, and bring cultural events to the college. This promised to be a major challenge with an annual budget of only two thousand dollars. The committee chairperson was Dr. Sheila Lawson. She gave Tyler an amused look as he took a seat at the table.

The first thing discussed was upcoming events. The Department of Fine Arts was planning a student art display in November. Tyler announced that Ms. Edna had scheduled a dance recital for the end of October. The Music Department was working on a holiday band concert for December. Tyler reported he had plans to direct the play PLAZA SUITE, by Neil Simon. He expected the production to open in mid-November.

Dr. Lawson requested suggestions for outside cultural activities. The committee discussed the possibility of bringing in professional artists and musicians. Dr. Lawson smiled, and reminded everyone of the limited budget. She suggested they give the matter more thought, and adjourned the meeting. Tyler approached her after the others had left.

"Good meeting, Madam Chairperson."

"Thank you, Mr. Richmond. I appreciated your input."

"Sheila, look...I'm sorry about Barry's party. Everything is happening so fast, I need to concentrate on getting settled." He hesitated. "That sounds stupid, doesn't it?"

"It certainly does," she agreed.

"What I'm saying, in my own bumbling way, is I just need some time. After the dust settles, may I take you out to dinner?"

She raised her eyebrows. "You want me to wait for your call?"

Tyler winced. "Ouch. I deserved that. I'm not doing very well."

She smiled. "You know, for an actor, you have a terrible command of language. Let's make this easy for you. Why don't you call me when you're ready? If I'm available, I'll go to dinner with you."

He smiled. "Thanks, Sheila." He took hold of her hand. "I promise to call soon."

"We'll see."

She squeezed his hand and walked briskly out of the room. He followed her with his eyes, until she was out of sight. He had underestimated her, and made a mental note to call her sooner than originally planned.

PLAZA SUITE rehearsals occupied most of his week-nights. Tyler had settled on the comedy for its wide audience appeal and its requirement for only one set. The stage crew was untested and he did not want to overtax their capabilities. He would need to supervise set construction, and had limited experience in this area. The drama instructor knew how to hold a hammer, but had never mastered the finer points of set design. He expected to spend long hours of research to develop this skill.

Auditions proved to be a great success. Molly Cross had done her best to beat the bushes, and forty students read for the parts. Fortunately, a number of them also volunteered to work on the set and costumes. He was gratified by the positive response, and thanked Molly.

"Glad to help, Mr. Richmond," she beamed. "I told you, theatre is my life."

"I do recall you saying something like that. Why don't you call me Tyler? I like to keep things informal on the set."

"Thanks...Tyler. I think we're going to have a great show."

"If we do, you'll be largely responsible. I need you in the cast, and working behind the scenes, too."

"Whatever it takes. I'll be here when you need me," she promised.

"Good. Now, get out of here and go work on your lines." She whooped and took off at a run.

Dean Henderson observed Tyler's progress with great interest and summoned him to the inner sanctum. "Well, Mr. Richmond, it seems you've been busy."

"I've been working hard to learn the ropes," he replied.

"So I've heard. It's a little unusual for new instructors to make office appointments with each member of our faculty." Dean Henderson waited for a response. There was none.

"I much prefer introductions to take place during social occasions. That's why we have faculty receptions. Your time could have been better spent preparing for your classes."

Tyler considered his reply. "I didn't neglect my work. I was just anxious to meet my colleagues. I found the experience to be highly informative."

"I'm sure you did. I just want to make sure you stay focused on your responsibilities. Your ultimate success depends on it."

Tyler began to seethe. "I realize that, sir. I intend to give full attention to my teaching duties."

"Good. There is one more thing. I was concerned to see your students lying in the grass several weeks ago. I'm sure you had your reasons for that episode, but it doesn't present a very good image. Teaching belongs in the classroom."

He clenched his fists. "I'm sorry, but I believe valuable lessons are learned outside the classroom, as well. Why should we confine ourselves to a single square room?"

The dean jumped to his feet and glared at him red-faced. "Because, Mr. Richmond, without rules we would have chaos. I will not have students running wild. I expect you to set a good example, and confine your teaching activities to assigned areas. Is that clear?"

37

"Very clear."

"Good. That's all." The dean sat back down, and turned his attention to some papers on his desk.

Tyler left the office without further comment. He thought back to Hugh Newsome's warning. The dean expected total submission from everyone on his staff. The young instructor would accept this condition for the time being, but there would be a day of reckoning. He needed to prepare himself for the possibility of having to find a new job.

CHAPTER 7

Molly felt ecstatic. Rehearsals for PLAZA SUITE had entered the second week. She relished her role in the production. The excitement on the set had become contagious. The student actors displayed growing enthusiasm as Tyler shaped each scene. He directed the comedy without any pressure and urged his cast members to have fun. The young thespians easily embraced this painless work ethic.

"Molly, try to enter the scene with less urgency. This is a hotel room, not a subway station," Tyler teased.

"I'm sorry, I couldn't wait to get started."

"Don't worry, we'll wait for you. Try it again with a little less energy, but I really like your enthusiasm. Take a deep breath and try it again."

"Sure," she blushed and ran off stage.

Molly had always loved performing. She had not been a pretty child, and her parents had resigned themselves to her plain appearance. Molly refused to accept any limitations. She organized neighborhood social activities and games. Her fertile imagination conceived treasure hunts, dance contests, haunted houses, ball games, historic dramas, plays, and costume parties. Parents endured her appeals for tools and supplies to support these ventures. They accepted the minor contributions as small payment for having their children gainfully occupied.

Irrepressible Molly never rested on her laurels and was not above organizing pranks to retaliate against injustice. Old Man Blauser found stones in his hubcaps after yelling at her gang for running through his back yard. Old Lady Lewis had her mailbox filled with shaving cream for not handing out candy at Halloween. Eddie Hopper, the neighborhood bully, became another victim. They hung a large banner over his front door proclaiming, 'Home of the Ape Man'. No one was safe from Molly's clandestine operations, but she only attacked those who deserved retribution. Remarkably, no one ever proved her complicity in any of the capers.

Molly's spirit of adventure continued throughout her teenage years. She took calculated risks for the right cause and embraced her role as a leader. Socially, she had to suffer disappointments. She longed for a boyfriend and had to intimidate Johnny Allison into taking her to the Junior Prom. Johnny hated dances and preferred working on his old car. Reluctantly, he cleaned the grease off his hands and rented a tuxedo for the occasion. He could not afford to reject Molly's invitation. He had participated in too many of her schemes. Johnny Allison swallowed hard and did his duty.

Molly's social life improved after she arrived at Stonewater. College life had a way of bringing all types of personalities into close contact. Molly found her niche in the Drama Department and with others who shared her passion for the theatre. She partied with kindred souls who followed the same dream. For the first time in her life she felt content, except for her relationship with Heather.

There had been a marked improvement since their last confrontation, but Heather remained secretive. The late night meetings still continued. She returned from them more depressed than ever. Molly entertained the notion of following her on one of these excursions, but decided against it. Heather had asked for time to put her life in order. Out of respect, Molly would wait, but not much longer.

******

Heather dreaded opening her mailbox. The thought of receiving another plain envelope, with her name typed in block letters, sent chills through her body. Her hand shook each time she dialed the combination. This time a letter was waiting.

Heather,
7 p.m. tonight!

That was all. Heather knew the implication of those few words. There was no need for further explanation. She had no choice but to comply. She drove the familiar route with trepidation. The professor had made no substantial demands of her since their first meeting. He seemed content to just toy with her. Heather sensed things were about to change. She rang the doorbell at 7 p.m.

"Heather, you look lovely tonight."

She was wearing slacks and a sweater. She had also taken pains with her hair and make-up. "Thank you," she replied.

"I'm pleased to see you've taken my advice. You look like your beautiful, charming self again." He applied his most engaging smile.

"Cut the bullshit," she snapped. "This isn't a social visit."

He seemed amused by her antagonism. "There's no need for rudeness. I enjoy your company. I wish we could have met under different circumstances." He stroked her hair as she passed by him.

"Don't touch me. What's this all about?" She glared into his eyes.

He retained his look of amusement. "Let's not make this difficult. I really do enjoy your company, but we have some business to discuss. Please sit down."

She refused to budge.

"The longer you fight against me, the longer you'll have to stay. Why not cooperate?"

She sat down on the sofa with her back rigid, and her knees clamped together.

"Thank you. May I get you something to drink? No tricks, I promise."

"No."

41

"You need to start trusting me. It will greatly improve our relationship."

"I don't trust you and we don't have a relationship."

"We're joined in a bond of mutual need. This forms the basis of our relationship."

"You're sick. I'm out of here." She jumped to her feet.

The professor grabbed her arm. "Sit down." He waited, until she stopped resisting. "Don't you see? I'm providing you with a valuable experience. This is the greatest challenge of your life. You're fighting for survival. What could be a better learning experience?"

"You're a real psycho. I hope you rot in hell!"

"So be it," he sighed, and brushed off her wrath with a manicured hand. "I'm sorry you have trouble accepting our pact. I could make things much easier for you, but you force me to play the heavy."

"Oh sure, I'm the one forcing you."

"All right, enough of this. The time has come for you to provide a little service for me. Are you ready to do what I request?"

Heather's mouth went dry. "Do I have a choice?"

"Frankly, no. Actually, it's not an unpleasant task, and you'll be well paid for your trouble."

"What is it?"

"There's a bar about twenty miles from here called the 'Fantasy Lounge'. I know the owner, Carl Russo. He needs young women as waitresses. If you work for Carl three months, and do a good job, our contract will expire. What do you say to that?"

Heather conjured up the image of a Playboy Bunny balancing a tray of drinks with a plastic smile painted on her face. "You want me to be a waitress in some dive called the 'Fantasy Lounge'. That's what this is all about?"

The professor's smile widened enough to flash his perfectly capped canines. "That's it."

"What do I have to do in this place? Date the drunks?"

"There's no pressure for you to do anything, except wait on tables. Of course, what you do on your own time is your business. You'll be paid well, and you get to keep all your tips."

"God, this is disgusting."

"Not really. You'll only work weekends, and you're far enough from the college never to be recognized. It's a perfect set-up."

"For who?"

"For all of us. What's your answer?"

She glared at him. There was no escape. She could run out the door, but he still held the upper hand. He could arrange to have her condemned for acts she did not commit. She had no defense, and needed time to develop a strategy.

"Okay, I guess I have to do it since you didn't give me a choice."

"We all have choices, Heather. You just made the right choice."

'The right choice?' Nothing seemed 'right' about the entire situation. She had to find a way to expose this smug bastard.

"Great, when do I report for work?"

"Friday night. Carl is expecting you to arrive at six o' clock. Here are the directions."

He handed her a 3 X 5 card containing typed instructions. The bar was located in a little town east of Stonewater called Fallbrook. Heather had been through it once before and was surprised a joint like the 'Fantasy Lounge' existed in such a quaint place.

"Do you mind if I leave now?"

"Of course. We're all finished here, but I expect you to be pleasant and cooperative with Carl. He gives me regular reports. I'll be very disappointed if you let me down. I'm sorry I had to break it to you this way. You left me no choice."

"We all have choices, and you chose to blackmail me."

"Such an ugly word. We have a contract and I'll live up to my part. Will you keep your end of the bargain?"

"I said I'd do it. May I leave?"

"Yes, but I'll be in touch."

Heather made a defiant exit and marched stiffly to her car. She refused to give the professor the satisfaction of seeing her run from him. However, once inside her car, she collapsed on the steering wheel. Her body convulsed in anguish, and tears gushed from her eyes.

She arrived at the bar a little after 6 p.m. on Friday night. The winding country roads had delayed her. During the long drive, her only consolation was the low probability of ever being discovered here by her friends.

The bar turned out to be worse than she imagined. A pink neon sign advertised the 'Fantasy Lounge'. A silhouette of a naked girl danced in a wineglass beneath the flashing letters. The building was a shack surrounded by a gravel parking lot. Once inside, she confronted an ape-like bouncer who weighed almost 300 pounds. His flat, expressionless face featured an ugly, broken nose. Her worst nightmare was about to come true.

"You must be the new girl."

"Yes," she managed.

"Carl's in back. He's expectin' ya."

"Thanks."

The bar was almost empty. She followed directions to the office and knocked on the door. Carl Russo sat behind his cluttered desk. Photos of nude dancers decorated his walls. Ashtrays were overflowing and stale cigar smoke polluted the air. Carl was overweight, middle aged, and balding. He looked like a low-life character from a 50s gangster movie.

"You're Heather." He gestured for her to take a seat.

Heather sat down in a worn overstuffed chair. It smelled of stale cigarette smoke, beer, and other mysterious odors.

"First thing we do is change your name. All of my girls have stage names. It keeps them anonymous. Let's call you...Candy. How's that?"

Heather winced.

"You met Tiny."

Heather remembered the ape. "You mean the man at the door?"

"Yeah. Tiny keeps the peace around here. If you have any trouble, you go to Tiny."

"Okay. What do I have to do?"

"Didn't the college guy tell you?"

"He said I had to wait on tables and be nice to the customers."

"That's right, real easy. Pretty girls bring in the suckers. Your job is to keep 'em happy and drinking. If they get too drunk, Tiny throws 'em out."

Heather glanced at the photos on the wall. "You mean I don't have to take off my clothes or dance?"

"Nah." Carl leaned forward. "To tell the truth, Heather...er, Candy, some of the girls do dance in the back room for the local hicks, but only if they want to. Nude dancing is illegal, so we can't advertise. We keep it real low-key."

She felt a wave of nausea grip her abdomen.

"Stand up, Candy. Let's have a look at you."

She got to her feet unsteadily.

"Nice body," Carl whistled. "Turn around slowly."

She clenched her fists, closed her eyes, and did as she was told.

"Oh baby, you got the goods. I'd love to...never mind. Go put this on and come right back." He handed her a plastic bag. "You can change in my bathroom." He pointed her to a door inside his office.

Heather walked into the small room and locked the door behind her. She inspected the contents of the bag and felt sickened. Inside, was a pair of platform shoes, a red mini skirt, and a skimpy brassiere. She slipped on the flimsy costume. She stared into the mirror, and had an uncomfortable sensation of being watched. After turning around several times, she realized the slightest bend at the waist would expose her panties. Her breasts were squeezed so tight, her cleavage protruded above the cups. Tears began to pour from her eyes. Her humiliation was complete. She took a deep breath, washed her face, and returned to Carl's office. He stared at her with undisguised lust.

"Baby, you're something else. That man is the greatest. He only sends me the best stuff. Turn around and let me enjoy the view."

She obeyed as she fought back the tears.

"Yeah, I'm going to enjoy having you around. Sit down, Candy."

She sat down and closed her legs together.

"We have a few rules around here. We got other girls in the place. It's okay to be friendly, but no real names and you can't discuss how you got here. Understand?"

She nodded.

"You work from 6 p.m. to 2 a.m. I don't care what you do after that, but you work until closing. Got it?"

"Yes."

"Tiny's here to protect you. He can be your best friend, but if you cross me, he's going to hurt you. He does everything I tell him. Let's not have any trouble, okay?"

Heather nodded.

"I want you to be real friendly with the suckers. Let 'em feel you up a little bit. It's good for business and you'll get good tips. If it gets too rough, call Tiny. Make 'em promises if you want, but keep 'em drinking. The idea is to keep their wallets open, get it?"

"I guess," she sniffed.

"Don't guess. I want you to do it!"

"I understand."

"That's the girl. Now, I told you about the back room. It's real private back there. We keep it that way. No one's going to make you dance, but if you do I'll give you an extra hundred bucks a night and you keep the tips."

She dropped her head in her hands.

"Think about it. No need to decide now. Any questions?"

46

She shook her head.

"Okay, great to have you with us, Candy. Get ready. The hicks will be here soon."

Heather retreated to the ladies restroom. She saw her reflection in the mirror and cringed. Tears began to stream down her cheeks. She pounded her fists into her forehead and looked for an escape. There was none. She found refuge inside one of the stalls, and collapsed on the toilet seat. There was nothing to do except tolerate the humiliation. She eventually got back on her feet and unlocked the stall door. She slowly returned to the lounge. Hungry eyes followed her every move.

CHAPTER 8

Tyler returned to the Farmers' Market on a regular basis. The dignity of the Mennonite people intrigued him. They had discovered a peaceful existence in the midst of a turbulent technological age. A good crop of apples or a healthy harvest of corn generated more excitement than the introduction of electric cars or all the computer advancements ever made. Political strife never entered into conversation. They lived for their religion, their families, and the land. Nothing else was worthy of their attention.

Tyler found the farmers warm and outgoing. They spoke freely about their lives and families, but never imposed their religious beliefs on anyone. They received compliments, but praise made them uncomfortable. It was acceptable for a Mennonite to extol the virtues of his prize pig, but he never spoke of personal accomplishments. These plain folk never tolerated vanity.

Tyler invited Sheila Lawson to accompany him on one of his Sunday excursions. He promised her a fun-filled afternoon of shopping at the Farmers' Market, touring the apple orchards, and general sightseeing. Lately, contacts with students occupied most of his days and nights. He enjoyed his teaching duties and play rehearsals, but desperately longed for a social life. He craved intimacy with a female companion.

It was early October. Bright sunshine cut through the crisp afternoon air and warmed the valley. Tyler met Sheila at her apartment. She had dressed in jeans and a white cashmere sweater. He had never seen her so informal. Her blonde hair fell to her shoulders, and she had shaded her lips in pale pink. The overall effect was stunning.

She observed his look of appreciation with a smile. "Well, Mr. Richmond, I'm ready for our little journey. What exactly do you have in mind for me...us?"

He grinned. "First of all, call me Tyler. It'll be tough to form a meaningful friendship unless we can cut through the formalities."

She hooked her arm through his. "I fully agree, Tyler. What's the plan? Do you lead, or shall I?"

"It's such a beautiful day, let's have a picnic. We can buy some bread and cheese at the Farmers' Market. I'm sure you can help me find a bottle of white wine somewhere, and then it's off to the hills. You can lead the way. After we eat and throw down the bottle of wine, I intend to read you long passages from Shakespeare."

"Yummy. I like your entire plan, except for Shakespeare. May we skip that part, please?" She squeezed his arm.

"Sure, no problem. I can always tell you the long, sad story of my life as a struggling actor."

"Why don't we just play the conversation part by ear. We might even find some topics of mutual interest to discuss."

"I certainly hope so." He sighed. "I need to hear your formula for success in dealing with Dean Henderson."

"No shop talk. I have no intention of spending the afternoon indulging in campus gossip. I want to get away from the ivory halls of learning and commune with nature."

"Yes ma'am, I'm with you. Let's go commune." He led her to his dented Toyota.

Their first stop was the Farmers' Market. He bought a loaf of homemade bread, and Sheila selected the cheese. A small bag of apples, and several ripe tomatoes rounded out their purchases. Sheila found a bottle of California Chardonay in a liquor store while he grabbed a bag of ice. Preparations were complete.

Sheila pointed the way to the Skyline Drive. She promised him an afternoon of sightseeing splendor and he was not disappointed. Engineers had constructed the mountain road to showcase the beauty of the valley. The red and gold of the autumn leaves splashed the landscape with brilliant color. The panoramic floor of the valley extended north and south below. Vast fields of green formed in geometric patterns. The purple mountain range on the far side of the valley stretched with endless majestic grace. Tyler observed the scene with breathless excitement.

They pulled off at a rest area designed for the tourists. Tyler suggested they find a more pastoral setting. Sheila agreed, and helped him unload their lunch. They left the sightseers behind and went off in search of a private site. Ten minutes later, she pointed to a grassy spot under a giant hickory tree. The location offered a spectacular view. He spread out the blanket, and they settled down to eat. Sheila arranged slices of bread and cheese on paper plates. He poured the chilled wine into plastic glasses and made a toast to the beautiful day. She nodded and added a toast to their new friendship.

"You know, for a city boy, I could get real used to this country living."

"You look like you fit right in, country boy." She smiled as he stretched out on the blanket. "You know, you haven't told me much about your life in New York."

Tyler raised himself up on an elbow. "That's right, I did promise to tell you that sad story. Let's see, where do I begin?"

Sheila passed him a plate. "Is this going to be a long story?"

He smiled and rolled over on his back. "Not at all, ma'am. I can give you the condensed version in less than one minute."

"Good. My ears are all yours." She settled down on the blanket beside him.

He took a deep breath as if preparing for a high dive. "Well, I jumped into the Broadway meat market right after earning my Masters Degree at Cornell. I spent every day running to acting classes, auditions, odd jobs, and rehearsals. I soon learned that most propositions didn't lead to real acting jobs. My money and patience ran thin. After two years in the rat race, I threw in the towel and escaped to Stonewater. Now, I'm lounging on top of a beautiful Virginia mountain with a gorgeous professor of biology."

Sheila blushed, and gently stroked his upper arm with her fingertips. "I'm glad you called me."

"This is the type of day that needs to be shared. Thanks for bringing me up here."

He turned and looked up into her deep, blue eyes. They held eye contact for several moments, until she bent over and kissed him lightly.

"A kiss is a good way to start a friendship."

"Nothing better," he agreed.

He reached for her and kissed her hungrily. She matched his intensity. He ran his hand beneath her soft cashmere sweater. She let out a moan and boldly took him in her grasp. Their breathing increased to a fever pitch. There were no more words. They made love with unrestrained passion. Their exertions continued until they collapsed, completely spent. Sheila rested her head on his chest. He wrapped his arms around her and held onto her warmth.

"I hope none of the tourists saw that," she sighed.

"It would make a great news story. *Naked professors shock tourists on Skyline Drive.*"

Tyler stroked the small of her back, and marveled at the beautiful shape of her figure. She adjusted herself to give him a better view. She seemed to delight in his admiration.

"I guess this makes us friends," she smiled.

"No doubt about it. We've reached new depths of understanding."

She playfully punched him in the stomach and rolled on top of him. "You have such a way with words and – other things."

They laughed and enjoyed the interplay.

The air turned cooler, forcing them to return to their clothes. Tyler wanted the whole experience to continue. There was nothing better than making love with a beautiful woman on a beautiful day. He helped her pack up the remains of their picnic and they returned to the car. They both regretted having to end such a perfect experience.

Sheila placed her hand on his thigh as they approached the outskirts of Stonewater. "I had a wonderful time."

"Me too," he agreed.

"Why don't you come home with me, and I'll make supper. Who knows, we might even find a way to expand on our friendship."

"I'd love to, but I've got play rehearsal tonight. PLAZA SUITE demands my undivided attention."

"I'm jealous," she pouted. "I hate sharing you."

"Theatre's a jealous mistress. There'll be other nights. I'd love to share supper with you."

Tyler drove up to her apartment and walked her to the door. He kissed her long and hard. "I hate to kiss and run."

"You know where I live. I'll keep a light on for you."

"Thanks. Today was special. I won't forget it."

"Just come back soon, okay?"

He promised he would, and returned to his car. He went to rehearsal, but found it difficult to concentrate. His mind kept wandering back to the Skyline Drive.

Molly noticed his distraction, and taunted him. "Hey, Tyler, what's next? You've got me hanging out here with no place to go."

"Sorry, Molly. Let's have you cross to the mirror while you deliver your lines."

He stumbled through the rest of the rehearsal until 10 p.m. He thanked everyone for their hard work and reminded them to learn their lines. Molly approached him as he collected his notes.

"There's someone I'd like you to meet. My roommate came to rehearsal. She's going through a rough time. She needs someone to talk to. I thought maybe you could..."

Tyler groaned. "Molly, it's really late."

"I know. I know. I'm sorry. Just say hello to her. I told her I trust you. She needs someone to trust."

"Oh, no. I mean…I'll talk to her if you want, but I can't get involved in her personal problems."

"Someone's got to. Just meet her, and see what happens."

He had no choice. It was impossible to resist Molly.

"Okay, I'll meet her."

"Thanks."

Molly led him to the back of the theatre. He was surprised that he had not noticed the young girl in the back row. She was beautiful, with large sad eyes. She appeared nervous.

"Tyler Richmond, this is Heather Andrews."

"Hello Heather." He extended his hand, and Heather accepted it with hesitation.

"Hello." She had difficulty looking at him.

"Is this your first time at rehearsal?"

She nodded.

"Your roommate, Molly, is quite a talent. She's become indispensable to me."

Molly punched his arm. "He's just saying that to keep me locked up in bondage."

Heather's head shot up and her features twisted. He observed the brief look of pain. The girl was suffering from some unknown ailment. He took a seat on an armrest across from her.

"Molly tells me you might be in some trouble."

"Molly talks too much," she snapped, and stood up.

He put up his hand. "I can't promise you anything, but I'll be glad to listen. I might even be able to help."

"I just wish everyone would leave me alone!" She began to sob, and rushed out the door.

"I'm really sorry," Molly apologized. "I shouldn't have dragged you into this."

"That's all right, but I don't think I'm the one she needs. You should take her to a professional counselor."

"She won't go, but I'll try to figure something out. Thanks, anyway. Goodnight." She left him alone in the theatre.

Tyler attempted to put the sad-eyed girl out of his thoughts during the drive home. The pain in Heather's face kept coming back to him. He could not shake off her momentary look of terror when Molly mentioned the word 'bondage'. There must be a connection. He conjured up the memory of his afternoon with Sheila. He smiled, as he remembered her parting words about leaving the light on for him. It was late on Sunday night, and they both had classes the next day. He shrugged, and turned his car in the direction of her apartment. She met him at the door wearing nothing but a long tee shirt and holding a glass of wine.

"Is it too late for supper?"

She smiled, and pulled him through the doorway.

CHAPTER 9

Heather established a new routine of disappearing Friday and Saturday nights. She departed with no explanation, and rarely returned to the dormitory before 3 a.m. Molly refrained from asking questions during those early morning hours, but it was difficult to control the impulse. She would listen as Heather showered off the stench of stale beer and cigarette smoke. However, the odor still clung to her clothing. The soiled garments remained scattered on the floor, until she got out of bed the next morning.

Molly navigated quietly around the room on those mornings. She realized Heather needed time for rest and recovery. The sight of the troubled girl moved her as she watched her sleeping. Heather seemed at peace during these moments. As soon as she awoke, the familiar look of anguish returned to her eyes.

Inexorably, she began to slip away from society. Relationships no longer existed. She managed obligatory contacts during classes, but had no outside communication with her classmates. She trusted no one. Molly, too, remained outside her circle of confidence. Letters and phone calls to her family became less frequent. Her parents took this as an ominous sign. Her father begged her to come home for a visit. She attempted to placate him with vague promises. Heather's father called Molly out of desperation.

"Molly, this is Bob Andrews."

"Hi, Mr. Andrews. Heather's not here," she replied.

"Molly, tell me the truth. What's going on with Heather? She rarely calls us anymore. Her mother and I are worried sick."

She struggled for the right words. "Heather is... under a lot of pressure lately. I'm not sure why."

"Come on. You're her roommate. You must have some idea."

"I really don't know. I've tried to find out, but she won't talk to me."

"You're best friends. I thought you shared everything."

"We did. Lately, I'm lucky to get two words out of her."

"When did all this start?"

"About six weeks ago. She went out to some fancy party, and hasn't been the same since."

"Do you think booze or drugs are involved?"

"No, I don't think so. She just seems mad at the world."

"What can we do?"

"I don't know. I tried to get her to talk to one of my professors, but it didn't work out. Now, she blames me for meddling."

"She needs to come home. If she doesn't, I'll drive down there. I've got to see her. Can you help me?"

"I'll try, but we don't talk much these days, and it'll be tough for her get away during the weekend. I think she just started a new job. She works Friday and Saturday nights."

"What job? She never said anything about a job."

"It just started."

There was a long pause at the other end of the line. "Talk to her, Molly. Tell her we love her, and want her to come home. Please call me back. I'll come to Stonewater if I have to."

"I'll do my best, Mr. Andrews. I'm worried about her, too."

Heather's father made a sound like soft weeping. "We used to be so close. I'm afraid she's slipping away from me."

Tears welled up in Molly's eyes. "Heather will be all right. I'm sure everything will work out."

"Just get her to come home. I need to see her."

"I'll do my best. I'll call you after we talk."

"Thanks, Molly. Heather needs you. We all do.

Goodbye."

Bob Andrews hung up, and she stared at the phone.

"Great! Now what?"

Molly felt the mantle of responsibility weigh upon her. She dreaded having another confrontation with her roommate. She attempted a casual approach with Heather after dinner on Wednesday evening.

"Oh, I almost forgot. Your father called this afternoon."

Heather shot her a questioning look. "What did he want?"

"You. He wanted to talk to you."

"I'll call him back." Heather turned away.

Molly pressed on. "He wants you to come home."

Heather turned. "What else did he say?"

"Oh, not much. He's just worried about you."

"What did you tell him?" Heather snapped.

"Nothing. I just said you've been under some pressure lately."

"Great! Now, he's going to worry himself to death. You know how protective he is. Why couldn't you keep your mouth shut?"

Molly lost her composure. "He's worried about you. He loves you. What was I supposed to say? Everything's great. I never see your daughter. She never talks to me. She's miserable and won't let anyone help. If she keeps it up, she's going to fall off the face of the earth."

"Stop it!" Heather yelled. "What gives you the right to judge me? Everything's ruined. I wanted to keep my parents out of it. Why can't you mind your own business?"

"Just for the record, your father called me. He was already worried about you. You did that, not me. You never call him anymore. What's he supposed to think?"

"I don't know, but I'm sure you gave him an ear full."

"I mostly just listened. He loves you, Heather. He wants you to come home. That's the only way he can be reassured. If you don't go home for a visit, he's going to drive down here."

"Shit! I can't get away." She banged her hand on the wall.

Molly was tempted to ask, 'Why not?' but resisted the urge.

"I just need three months," Heather seemed to forget Molly was in the room. "If I can explain, maybe..." She turned to her roommate. "Never mind. I'll take care of it. Do you have any more good news?"

"No."

"Next time, I'll talk to my father. You stay out of my life." She stomped out of the room.

Heather considered her options. She needed to confront her parents to minimize the damage. She could concoct a number of excuses justifying her behavior – that was the easy part. The difficult part would be persuading Carl to give her the time to go home. She had only worked two weekends for him. She picked up the phone in the lobby, and dialed his unlisted number.

"Carl? This is Heather ... er, Candy."

"Hey, baby. How they shaking?"

"Listen, Carl, I need a favor."

"Sure, baby. What can I do for you?"

"My parents are making a stink. They're worried about me. If I don't go home for a visit, my father's threatened to come after me."

"Ho, Ho," he snorted. "Parents can be a real pain in the ass. What do you want from me?"

She took a deep breath. "I need to go home this weekend. Can you give me the time off?"

"I don't know, baby. That's a rough one. The suckers really like you. It won't be good for business."

"I'm sorry. I hate to ask. I don't know what else to do."

"Hey, baby, I understand. I'd like to help you out." He paused for a moment. "What the hell – go ahead and go home. We'll get by for two nights."

"Thank you so much. I really appreciate it."

"No problem, baby. But I might need to ask you for a favor when you get back. We've got to help each other out, right?"

She felt a prick of dread in her stomach. "Sure ... I guess."

"Go visit your daddy. I'll see you here next weekend. Don't let me down, baby."

"I won't," she assured him. She hated the thought of returning the favor.

Life at the 'Fantasy Lounge' was nearly unbearable. Heather had to endure lewd comments and wandering hands. She was fair game whenever she entered the lounge. Drunken patrons mauled and propositioned her. Tiny had to intervene on several occasions to protect her from harm. One ugly trucker forced her down on a table, and attempted to rip off her panties. Tiny rushed him outside and beat him to a bloody pulp. The rest of the customers treated her with more respect for the remainder of the evening. Her only friend in the joint was Claudia, the bartender. Claudia sported a number of tattoos, spoke loudly, and appeared well over forty. In spite of her rough edges, she had a sympathetic nature. She saw herself as a mother figure to all the girls and took Heather under her wing.

"Don't you worry none, honey. Most of these bums are decent guys with wives and kids. They wouldn't hurt you for anything. Tiny'll take care of the few that try."

"Thanks," Heather replied.

"That's okay. If you ever need anything – ask me. If you get too uptight, I've got some pills to help calm you down, but don't take them while you're drinking booze. In fact, don't drink around here at all. You need to keep a clear head at all times."

"I won't."

"Good for you. Do you need something to help you relax?"

"No thanks. I'll be all right."

"Okay, just let me know. These little babies work miracles." She held up a small brown bottle.

Heather shook her head and entered the lounge area. Carl had been right about the pay. She usually left with $300 in her purse. Patrons tipped with twenty and fifty-dollar bills. She wondered how they could afford such extravagance. The money did nothing to alleviate her distaste for the job, but she accepted it as partial retribution. She tolerated the pinching, the bruises, and the indignities for reasons more substantial than money.

Initially, Heather had little contact with the other girls. The waitresses were all about her age and beautiful. However, their smiles seemed forced and they displayed little enthusiasm for their work. They flirted with the clientele because Tiny was watching. Fear of the big man caused them to perform their roles. Occasionally, one or two of them would slip into the back room with a customer. Heather had no intention of following. She wanted to communicate with her counterparts, but was determined to minimize her contact with the customers. If she was going to find a release from purgatory, she needed help. She prayed it would come from others also desperate to escape.

Heather turned her thoughts from the 'Fantasy Lounge' to the immediate problem at hand. She had to face her parents. Carl had given her an opportunity to make the visit, but she would pay a price for his generosity. That would come later. At this point, nothing terrified her more than the trip home. She needed to convince her father nothing threatened her well–being. After accomplishing that feat, she would try to recover her freedom.

CHAPTER 10

Tyler had difficulty getting the image of the troubled Heather out of his mind. It bothered him that a young woman could seem so distressed. He shared his concern with Sheila.

"I tried to reach out to her, but she refused. I've never seen a more troubled girl."

"You shouldn't get involved with female students in any capacity. It leaves you open to criticism."

"I understand that," he replied. "But how can I ignore someone in trouble, male or female?"

"You need to protect yourself," she warned. "We all live under a microscope at the college. The administration will never tolerate scandal, no matter what the circumstances. If you're really worried, report her to the clinic. They're the ones who can help her. You stay out of it."

He wondered if she had ever gone out of her way to help anyone. "By the administration, I assume you mean Dean Henderson. You're not the first person to warn me about scandal. Hugh Newsome gave me a shot of the same medicine soon after I arrived."

"Hugh's an old oaf, but he's learned how to survive."

"Is that what this is all about – survival? I thought we were here for more noble pursuits."

"We are, darling." She wrapped her arms around him and nuzzled his neck. "It doesn't hurt to stay out of trouble. Otherwise, you won't have the opportunity to exercise those noble pursuits of yours."

"Dean Henderson strikes again. Thanks for the warning." He pulled away from her.

"Don't be angry with me," she pleaded. "I don't want to see you get hurt. I have selfish reasons for wanting to keep you around."

"It's not you. I'm just not used to running scared."

"You're still new at the college. You'll adjust to our unique environment...in time."

"I hope so, but I'm getting real tired of kissing ass."

"I certainly hope you're not going to include mine on your list," she teased.

"No, not yours," he replied, half-heartedly.

He wondered if he could ever accept Sheila's prescription for survival. Some compromise was possible, but total submission was not an option. He could never ignore his responsibilities. The pain in Heather's face was still a vivid memory.

******

PLAZA SUITE entered the final two weeks of rehearsal. The pace accelerated as the production got closer to opening. The show required an increased number of late nights, and work on the set stretched into the weekends. Tyler was pleased with the play's progress and the dedication of his crew. If he maintained this core of workers, greater theatrical endeavors were possible in the future.

He often remained in the theatre after each rehearsal. Molly made a habit of being the last cast member to leave. She took the opportunity to update him on Heather. The news had not improved, but at least Heather had agreed to go home for a visit. Molly hoped the visit would result in a breakthrough. Tyler agreed, and sent her off to the dorm. He used the quiet time to organize his notes and make plans for the next rehearsal. He had just about finished when he heard a voice boom from the back of the theatre.

"You work real late. Not many keep your hours."

He observed one of the campus cops moving toward him. He recognized the policeman from a previous meeting, but could not remember his name.

"I'm sorry. Is it all right if I stay in the building this late?" He looked at his watch. "I didn't realize it was after eleven."

"It's okay with me, Doc. You've got a key. I'm just checking things out. I've seen you around, but we haven't met."

"I'm Tyler Richmond – you don't need to call me, Doc. I'm not a professor, and I don't have a doctoral degree."

"That doesn't matter. I call everyone, Doc. It keeps things simple. My name's Ben Grubb." He was a big man, and appeared to be a shade over fifty. He smiled, and shook hands like a professional wrestler. "I like to meet all the new faculty. I'm the one to call if you have trouble, not the local cops. I'll bring them in if I have to, but it's best to keep our problems in the family."

"I understand," Tyler replied.

"We've had trouble with the local law in the past. They've gotten pretty rough with some of our kids. If I handle things, no one gets hurt." Ben settled himself on one of the theatre seats.

Tyler put away his notes. "Well, is it quiet tonight?"

"Sure. It's the middle of the week. There aren't any big parties. Almost everyone is at home, except you and me."

"I guess you're right, but I'm all done. I need to lock things up and get out of here."

"No hurry, but I won't hold you up. I just wanted to introduce myself."

Tyler made a move to leave, but stopped. "Can you tell me something?"

"Sure." Ben still lounged in the theatre seat.

"Do you have much crime around here? I mean do many college students get in trouble?"

"Not many. It's pretty quiet. We have the usual pranks and beer parties. Every once in a while I stumble on some drugs, but not often. Beer seems to be the drug of choice."

"That's good. I didn't exactly figure crime was running

rampant on the campus."

"You got that right. Old Dean Henderson wants this to stay a nice clean college. It's my job to keep it that way."

"So, if I run into something I can't handle, should I tell you or the dean?"

Ben pulled his bulky frame out of the seat, and patted him on the shoulder. "If you have a problem around here, see me first," he winked. "I'll help you work things out. We'll try to keep the dean out of it."

"Thanks. It was nice meeting you." He shook Ben's hand and recoiled from the pressure. The big man had a vice-like grip.

"You, too." The cop slapped him on the back. "I think you're going to do all right."

"I hope so. I've got some obstacles ahead."

"Who don't?" Ben laughed. "Hang in there, Doc." He waved and left Tyler to turn off the lights.

Tyler made an effort to avoid confrontations with the dean, especially since their last meeting. Ms. Edna, however, would not let him forget his pledge to request funds for her program. She reminded him daily of his obligation.

"You get over there and get me that money. How can you expect me to run a quality program without the proper equipment?"

"I can't."

"There, that settles it. Do your duty and go see the old bastard."

"Ms. Plum, you are the most determined woman I've ever met."

"Nonsense. It has nothing to do with me being a woman. Everyone should be willing to fight for what's right."

"I can't fault your logic. I'll go see the dean."

He made an appointment the next day.

The dean greeted him as he entered his office. "I didn't expect to see you so soon."

"Thank you for agreeing to meet with me."

"My door is always open to members of our faculty. How are you getting along?"

"I'm doing fine. PLAZA SUITE opens in ten days. I hope you can come see it?"

"Of course. I'm very interested in your work. Now, what can I do for you today?"

"This is a little awkward, but I promised Ms. Plum I'd see you."

The dean grimaced and got out from behind his desk. "So, Ms. Plum is at it again. It didn't take her long to get to you." He sat in a chair opposite Tyler and crossed his arms.

"She asked me to request some money for her dance program. She needs an extra one thousand dollars to purchase books, tapes, and videos."

"You already have an approved budget. Dr. Kimball completed it before he left. Have you seen it?"

"Yes, I have. Somehow, the items Ms. Plum needs were not included."

"In case you haven't heard, funds are extremely limited. That's why we use the budget system. The process is over for this year. Ms. Plum will have to wait until the next budget cycle. Please tell her that."

"She'll be disappointed."

"She's fortunate to have a job. The dance program has been marginal for years. It's obvious she neglected to request her supplies at the proper time. She's taking advantage of you, young man."

Tyler felt stung by the comment. "I'm sorry, I don't see it that way. I'm concerned about the students. They deserve our support."

Dean Henderson banged his fist on the chair arm. "Our students receive outstanding support. Why do you insist on antagonizing me?"

"I intended no offense. I just want the best for our Performing Arts programs."

"Your programs get everything they deserve. I owe you

nothing more. I suggest you accept our established administrative procedures. You're too new to challenge the system."

Tyler got to his feet. "Thank you for your time, sir. I won't forget your advice."

"Please don't. We expect everyone on the staff to cooperate and accept our policies."

He felt anxious to escape. "Yes, sir."

"I expect more out of you than I've seen so far. I hope you can make the adjustment. Good day, Mr. Richmond."

Tyler left the dean's office without further comment.

Dean Henderson remained in his chair for several minutes. The drama instructor puzzled him. Most new faculty members kept a low profile during their first year. Mr. Richmond seemed determined to question authority. The dean had seen this type of behavior only once in the past. The other instructor had not survived probation. Tyler Richmond was in jeopardy of meeting the same fate.

CHAPTER 11

Heather left for her home in Bellville, Maryland following her last class on Friday. She agonized over what to tell her parents during the entire two-hour drive. She tested several different scenarios, but none seemed plausible. Eventually, she settled on a story that sounded almost reasonable. Initially, the reunion was strained. Heather did her best to put up a brave front. She hugged her mother.

"It's great to be home."

"You look really tired, darling."

"I'm fine, just studying too hard."

Her father looked skeptical. "Why didn't you call?"

Heather kissed him, and poked his ribs. "Come on, Dad, you know how it is. College life is so hectic. I'm really busy."

"You found time to call us last year."

"I know. I'm really sorry. You must think I'm a terrible daughter."

"No, but I miss your calls."

"I'll do better, I promise." She gave him a hug.

Her father managed a tentative smile.

"Let's eat," Heather's mother announced.

The family sat around the dinner table like they had in the old days. Heather gave her best imitation of a famished college student, but the food settled uncomfortably in her stomach. Later, in the living room, the main topic of concern came into the open.

"I'm sorry I haven't called home much," she apologized.

"You had us terribly worried, dear," her mother replied.

"I know, but I didn't know what to do, or what to tell you." Heather paused. "I've had some...some trouble. It started off innocently, but things got out of hand."

Bob leaned forward with concern etched on his face. "I want you tell us everything."

Heather took a deep breath. "I met a guy. He seemed real nice at first, but then he started asking lots of questions. He wanted to know where I was all the time. He'd get real jealous when I talked to someone else. Finally, I had enough and told him to leave me alone. He got real mad – I thought he was going to hit me. He started to cry instead, and told me he loved me. I didn't know what to say. I had no idea he felt that way. I started to feel sorry for him. Anyway, I told him we could go out again."

"You didn't," her mother gasped.

"I know it was stupid, but I didn't know what to do. He looked so crushed. After that, he kept calling. I kept giving him excuses why I couldn't see him. He started following me after that. Every time I looked around, he'd be there."

"Why didn't you report him?" her father asked.

"I thought about it, but he wasn't doing anything real bad. I mean he wasn't looking through my window or anything. I hoped if I ignored him long enough, he'd finally give up."

"Did he?"

Heather squirmed in her chair. "No. He kept it up for weeks. One night, when Molly was at rehearsal, he followed me into my room. He put his arms around me and begged me to love him. It wasn't like rape or anything...more like an obsession. I wasn't afraid. I knew he wouldn't hurt me."

"How did you know that? He could have killed you."

"No, but he talked about killing himself. That's when I got scared. I really believed he might do it."

"I hope you told someone."

"I started to, but he seemed to get better. I thought he was doing okay. He apologized for scaring me, and promised not to bother me again. Then, last week, he said he was leaving school. He mumbled something about joining the army and starting a new life. I haven't seen him since."

"Are you sure he won't bother you again?"

"Pretty sure. If he comes back, I'll call the police."

"You'd better," her father warned. "What's this about a night job? Molly told me you're out late on the weekends."

"Molly worries too much. I started a night job at the Stonewater Inn to get away from this guy. I work on the front desk. I didn't plan to keep the job very long, but I really like it. The people are nice and the extra money comes in handy. I've bought some great new clothes."

"What about your grades?"

"Don't worry, my grades are fine."

"What about Molly?" her mother inquired. "You used to be such good friends."

"Don't worry. Molly and I will be fine. You know how roommates are. We had a fight because I wouldn't tell her about my problem. We'll patch things up."

"I hope so," her mother replied.

"Are there anything other things going on?" Her father asked, cautiously.

"No, Pop. Nothing, I swear." The lie caught in her throat, and she swallowed hard.

"We're glad you're home, sweetheart." He took her in his arms and held her against his chest.

"Me too, Daddy. Me, too."

Heather slept late the next morning. She found it difficult to relinquish the comfort and security of her childhood bed. The room filled her with memories of a carefree past. Photographs of friends, cheerleader pom-poms, school pennants, sports trophies, stuffed animals, and an old music box increased her nostalgia. This room offered peace and safety. She touched each item and hugged a stuffed teddy bear. For a few minutes, she felt like a little girl safe in the bosom of her family. She held onto the moment for as long as possible. After a while, she made her bed and joined her parents for breakfast.

Heather excused herself after breakfast to drive around town. She needed time to revisit her past. Her father encouraged her to return in time for lunch. She promised to be back in a few hours, and made her escape. The conflict between craving family security, and having to lie to her parents caused her great emotional pain. She needed time to vent her frustrations.

She drove around the little town and made several stops. She visited the supermarket where she had worked during summer vacations. She paused at the Dairy Queen for a hot fudge sundae. Her final stop was Bellville High School. She sat on the bleachers for over an hour watching the football team practice. She recalled the soccer games she had played on the same field. Life had been so simple back then. It saddened her to leave the stands and make the transition back to reality.

Heather began the return trip to Stonewater after church services on Sunday. The parting from her parents was difficult. Her mother looked distressed. Her father begged her to call home regularly. She held off the tears until she had backed out of the driveway.

Molly was waiting when Heather returned to the dorm. "Well, I'm back."

"I can see that. Are you okay?"

"Sure. Mom and Dad send their love."

"Thanks. Did you patch things up?"

"Of course – piece of cake. We shed some tears, but everything's fine."

"I'm really happy to hear that. Your dad was close to panic last week."

"He gets like that sometimes. I'm still his baby."

Molly paused, and took a deep breath. "What about us? Are we okay?"

Heather dropped her overnight bag on the bed. She moved to Molly and took her hand. "We're fine. Give me a few more months, and I promise we can get back to normal. Be patient with me, babe." She gave her a hug.

"Why do we have to wait? Let's go back to normal now."

Heather shook her head. "I wish we could. I need to work some things out first – until then, no questions. Promise?"

"I'll try."

"Good. Let's get some supper. I'm hungry."

Molly followed her roommate out the door.

Heather spent the next five days dreading her return to the 'Fantasy Lounge'. As Friday loomed closer, her anxiety level increased. She remembered Carl's request for a special favor. The price for his generosity would be steep. She hoped she could repay the debt without losing too much more of her dignity.

Carl was waiting in his office, when she reported back to work on Friday night. "Hey, baby, we missed you. Several of the suckers asked me where you were last week."

"Thanks a lot for the time off. My parents aren't so worried about me any more."

"Good. We need to keep everyone happy. Ain't that right?"

"Sure," she replied.

Carl leaned forward. "Listen, I need your help tonight. I've got some high rollers coming in. They asked for a private dance in the back room. No big deal. There're four of them and they've got money to burn. I'll give you an extra hundred bucks and you've only got to dance twice. Some other girls will dance, too, and you keep all your tips. What do you say?"

"Do I have to take off my clothes?"

"Nah, only your top. It's up to you if you want to take off more."

She swallowed. "I thought I didn't have to dance. You said I only had to wait on tables."

He chomped down on his cigar. "Listen, baby, I did you a favor. I need you to help me out here. Are you going to do it, or not?"

Heather trembled under his intense glare. "I'll do it."

His stern expression vanished. "Good girl. I knew I could count on you. Go cool your heels for a while. I'll call you in a couple of hours."

"Just this once, okay?"

"Sure, baby, sure. Go relax and have a few drinks on me."

Claudia welcomed her at the bar. "Hi, honey. I missed you last weekend."

"Carl gave me some time off to go home."

"Yeah, he told me. He can be a real nice guy, but don't piss him off."

"I found that out. He wants me to dance tonight in the back. I tried to get out of it."

"Are you going to do it?"

"I've got to. I've never done anything like this before."

"It's not so bad. Just pretend you're somewhere else the whole time you're dancing. Let them look, but pretend they can't see you. Tiny will be close by if anyone tries to grab you."

"I don't know, Claudia. I'm really scared."

"Take it easy. Try to relax. Here, take one of these." She reached for her bottle of pills. "One is all you need to take the edge off."

"What is it?"

"It's sort of like Valium. One won't hurt you. I promise."

"Okay, thanks." She swallowed the little pill with a drink of ice water.

"Come back in a few hours if you need another one. I've got plenty more."

"Thanks." Heather left the bar and wandered into the lounge.

It took thirty minutes for the pill to take effect. Initially, she felt some light-headedness and later her metabolism began to slow down. The drug had a powerful calming effect on her brain. She experienced a sense of security in spite of her emotional torment. The thought of dancing naked in front of strangers seemed less repugnant. She waited for Carl to summon her to the back room. Her mind drifted back to her home and the comfort of her stuffed animals.

CHAPTER 12

Molly felt temporarily cheered by her friend's upbeat attitude. Initially, she exhibited brief glimpses of her old self, but her mood worsened as Friday approached. It was obvious the strain of preparing for the weekend caused her to become distant and morose. Molly had promised not to ask questions, but had not agreed to ignore the problem. Heather needed help, whether she admitted it or not. Molly was ready to spring into action, but needed to clear her schedule with Tyler. PLAZA SUITE was going to open in ten days.

"You want to do what?" Tyler was astounded.

"I need to skip Saturday night rehearsal. I've got to help Heather."

"You're not serious. Saturday is our first technical run-through. We're doing sets, lights and costumes. I need you here."

"I'll do what I can in the morning and afternoon. I just have to miss Saturday night."

"Listen, Molly, you made a commitment to me. What happened to 'the theatre is my life'?"

She bit her lip. "I'm sorry. This can't wait. You saw what kind of shape she's in. How can I not help her?"

His anger turned into frustration. "This is not the time. What are you planning to do?"

"I'm not sure. I've got to find out where she's going, and what she's gotten herself into."

"Why now? Why this Saturday? You could be getting in way over your head."

"I'll be careful. The show won't be over for two weeks. That's too long to wait."

Tyler resisted the urge to lecture on loyalty to the production. He, too, shared Molly's curiosity about Heather's mysterious weekends.

"You're asking for a huge favor. I can't afford to let any of my actors miss final rehearsals."

"I know. I'm sorry. You understand, don't you?"

His resistance collapsed. "Yes, I do. I want you to call me as soon as you get back. Do you promise?"

"I promise." She gave him a hug. "Don't worry, I'll be careful."

He held both her arms. "You'd better. I need you in the show. There's no understudy."

She smiled. "I know you only care about the play, but I'll be careful anyway."

"Get out of here. I've got work to do."

Tyler smiled after she left his office. Molly had unique powers of persuasion. He accepted his fate with resignation. He admired Molly's determination to help her friend.

Molly spent three restless days waiting for Saturday. Heather had lapsed into another funk, making conversation impossible. She went through the motions of going to class and attending rehearsals, but her focus remained on her roommate. Tyler noted the distraction, but let it pass. He had no doubt she would be ready to perform once the curtain opened. Molly could not ignore her responsibility to the theatre for any length of time. He had total confidence in her ability to bounce back.

Tyler had seen little of Sheila during the past two weeks. They managed one brief interlude on a Sunday afternoon and one late night meeting after a rehearsal. He chalked it up to his busy schedule, and promised to do better once PLAZA SUITE closed. She accepted the explanation, but he suspected she knew his interest in their relationship had begun to wane.

The pressure of a hectic schedule and the long hours spent

in rehearsals were beginning to take a toll on Tyler's nerves. PLAZA SUITE had become more than a theatrical production. He needed a major success to improve his standing with the dean and secure a permanent place on the faculty. He had lost some ground since his arrival and his future was uncertain. It would take substantial effort to convince the dean of his worth. A successful production might help his cause, but it would take more than just a good play to win the dean's favor. Dean Henderson needed to feel convinced Tyler was not a threat to good order and harmony. Ultimately, he needed the dean's endorsement to survive probation.

Stonewater College remained an enigma to him. She kept her traditions alive and her secrets hidden, but he had grown to love the place. The college, the town, and the valley were becoming part of his inner being. The purple hue of the mountains enriched his soul. The sincerity of the Mennonite people warmed his heart. He longed to become a permanent part of the landscape. However, his future in the valley was yet to be decided.

******

Molly spent most of Saturday afternoon assisting with final preparations for the technical rehearsal. Lighting technicians checked and re-checked the focus of the lights. Props were inventoried and put in their proper place. The costume crew pressed all the costumes and hung them on racks. Carpenters inspected set pieces and doors for durability. By 4 p.m., everything appeared ready for the evening rehearsal. At that point, Molly spoke to Tyler.

"I've got to shove off."

He eyed her. "Thanks for your help today. Get out of here before I change my mind."

"Thanks."

"Molly." She turned back to him. "Be careful, and call me."

"I will." She hurried out of the theatre without turning around.

Molly waited for Heather in the parking lot after dark. She had borrowed a friend's car. She focused on the red Geo Prizm while waiting for her friend to appear. Knots of anxiety twisted inside her stomach. Her breathing increased with each passing minute and fogged the windshield. The outside temperature plunged toward the freezing mark in the brisk November night. She stomped her feet and rubbed her legs to stimulate warmth.

Heather arrived twenty minutes later and unlocked her car. She wore a sweat suit and ski parka. She surveyed the parking lot and got into her car.

Molly waited until the Prizm roared to life before starting her borrowed automobile. She followed no closer than six car lengths while driving through Stonewater. She attempted to keep one vehicle between her car and Heather's at all times. Once her friend left the town limits, this strategy was no longer possible. She adjusted her speed to keep the Prizm's taillights in view. Heather seemed in no particular hurry as she traveled east through the countryside. In twenty minutes they arrived at the outskirts of Fallbrook. Molly could not contain her curiosity as they entered the quaint village. Nothing seemed threatening about the place. Heather passed through town and then turned down a narrow county road. Molly paused until she felt it was safe. She made the turn and caught a glimpse of Heather's car going around a curve. She followed for another mile before Heather drove into a lighted parking lot. She pulled off the road and waited. Several minutes later, she found Heather's car parked in front of the 'Fantasy Lounge'.

It took a while for Molly to fully comprehend the scene. The cheap appearance of the establishment not only seemed out of place in Fallbrook, it contrasted sharply with Heather's character. She could find no rational explanation for this. She snorted in disgust as she moved her car to the rear of the lot. It would not be possible to go inside. She decided to observe the activity from the shadows.

The temperature had fallen below freezing by the time Molly parked her car. She hated to turn off the ignition, but had no choice. A car left running in the parking lot would attract attention. Reluctantly, she switched off the engine, and took advantage of the remaining heat. She crouched behind the steering wheel and waited. Several hours passed. Automobiles, driven by men in rough farm clothes, arrived and departed. Molly shivered and her teeth chattered from the cold. She had almost reached the limit of her endurance when the lounge door opened. A huge bear-like man stepped outside. He lit a cigarette, oblivious to the cold. He smoked casually and observed the cars in the lot. She slid lower behind the wheel. The lounge door opened again and Heather appeared briefly to give him a message. Molly was outraged at seeing her friend's skimpy attire. The large man crushed the cigarette with the heel of his shoe and returned inside.

The whole scene only lasted two minutes, but the impact devastated Molly. Heather worked in this dump as a bar girl, or worse. She pounded her hand on the steering wheel. Desperately cold and confused, she turned on the ignition and headed back toward Stonewater. The car heater kicked into action after a few miles. The warmth was a welcome relief to her frozen fingers and toes. It took some time for her body temperature to return to normal. Once she achieved proper circulation, her mind began working furiously. A portion of the mystery had been revealed. Molly knew where Heather spent her weekends, but why was she there? How could she get her back?

It was after 11 p.m. Tyler should be back home after rehearsal. She decided to pay him a visit. The details were too shocking to discuss over the phone. She turned her car toward his apartment complex and hoped he did not have company.

Tyler was drinking a beer when Molly knocked on his door. The evening rehearsal had lasted four hours and he was fatigued. One beer and he planned to sleep for at least eight hours. Molly's knocking interrupted his plans.

"I thought you were going to call."

"It couldn't wait. Can I come in? It's freezing out here."

He ushered her inside. "Just for a minute. What's going on?"

"Can I have something hot to drink? Tea or coffee would be great. I was out in the cold for hours."

He groaned. "Is instant coffee, all right?"

"Perfect, thanks."

He left for the kitchen. She removed her coat and rubbed her hands together. She observed the interior of his apartment and noted the sparse furnishings. He was a man who required only the basics for survival. There were no frills or excesses anywhere. She viewed his extensive collection of theatre books and scripts with interest. She would ask to go through his library at some later date. Tyler returned with the coffee.

She sipped it. "Thanks. I thought I'd never get warm again."

"Where have you been?"

She told him the story of her exploits. She described the 'Fantasy Lounge' in detail, and how she had followed Heather. She included a description of the bouncer and Heather's sleazy appearance. He listened with total fascination.

"Are you sure it was Heather?"

"Of course. She was standing in a lighted doorway. There's no doubt who it was."

"This is crazy." He paced the floor. "It doesn't make sense, but she did drive there by herself. No one forced her, right?"

"How do I know? It's not like Heather. She would never work in a place like that."

"I don't know what to tell you. If she wants to be there, we don't have many options."

"She doesn't. I'm sure of it. You've got to help me get her out."

"How? It sounds like she might be in with a rough crowd."

"That's the point. I think she's in trouble. Please help her."

Tyler rubbed his forehead. "Listen, Molly. I've got a play ready to open in a few days. I've got a full teaching schedule and a career on the ropes. One major screw-up and I'm out of here. Do you still want me to get involved?"

She looked at him with compassion and desperation. "There's no one else. Heather would kill me if I went to her parents, or the police."

"Damn it, I can't! There's too much at stake."

Molly collapsed in a chair. "I can't do it myself. Look, if you could just get inside and check the place out, we could decide what to do after that. Maybe we'll need to bring in the police."

"When? The show plays through the weekend. I couldn't do it for two weeks. Besides, Heather knows me. She'd freak out if I showed up."

"Aren't you a master of disguise? I bet you could fool your own mother, if necessary."

"I might, but it's still risky."

She jumped up, and grabbed his arm. "One night is all I ask. No one will ever know. You do want to help, don't you?"

He shook his head. "I just see too many complications."

"You'll do it?"

Tyler's shoulders slumped. "Yes, but only after the play, and for one night only. Agreed?"

Molly wrapped her arms around him. "Thank you. I knew you'd do it."

"Don't get too excited. My involvement will be limited. Now go home. I need to get some sleep."

She put on her coat and left his apartment smiling.

Tyler could not fall asleep. He attempted to put Heather out of his mind, but the image would not go away. In spite of the obstacles, he had committed himself to action. There were plans to make and a date to keep with the 'Fantasy Lounge'.

CHAPTER 13

Carl reacted violently to Heather's lack of cooperation. She had danced in the back room as promised, but without any enthusiasm. The raucous crowd jeered at her stilted efforts to endure the humiliation. She managed to remove her halter-top, but covered herself with her hands. The jilted men booed and banged on their tables until Tiny appeared. He dragged her into the office. Carl slapped her across the face and threw her into a chair.

"You bitch! Are you trying to ruin me?"

Heather sobbed and kept her head down.

Carl roughly grabbed her face. "Answer me. If the word gets around my girls are duds, I'm finished. I'm not going to let that happen. Are you trying to wreck my business?"

"No," she whimpered.

"You promised to help me out. Instead, you stick a knife in my back. What am I supposed to do with you?"

"I don't know. I tried."

"Not good enough. You've got to heat those hicks up, and give 'em what they paid for."

"I don't think I can," she moaned.

Carl rubbed his head and paced the floor. "You're on real thin ice here. If you don't want to help me out, then Tiny'll have to convince you to do the right thing."

Heather held up her hands to protect her face. "Please don't hurt me."

Tiny grabbed both her arms from behind and twisted hard. She screamed in pain.

80

"Don't make her yell, stupid," Carl warned. "We don't want to attract no attention."

Carl put his face next to Heather's. His breath smelled of stale onions and beer. "If I really wanted Tiny to hurt you, he'd take you deep into the woods. He could cause you pain like you never felt before. You could scream all you wanted to and no one would hear you. Tiny can hurt you real bad and not leave any marks. He likes to hurt people, don't you Tiny?"

Tiny grinned, and nodded. She cringed in fright.

"Tiny especially likes to hurt pretty girls. He has a special treatment for them. Do you want to hear about it?"

"No, please." She covered her ears with her hands.

Carl removed her hands and stroked her hair. "Listen, Candy, I like you. I think you want to do the right thing. I'm going to give you one more chance. Take a break for thirty minutes, and I'll send you back in. You'd better not screw up this time."

Heather prayed for escape. Tiny stood grinning above her. He placed one of his big paws on her right shoulder and squeezed.

"Can't I just wait on tables?" she begged.

"It's too late for that. You promised to dance for the boys, and you're going to dance."

"I don't know if I can do it. I'm so scared," she cried.

"Scared, huh. In that case, I can help you feel better." Carl turned to Tiny. "Hold her down."

Tiny clamped both hands down on Heather's shoulders and held her fast.

"What are you doing?"

Carl moved to his desk and opened the bottom drawer. He removed a small metal case and held it up to her.

"This is the stuff dreams are made of. One little shot, and you'll feel like you could dance all night. Hold her tight."

He removed a glass vial and a syringe. He withdrew a small amount of liquid and tapped the needle. He tore open a sterile gauze packet, and picked up a piece of rubber tubing. He moved toward her. Heather stared at him with wide-eyed fear.

"Please, don't do this. I'll dance. I'll do anything. Please, don't."

"Too late, Candy. You blew it. This is your last chance. You'd better take it quietly."

Tiny increased his grip on her upper body. Carl grabbed one of her bare arms, and secured the rubber tourniquet around her bicep. He twisted her wrist to expose the underside of her arm and wiped the area with the gauze.

"Don't move," he warned.

Carl slipped the needle under her skin and punctured a vein. He hit the plunger and withdrew the syringe. Then, he removed the tourniquet and rubbed her arm.

"There, that'll get things going."

Heather felt a hot stinging sensation run up her arm. Carl continued to massage the area. She attempted to squirm out of Tiny's grasp, but he held her fast. Eventually, the pain went away and she slumped in the chair. Tiny relaxed his hold on her upper body.

"Now, you'll feel better," Carl retrieved his instruments and replaced them in the container. "Sometimes we all need a little pick-me-up. Don't fight it, baby. Let it happen, and you'll be all right."

Heather felt numb. She had never experienced anything of this magnitude. Her entire body seemed to melt into the chair. She recalled the sensation of being drugged at the professor's place. That had been painful and nauseating. This contained none of those elements. She felt calm and blissful.

"Just sit for a while, baby. When you go back in, you're gonna dance real nice for the boys. You're gonna smile and wiggle your ass like you really mean it. Do you understand me?"

Heather nodded limply.

"Good, and this time everything comes off – got it?"

Heather looked at Carl and had trouble focusing on his features. She wanted to run, but the drug had stolen her resolve. She agreed without understanding the question.

He patted her face. "That's my girl. Just to make sure you don't screw up again, I'm gonna send Tiny in there with you. You'd better not make him mad. He'd love to spend some time with you – alone. Are you afraid? Do you believe me?" She covered her eyes and nodded.

"Good. Don't let me down."

Pride and resistance had disappeared. The danger was real. She did the dance with all the enthusiasm she could muster. The customers showered her with money. Carl praised her efforts.

Heather awoke the next morning with a monstrous hangover. Her mouth felt parched and her head throbbed. She sat up, and waited for the dizziness to subside before standing. Thankfully, Molly had already left for breakfast. She was free to endure the agony alone.

A note waited in her mailbox on Monday morning with a familiar message.

Tonight. 7 pm.

The professor must have heard about her weekend. She expected a flurry of threats from him. The routine had become all too familiar. She was almost past caring. She had suffered so many indignities his threats had lost their shock value. Sensitivity and fair play were luxuries that lived in the past. Even the thought of committing murder seemed entirely within reason and not the least bit distasteful. She wanted to kill everyone who had abused her. Heather kept the appointment.

The professor glared at her. "What am I going to do with you, Heather?"

"Tear up the photographs, and give me my life back," she snarled.

"I can't help you any longer. You made some dangerous men very angry. It's out of my hands."

She stared at him in stunned silence. "You could stop all this, if you wanted to."

He gave her a helpless gesture. "No, I can't. Once I turned you over to them, I was out of it."

"Don't you see how sick this is?" she shouted. "I've been raped, drugged, turned over to gangsters, and forced to dance naked. What's next? You're responsible for all of it."

"Calm down," he warned. "It will serve no purpose to fix blame on anyone. Your only hope is to do what you're told. If you don't, you can only blame yourself."

"Real slick. I don't know how you sleep at night. You're worse than Carl and Tiny. At least they admit to being criminals."

"You need to worry about yourself. I didn't have to bring you here tonight. I could have let you sink on your own."

"You're a real prince. How can I repay all your kindness to me?"

The professor sighed and shook his head. "There's no way out of this for you. We have the photographs you already know about, and Carl has some nice new shots of you dancing nude. Who's going to believe you're an innocent victim after seeing those?"

"Oh, God!" Heather swung her fist at him.

He grabbed her wrist and twisted hard. "Listen here, young lady. I've had enough of your crap. You have one choice. Go back to work, and do what you're told. If not, I'll expose you to the world as a cheap slut. You've only got two months left. Don't blow it."

Heather squirmed in pain. He loosened his grip.

"I could kill you," she wheezed.

"Get in line," he scoffed. "There are many others who share your sentiments."

"When this is over, I'm going to bring you down."

"I doubt it. Others have tried and failed. Remember, I'll still have the photographs as insurance."

"You promised they'd be destroyed."

"My dear girl, do you really think I'd destroy that which gives me protection? My only promise is your service to me is over in two months. If you keep your end of the deal, no one will ever see the photographs. That's as far as I go."

"Somehow..."

"Don't waste your time. You're making things too hard on yourself. Do what you're told, and it will all be over."

"How do I know that?"

"You don't. You have to believe it, or you'd go insane."

"I think I've already gone crazy."

"You're fine. You have hate and hope to keep you going. Those are powerful emotions."

She stared back at him in silence.

"Go home and get some rest. If everything goes all right, you won't need to come back here again. Make it easy on yourself. I don't want to see you get hurt."

"I've already been hurt. It can't get much worse."

"It can, Heather, believe me. There is pain that never goes away. So far, you have no permanent scars."

"I have scars that will last for the rest of my life."

"You have your life, everything else will heal in time. Go home and think about it. You'll see I'm right."

Heather glared at him. "Go to hell! If anything happens to me, the trail will lead straight to you. Now, it's your turn to sweat."

"What do you mean?"

She had no idea how to respond. The threat had been invented spontaneously. However, the ruse gave her a momentary feeling of power.

"I've made some arrangements. Let it go at that. You'd better make certain nothing happens to me."

The professor appeared unfazed. "Don't do anything foolish. You already have enough trouble."

"We both have trouble. You'd better let me off the hook, right now. Think about it."

"I don't have to. Two months is the agreement. I have too much invested to let go. Do your time, and you won't get hurt. Don't threaten me again. Tiny wouldn't like it." He pushed her out the door before she could reply.

The professor clenched his fists after her departure. The

girl had become a danger to the entire operation. He wondered if he should advise Carl about her defiance. He decided to wait and see what developed. The idea that Heather might implicate him in the scheme was unsettling, but he considered the risk manageable. She had no proof and could only make empty accusations. This girl was more rebellious than the others. The professor cursed her audacity and regretted ever having met Heather Andrews.

CHAPTER 14

Opening night. The excitement backstage built to a feverish pitch as it got closer to curtain time. Tyler paced the floor in the dressing room as his actors applied their make-up. He kept his remarks to a minimum. He settled for random words of encouragement to the cast and crew. Nothing else needed to be done. The show was ready to open. Once the curtain went up, a director had little else to contribute. His final speech was brief and to the point.

"You've all worked hard. There's nothing else to do, except get out there and have fun. Break a leg, everyone. I'm proud of you all."

Molly beamed. She was in her element. She gave him a hug and gloried in his smile. Nothing was as important as this moment in time and she felt totally focused. Tyler returned her hug with appreciation. After that, he retreated to the lobby.

Most of the 400 seats were filled for his first production at Stonewater. Dean Henderson nodded as he passed through the lobby. The dean took his reserved seat in the fourth row. A theatre critic from Staunton settled into his usual aisle seat in the third row. He had been covering productions at Stonewater College for over ten years. His newspaper reviews were bland and forgiving. Southern manners dictated he should be gracious at all costs.

Sheila arrived fifteen minutes before the first act. She breezed into the lobby dressed in a full-length, light blue evening gown with a string of pearls adorning her graceful neck. She looked radiant. Tyler smiled appreciatively as she took his arm and kissed him on the cheek.

"This is your night, darling," she purred.

"Thanks. I'm glad you could be here."

"I wouldn't miss it. I know how important it is to you."

"It's not that important. My whole career just hinges on its success."

"Nonsense. You're already important to this fine institution. Where are we going to sit?"

"I sit in the back by the exit door. I might have to make a hasty retreat."

"Come on then, I'll guard your flank." She joined him in the rear row on the aisle.

The play opened with applause for the lush look of the set. It had been built to resemble an elegant hotel suite. Tyler felt a surge of satisfaction for the praise, and settled in to view the first act. The entire play went off without a hitch. He agonized as each new scene approached, but there was no need for worry. The cast and crew had rehearsed how to handle the multitude of cues. The audience loved the comedy and roared with laughter at the appropriate moments. Their enthusiastic response left no doubt his first production at Stonewater College was a resounding success. He accepted congratulations between each act, and the actors received a standing ovation at the curtain call. Sheila squeezed his arm as the audience exited from the theatre. Even Dean Henderson paused to comment before leaving.

"A very enjoyable play, Mr. Richmond. Please thank the cast for me."

"Thank you, I will."

"Good night Mr. Richmond, and to you Dr. Lawson."

The dean's parting look acknowledged their relationship. He did not seem to disapprove. Legitimate personal contacts between faculty members must adhere to his strict code of conduct.

Molly looked flushed when Tyler arrived backstage. She brushed past Sheila and embraced him. The other cast members joined her to participate in the celebration. He had a special word of praise for each individual and then addressed the entire ensemble.

"Something special happened tonight. You brought joy and laughter into the lives of 400 people for two hours. They are grateful to you. I am proud to be associated with such a fine group of professionals. We have three more performances. Let's make each one more memorable than the last. We'll save the celebration for the cast party on Saturday night. Enjoy the moment. Hopefully, you'll never forget this night— I won't. Thank you."

The students cheered and praised each other. Tyler let them savor the accomplishment. Very few human beings ever got to experience this level of inner satisfaction. Most of the young actors had never feasted on the rewards of artistic success before tonight. He envied their innocence and the thrill of their discovery. It was their night. He and Sheila slipped out the back door.

The word passed quickly about the success of PLAZA SUITE. The seats filled each night and the audiences responded favorably. Tyler had a hit on his hands and was besieged with questions about his next play. He fended off the inquiries with vague responses, but promised to announce the title of the spring production soon.

Barry Zucker attended the Friday night performance and invited Tyler and Sheila to an impromptu gathering at his place after the show. Barry and his friends toasted the director. Sheila beamed and hung onto his arm.

Barry pulled him into a corner.

"I'm proud of you, boy. You made your mark tonight."

"A temporary coup, but it still feels good."

"Temporary? Why son, a few more blockbusters like this one, and you can write your own ticket. We're starved for culture at the ol' Bible College."

"I'm still a dissident to the dean. He'll accept nothing less than total conformity."

"The old boy's a control freak, there's no doubt about that. So give a little, take a little. I've thrown so much bullshit at him over the years he leaves me alone. I used to dazzle him with my psychological insights. I've bored him so much and so often, he avoids me."

"A novel approach," Tyler replied, smiling.

"It works. Once he's convinced you're not a threat to his empire, he won't bother you."

"I'll have to try it."

"Relax, boy. Spend more time enjoying Dr. Lawson's considerable charms and less worrying about the dean. You've already made friends here, and we'll stand by you." Barry slapped him on the back.

"Thanks, Barry."

"Let's get back to our women. They deserve our undivided attention." He winked.

Ben Grubb came to the final performance on Saturday night. He wore his uniform and viewed most of the play from the rear of the theatre. The roar of his laughter was unmistakable, and Tyler smiled at the sound of his booming voice. Ben pumped his hand at the end of the show.

"I don't go to many plays, but this one was great. Good job, Doc."

"Thanks, Ben. I'll save you a seat for the next one."

"Hell, I'll come to 'em all. You can put me down as a regular customer."

"Glad to hear it. Thanks for the support." Tyler grinned.

"No sweat. Come see me sometime. I keep the coffeepot on and I can bore you with stories about the college. I don't get much company."

"I'll do that."

"Great. Good night, Doc." Ben squeezed his arm and made his way out of the building.

Tyler remained in the lobby until everyone had departed.

Many of them stopped to congratulate him, and others just smiled and nodded. PLAZA SUITE was history. The only thing left to do was tear down the set and celebrate the success with a cast party.

Tyler returned home from the party as the early morning sun inched over the mountaintops. He could not help but feel pleased. Exhaustion gnawed at him, but exhilaration kept him awake. Maybe, he could count on a future at Stonewater College after all. Nagging doubts interrupted his reflections, but he eventually slipped off into sleep.

CHAPTER 15

The pace of Tyler's life slowed considerably after PLAZA SUITE. He had time in the evenings to read and listen to music. He also looked forward to exploring more of a social life and expanding his circle of friends. He no longer viewed Sheila as a partner in a full-time relationship. Her tactics for survival were unsettling and in direct opposition to his approach. It seemed fruitless to pursue the relationship beyond occasional contact.

The matter of Heather Andrews was a piece of unfinished business. He cursed Molly for involving him in it, but then chastised himself for being insensitive. He recognized the potential for danger, but harbored a secret fascination for the intrigue. He invited Molly to his apartment to help him prepare as an undercover sleuth. She offered encouragement while applying a fake beard.

"No one will recognize you behind this beard."

"You do good work. Who taught you how to do make-up?"

"I learned mostly out of books, and lots of experimentation. I've tried to learn everything I can about the theatre."

"You've got a good touch. Let's put some shadow under the eyes and make the eyebrows a little bushier. I'll wear some old work clothes, a pair of glasses, and a farmer's hat. That should complete the disguise."

"You'll blend right in with the rednecks," she teased.

"Thanks a lot. I just need to make sure Heather doesn't recognize me."

"Don't worry, I don't recognize you, and she only met you once."

"Let's hope you're right. I guess that's it. How do I look?" He stood up for inspection.

She whistled in appreciation. "We did it."

"Let me finish getting dressed and you can judge the final results."

He retreated to his bedroom. Ten minutes later, he returned dressed in wrinkled work clothes, and a hat from a local feed store.

"You look positively...gruesome," she laughed.

"Good. That's the look I wanted. Where are my keys?" He patted his pockets and looked around the room.

"Here, on the table." She handed them to him. "Do you have everything you need?"

He patted his pockets once more and did a mental inventory. "I guess so. Wish me luck."

"I wish you luck. I can't thank you enough."

"I must be out of my mind."

"It's the right thing to do. You know it is."

"I'll let you know after I get back."

"Can I call you tonight?"

"I'll be home around midnight. Call me then."

"I will and good luck. I mean...break a leg."

"This isn't a performance, but thanks for the sentiment. Go back to the dorm."

Tyler squeezed her shoulder and walked her to the parking lot.

He got into his car and waved as he pulled away. He followed Molly's directions to the 'Fantasy Lounge'. It was 9 p.m. and the parking lot was half full. He waited in his car while studying the exterior of the place. He felt sickened by the look of it. The invitation to sin was unmistakable. He emerged from his automobile and trudged toward the entrance. He pulled the door open and stepped inside.

It took thirty seconds for his eyes to adjust to the dim light in the smoke-filled lounge. Country music played loudly from a jukebox. When the fog cleared, he observed several scantily clad waitresses moving between the tables. They teased and toyed with their rough looking customers. One precocious young woman bounced on a farmer's lap while he clung to her halter-top. His buddies encouraged her to bounce higher. Tyler scanned the room for Heather, but she was not in sight. He became so absorbed in his search he failed to notice the gorilla standing next to him. The 300-pound ape nudged him.

"Five bucks cover charge."

He made a concerted effort to slouch and appear non-threatening. "Oh, really? Is there entertainment tonight?"

The primate sneered and held out his hand. "Yeah, me. I'm the floorshow. Five bucks."

"Of course."

He dug for some cash in his pocket. He had left his wallet locked in the car. He peeled off a five-dollar bill and handed it to the bouncer. The bill disappeared inside Tiny's huge paw.

"Okay, have fun." The bouncer crossed his arms and resumed a vigilant pose.

Tyler moved to a table on the far side of the room. A perky, young waitress accosted him. She took off his hat and ran her fingers through his hair. His heart began to beat wildly at the thought of her touching the fake beard. He removed her hand and pushed his chair away.

"What's the matter, darlin'? I won't hurt you."

"Oh, I know that," he stammered. "I'm jest a might ticklish."

"You poor ol' thing," she teased. "I wasn't even touching your most ticklish parts."

Tyler laughed, and feigned embarrassment. "You're right about that."

"Well, if I can't touch you, what can I do for you?"

"You could bring me a beer. I'm real thirsty."

"Beer? Is that all?"

"Yes, ma'am, but you're real pretty to look at."

"Just for that, I'll bring you a beer. I like a man with good manners." She winked and skipped off.

Tyler resumed his search for Heather. She was nowhere in sight. He wondered if she had taken off for the night. The noise level increased as more customers stomped into the lounge. They seemed like regulars and knew the territory. One of them shouted for a waitress, while another yelled, "Where's Candy?"

"She's in the office. She'll be out in a little while," one of the girls replied.

"She'd better. I just love that woman."

Tyler's perky waitress returned with the beer. "The beer's two bucks, but I add on a little delivery charge. How's this for service?"

She moved behind his chair and pressed her breasts into the back of his neck. The pressure increased, as she bent over to place his beer on the table. He felt trapped by the weight of her body.

"That's, ah, quite a delivery system you've got."

"I thought you'd like it." She waited for her tip.

He pulled out a five-dollar bill and passed it to her. She tucked it neatly into her halter-top.

"If you need anything more, just yell. Everyone else does around here. I promise not to tickle you, at least not too much." She poked him in the ribs and scooted away.

The din in the lounge increased as more tables filled with working men. There was not a business-type visible anywhere in the joint. This was a refuge for the farmer, the truck driver, and the working man. The 'Fantasy Lounge' provided temporary escape from families and obligations. It offered an opportunity to bond with peers, and dream of savoring the pleasures of young flesh. Most realized their rough, callused hands would never caress the objects of their desire, but the fantasy was enough to sustain them.

Tyler observed this activity with mixed feelings of sympathy and resentment. He understood the need to escape from reality, but was disgusted by the exploitation. Most of the waitresses appeared more refined than their customers. They made attempts to sound earthy, but the effort was a facade to manipulate the lounge clientele. Tyler's waitress returned.

"Are you ready for another beer, or would you like some other type of refreshment?"

"No thanks, I haven't finished this one."

The waitress studied him intently and leaned forward on her elbows. "You're different."

"Why do you say that?" He shifted in his chair.

"For one thing, you're polite. None of the rest of these goons ever shows any manners."

"I'm not so different."

"Oh, really? Those hands of yours have never seen any hard work."

He removed his hands from the table and hid them in his lap. "You don't miss much, do you?"

"Not too much. It's obvious you don't fit in here. What's the story? You must be some rich guy out for a cheap thrill."

Tyler nearly choked on his beer. "No, I'm not rich—not by a long shot. I was just curious about this place and decided to drop in."

"You're not a tourist. In fact, there's something very familiar about you. I'm almost sure I've seen you before."

"Not a chance. I've never been in this place."

"Not here, but somewhere else. I never forget a face." The waitress stared at him.

He coughed. "What's your name?"

"Amber. That's what they call me here."

"What do they call you away from here?"

"Let's stick to Amber. It's safer that way." She looked around the room.

"Well, I'm ready for another beer. Can you get me one, please?"

"There you go again being polite."

"I can't help it. I've been brainwashed. By the way, you

can skip the special delivery routine this time. You'll still get your tip."

Amber got up from the table. "We don't get many like you in here. I sure wish we did."

"Hey, Candy! There you are baby. Come see me."

A young redneck on the other side of the room held out his arms. A new girl had just entered the lounge. It was Heather. She forced a smile and moved toward her admirer. He grabbed her and rubbed his hands over her body. She endured his groping with as much dignity as possible. Tyler resented this humiliation. Chivalry demanded that he rush to her rescue, but discretion took hold of the impulse. He would have to wait for a better opportunity.

Amber returned with his beer. "That will be two dollars, sir." She curtsied and placed the bottle on the table.

"You make me feel like an idiot." He reached into his pocket and pulled out another five-dollar bill.

"Thank you, sir. It's been a pleasure serving you."

"Get out of here, before you get me in trouble." He slumped in his chair.

"I live to serve. I'll be back." She smiled and wiggled off to another table.

Tyler's attention kept going back to Heather. She still endured mauling from the redneck and his friends. He picked up his beer and moved closer. He sat down at an empty table. There was nothing he could do, but at least he was in the right vicinity. He waited for the right opening.

CHAPTER 16

Heather cringed as rough hands squeezed the soft flesh of her thighs. She knew the culprit only as "Ronnie". He had exhibited a penchant for cruelty, and the level of torment he inflicted on others increased in direct relation to his intake of beer. Ronnie delighted in playing to the crowd at Heather's expense. She would be at his mercy until one of the customers or Tiny intervened. She made a feeble attempt at good reason and logic.

"Come on, Ronnie, let me go. I need to get your friends a beer."

"You stay here, baby. I don't want none of them other boys messing with you."

"I'll be right back. Don't I always come back?"

"Not fast enough. I need to put you on a leash or something." He thought this was hilarious and elbowed one of his friends.

Heather attempted to reason with the bully. "You know I've got a job to do. We don't want to make that big man by the door mad, do we?"

Ronnie glanced over his shoulder. He had had a run-in with Tiny once before.

"C'mon, Ronnie, let her go. I need a beer," one of his friends pleaded.

"Shut yur mouth, Frank. She ain't leaving here until I say so," he replied.

"C'mon let her go, and I'll buy the beer," Frank offered. Ronnie turned to face Heather.

"You promise to run right back?"

"I won't be long, promise."

"I'll come git you if you stall on me."

"I won't stall."

"Okay, but I'm watching you. Hurry back, you hear?"

He loosened his grip.

Tyler overheard most of the conversation. Heather had done nothing to encourage Ronnie and had used her guile to make an escape. He watched sadly as she loaded beer on her tray at the bar. He felt sympathy for the beautiful girl and sensed her dread as she prepared to return to the bully. Ronnie waited breathlessly.

"Good girl. You came right back. Pay her, Frank."

Frank passed her a ten-dollar bill.

"I'll get your change," she replied.

"No, you don't. Keep it. Sit down here with me." Ronnie swung his knee out from under the table and gestured for her to sit on his lap.

"I can't. I've got to wait on other customers."

"I'm your customer. Take care of me first. Sit here for one minute, and I'll let you up." He held up his hand as if taking a sacred oath.

She looked skeptical. "Do you promise?"

He crossed his heart with mock sincerity and attempted an innocent smile. It came across as an overt leer. Heather settled on his lap. Ronnie clamped his arms around her bare waist.

"Oh, that feels so good." He squirmed beneath her, and attempted to run his hand under her short skirt.

"No!" she screamed.

Tyler leaped to his feet, but Tiny was already there. He grabbed Ronnie's ear and squeezed.

"Let her go. She has work to do."

Ronnie's arms shot into the air. Heather jumped up and ran from the table.

"Next time, I'll beat the crap out of you – get it?"

Ronnie groaned and shook his head.

"Good, now have fun." Tiny released his ear, and returned to his station by the door.

Tyler caught his breath and sat down. Ronnie moaned and rubbed his injured ear. Heather sighed and returned to the bar. Tyler strained to hear the conversation at Ronnie's table. He wanted to make sure Heather was out of danger.

"Come on, let's get out of here. You can't mess with that girl no more. Tiny'll beat the shit out of you." Frank pleaded.

Ronnie massaged his sore ear and glared back at Frank. "She's mine. Tiny can't protect her outside. I want that girl real bad. I'll be waitin' when she gets off work. I'll take her away in my car and get what I want. She'll pay for this." He pointed to his swollen ear. "Are you with me, or not?"

"You're crazy," Frank shot back. "If you get caught, you'll go to jail."

The others nodded.

"Screw ya'll. I'll do it alone. But first, I'm going to finish my beer." He raised his glass defiantly.

Tyler grabbed a bar napkin and wrote a hasty note on the backside.

Heather,
Get out of here now! You are going to be attacked tonight.
A Friend

He folded the napkin in quarters and waited for a chance to hand it to her. Ten minutes ticked away before he saw an opportunity. She finally passed close enough for him to get her attention.

"Excuse me, ma'am. Could I get a beer...and could you take care of this for me." He passed her the folded napkin.

Heather stared at him. "Sure. Is there anything else I can get for you?"

"No thanks, but please take care of that for me." He nodded toward the note in her hand.

"Yes sir, I'll be right back." She moved to get his order.

Tyler watched her walk to the bar. She left the tray with

the bartender and exited into the ladies room. She seemed shaken when she emerged three minutes later. Heather glared in his direction before retrieving her tray. His body tensed as she approached his table. Her eyes shot darts at him.

"Who are you?" she hissed.

"It doesn't matter. You're in danger. Get out of here fast," he whispered.

"How do you know that?"

"I heard them talking at the next table."

Heather took a quick look over her shoulder. "Ronnie?"

"Yes. He sounded serious."

It took a minute for her to regain control. She passed the beer bottle to Tyler. "How did you know my name was Heather?"

He put his finger to his lips.

She frowned. "Drink your beer and meet me outside in ten minutes."

He nodded and paid for his drink. Heather tucked the money away and left his table.

"Hey, Candy. Bring us another round!" Ronnie yelled. He looked dangerously drunk.

She forced a smile. "Sure, Ronnie. I'll be right back." She rushed to the bar.

Tyler made an effort not to gulp his beer. He felt compelled to get Heather out of danger and struggled to control his anxiety. He leaned forward to listen to the conversation between Ronnie and his friends.

"One more beer and I'm gone," Ronnie announced. "I've got a date with a pretty little gal."

"Shoot, you're too drunk to do anything except puke," one of his companions taunted.

"Don't you worry none, boy. When the time comes, I'll be ready." The banter died when Heather returned with the beer.

"That will be eight dollars," she requested.

Ronnie pulled out a ten-dollar bill. "Keep the change, darlin'. You can thank me for it later."

One of the good old boys covered his mouth and snickered. Heather's hand shook as she accepted the bill. Tyler gave her a look of encouragement when she turned toward him. She nodded and rushed off to the ladies' room.

Tyler finished his beer and waited. He needed to appear unhurried. He watched Heather, as she buttoned her coat and moved to the front door. She spoke to Tiny and slipped outside. Tyler permitted the clock to tick off two minutes before following her. Fortunately, no one noticed him.

Tiny glared at him when he got to the front door, but did nothing to prevent his exit. Tyler muttered some words of parting and stepped into the parking lot. Heather was not visible. He wondered if she had escaped without waiting for him. He found her crouched beside her car. He could see she was breathing rapidly by the cold bursts of vapor coming from her mouth.

"Tell me what this is all about. How do you know my name?"

Tyler knelt beside her. "I heard Ronnie bragging he was going to attack you after work. You need to get away from here."

She slumped against her car. "Who are you? Your voice sounds familiar."

He hesitated before answering. "I'm Molly's friend, Tyler Richmond. Please leave now."

"Oh, God!" She stumbled to her feet. "How did you find me?"

"It doesn't matter. We'll talk later. Please drive away, before it's too late."

"I can't just leave. They'll come after me."

"Ronnie and those bums won't be able find you once you get back to the college."

"Not them. It's the others. You have no idea what this is all about. Why did you have to come after me?" she sobbed.

"What's going on here?" Tiny's voice cut through the cold night air.

Heather shrieked in surprise. Tyler's heart jumped as he

turned to face the huge bouncer. His mind raced to fabricate an alibi.

"She's...She's sick. I just stopped to help her out. She needs to go home right away."

"She ain't goin' nowhere. I've been watching you two. Something fishy's going on." He grabbed Tyler by the coat, and pushed him against Heather's car. "I ain't seen you before. What are you trying to pull?"

"Nothing. I was just trying to help." He gasped as he felt the force of Tiny's power against his chest.

"Bullshit! You two are planning something. We're going back inside."

Tiny grabbed Tyler's coat collar and Heather's wrist. He dragged them into the lounge, past astonished patrons, and into Carl's office. Carl was counting money at his desk. He looked up in surprise.

"What's going on?"

"I've been watching these two. He passed her a note and I found 'em outside trying to leave."

"Who the hell are you? What do you want with Candy?" Carl glared at him.

"Nothing. She was sick and I was just trying to help."

"He's lying," Tiny replied.

"Are you a cop?"

"No, I was just trying to help her."

Carl looked at Tiny, and nodded. The bouncer slapped Tyler across the face with astonishing speed and slammed his huge fist into his stomach. Tyler hit the floor gasping for air. The force of the slap tore off a large section of fake beard. Carl jumped up and ripped the rest of the disguise from his face.

"Who the hell are you?"

Tyler remained on the floor fighting for oxygen.

Carl ground his shoe down on his head. "Why the fake whiskers? Who are you working for?"

"No one. I'm alone." Tyler found it difficult to speak with his face mashed into the carpet.

Carl increased the pressure on Tyler's head. "Last chance, shit head. Tell me who you are, or you're tomorrow's garbage."

"I...I didn't mean any harm. I wore a disguise so my wife wouldn't find out I was in this place."

Carl removed his foot and knelt down beside him. "Listen here, I don't like people sneaking into my club and messing with my girls. If I ever see you again, you're a dead man. Do you understand me?"

"Yes," he wheezed.

"Tiny's gonna give you a little lesson to help you remember. There won't be no next time. Get him outa here. Candy and me are gonna have a little talk."

Tiny pulled him off the floor and muscled him into the parking lot. "Where's your car?"

Tyler's hand shook as he pointed it out.

"Give me the keys."

He reached into his pocket and handed them over. He considered escape, but the bouncer had a firm grasp on his collar. The pain in his stomach made running impossible. Tiny fumbled with the car keys and opened the trunk of the Toyota.

"Get in."

The trunk was small, but Tiny forced him into the tight space and closed the lid. There was little room to move or breathe. The car started and pulled out of the parking lot. Tyler tried to focus on the outside sounds and the passage of time, but dread interfered with his concentration. There was no doubt he was going to get a beating. He had not been in many fights, but needed to prepare for one now. He groped for a weapon. His fingers strained to locate something heavy. The only thing he could reach was his flashlight. He wrapped his hand around it and waited.

The car left the pavement and turned onto a dirt road. Tyler's heart skipped as the little car hit each bump and rut. The bouncing continued for several minutes before the Toyota came to halt. He banged his head and gripped the flashlight. The big man unlocked the trunk.

"Okay, shit head, get out. It's time for your lesson."

Tyler unfolded his legs and climbed out. Tiny seemed to enjoy watching his awkward exit from the trunk, and waited for him to get on his feet. Tyler exaggerated his discomfort and moved slowly.

"Do we have to do this? Can't we just..."

He never finished the sentence. He swung the plastic flashlight and it shattered against the bouncer's head. Tiny blinked and grabbed him by the throat. Blood poured down the side of the big man's face.

"Dumb shit! I was gonna go easy on you – not now."

The first blow caught Tyler on the side of the head. The pain exploded in his brain, and the force of the punch drove him to the ground. There were more blows to his face, stomach, and ribs. The whole nightmare became a blur of agony. The beating ended after he collapsed, bloody and dazed. Tiny kicked him in the ribs for good measure.

"Dumb shit."

He wiped the blood from his hands on Tyler's coat and got into the Corolla. He drove away leaving the college instructor crumpled on the ground. Tyler sank deeper into unconsciousness. Blood from his broken nose seeped onto the wet leaves.

CHAPTER 17

The musty odor of rotting leaves and damp earth was the first indication of awareness. Consciousness was a cruel reminder of recent suffering. Time and place were irrelevant. The intense cold and unbearable pain were all–consuming.

The mental fog cleared, and Tyler realized his injuries were serious. A sharp jolt of pain accompanied each labored breath. His head throbbed, and his nose stung from the ferocious beating. The burning agony in his stomach spread deep into his groin and legs. No portion of his body was unaffected by the assault. The specter of death hovered above him. He needed to find help, and shelter.

It took great effort to maneuver to his knees. Each motion increased the agony and taxed his endurance. He utilized a small tree to pull himself off the ground. Once on his feet, he wobbled and fought off waves of nausea. His nose was broken and one eye had swollen shut. His jaw was sore, but it moved. Several ribs seemed cracked, and his groin ached with burning intensity. In spite of the pain, he forced his body to start moving.

He located a sturdy stick and used it as a crutch. The darkness hindered his progress. He took his first few steps with hesitation, until he found an opening through the trees. The opening became more pronounced as he limped forward and adjusted the focus of his one good eye. He had found the route back to civilization.

The cold night air stuck in his throat and burned into his

heaving lungs. The beating had crushed his nose, and rendered it useless. All forward progress became a cautious exploration into an unknown void. The road was teeming with hidden danger: rocks, ruts, and tree limbs all conspired to block his path. Tyler maneuvered his damaged body over the obstacle course like a soldier negotiating a minefield. Every stumble sent shock waves of pain through his brain.

He had no way to record the passage of time. The sound of a distant truck offered the only sign of hope. If he could make it to the highway, he could flag down a passing vehicle. His extensive injuries and the blackness of night hampered an impulse to rush forward. His trek continued at an unsteady pace. Each step brought him closer to his destination, but the effort sapped his energy. The cold and pain intertwined to accentuate his suffering. Anger helped sustain him and thoughts of revenge drove him forward, but time was running out. His body would soon succumb to the elements, in spite of his strength of will. He stumbled onto the county road and collapsed. He had never been so happy in his life to see pavement. He settled down and waited for rescue.

The temperature dipped below freezing. The Shenandoah Valley braced itself for the first blasts of winter. Snow would arrive in a few days. Nature moved at her own pace and cared nothing for the whims of mankind. Every season had a purpose. Now was the time for living things to go dormant. Renewal would come in the spring. Until then, cold and snow would hold the upper hand.

Tyler shivered and waited. Long minutes crawled by. No vehicles appeared. Waiting for rescue was becoming a dangerous option. His body began to stiffen. He moved his fingers and toes to generate warmth, without success. He needed to move along or risk frostbite.

He made a visual search of the area and observed lights in the distance. He estimated them to be a half-mile away. There would be great risk in attempting the journey, but waiting seemed more dangerous. He staggered to his feet, and pointed himself in the direction of the farmhouse. He decided to take a straight line. It would be safer traveling along the road, but he needed to shorten the trip. Of course, he faced the possibility of attack from disgruntled farm animals, but that was the least of his worries. After what he had just been through, a confrontation with an angry cow seemed manageable.

The first challenge came from a barbed wire fence. He stretched it and navigated his large frame through the opening. Fortunately, the wire was loose enough to manipulate. Nothing stood ahead but a large open field leading to the lights. At least, the way appeared open to his one undamaged eye. He changed his mind as he stumbled over rocks and thistles. This was going to take longer than expected. He traveled up hills and through open gullies. Nothing major impeded his progress, but the effort of moving cross-country increased his exhaustion. He made frequent rest stops.

The farmhouse loomed large as he climbed through the last fence and stepped onto the driveway. The house was constructed of gray stone, and protected by a green metal roof. Outside lights revealed attractive landscaping. Tyler moved toward the front door. He was afraid of meeting an angry farmer with a shotgun. His hand quivered as he rang the doorbell.

A dog barked. Voices. Lights came on. He heard a man and woman discussing the disturbance. Someone tiptoed down the front stairs.

"Who's there?" A man called from inside the house.

"Can you help me, please? I've had an accident," Tyler pleaded, with a raspy voice.

A lock turned and the door opened. A man in his sixties poked his balding head through the opening. His face looked leathery and lined from long hours in the sun. His steel blue eyes, still blurry from sleep, squinted in the light. There seemed to be no threat in his demeanor. He appraised Tyler and inspected his injuries.

"What happened to you?"

Tyler searched for an explanation. "I...ah...had an accident. I mean my car was stolen. Someone beat me up and stole my car."

The man listened sympathetically. If he had any doubts about Tyler's veracity, he did not show it. He seemed primarily concerned about the condition of his visitor.

"Come inside. You need attention." He took Tyler's hand, and recoiled. "You're frozen. How long were you outside?"

"I don't know. It seems like hours."

"Let's get you to the stove. You need to warm up." He called up the stairs. "Rebecca, come down. We need you."

The farmer guided Tyler into a cozy kitchen with oak cabinets and a hardwood floor. A potbellied stove in the corner of the room radiated heat. He settled him into a rocking chair near the stove and threw a log onto the coals. Tyler felt a surge of heat flow over him. He held out his hands to speed the thawing process.

Tyler looked up at his gentle host. "Thank you. I thought I might die out there."

The farmer smiled. "You're safe now."

A plump woman entered the kitchen in a quilted bathrobe. Her gray hair flowed over her shoulders. She had a round face and rosy cheeks. She exhibited shock at Tyler's battered face.

"What happened?"

"He had an accident. He's been outside in the cold for hours." The farmer turned to Tyler. "This is my wife, Rebecca. I'm George Weaver. Rebecca, please get some warm water, bandages, soap, and alcohol."

She left to collect the items.

"I'm afraid all we can do is clean you up. I think you need to go to a hospital."

He looked up at the farmer. "I'm Tyler Richmond. I appreciate anything you can do for me. It just feels good to be warm."

"I know you hurt, Mr. Richmond. Your nose is broken. What else did they do to you?"

"Head, jaw, ribs, stomach. I don't know what else. I was unconscious for a while."

"You're lucky to be alive. Let's check out the damage."

George removed Tyler's sweater and shirt. There were angry red welts covering his torso and ribs. Rebecca returned with a basin of water and some towels. She washed the blood off Tyler's face, and gave him a wet cloth to hold over his nose. George dabbed his cuts with alcohol swabs and covered them with bandages. "There's not much else we can do for you. There may be bleeding inside, or you could have a cracked skull. We should take you to the County Hospital in Stonewater."

"Thank you," Tyler replied.

"Rebecca, get dressed. I may need your help. We'll be right back, Mr. Richmond. Stay warm by the fire."

Tyler huddled by the blaze. There were parts of his body still numb from the cold. His fingers and toes moved with effort, but appeared unaffected by exposure. The pain in his head and nose eclipsed his other injuries. The relentless pounding in his brain had not subsided.

His thoughts turned to Heather. He hated being dragged away from her at the 'Fantasy Lounge'. He hoped the two thugs had released her. Carl could not afford to endanger his operation by allowing Tiny to attack her. A disfigured college girl would attract more attention than a battered college instructor would. Tyler figured they had set her free, but would call Molly as soon as possible for verification.

George and Rebecca returned. Rebecca had arranged her long gray hair into a tight bun.

"I'll go bring the car around to the front of the house," George grabbed his coat by the kitchen door and hurried outside.

Rebecca remained with Tyler. "I wish there was more we could do for you."

"You've saved my life."

"We're happy you found us. Please don't talk anymore. You need to rest. I'll get you a bag of ice for your nose. We need to keep the swelling down."

She put ice cubes into a plastic bag, and wrapped the bag in a small towel. Tyler leaned backward, and placed the ice bag over his nose and forehead.

George returned to the kitchen. "Let's go."

The farmer and his wife assisted him out of the rocking chair. Tyler steadied the ice bag on his nose as they moved him toward the front door. When they reached the car, George opened the rear door and guided him onto the back seat. There was just enough room to stretch out. George waited for his wife to fasten her seat belt before putting the car in gear. The car tires crunched on the loose gravel as they drove down the driveway. The car heater pumped warm air into the back seat. The ice bag soothed the throbbing ache in Tyler's nose. George and Rebecca spoke in low tones. Tyler attempted to stay alert, but the warmth and motion of the car soon lulled him to sleep. He awoke with a start as the car door opened.

A hospital attendant reached for him. "We're going to take you into the Emergency Room. Are you able to move your legs?"

He shifted himself. The attendant helped him out of the car, and wheeled him into the treatment room. Tyler answered questions about his injuries and medical history. The doctor ordered x-rays of his skull and ribs. He wondered if George and Rebecca had gone back to their farm. The attendant pushed his gurney to the X-ray room and lifted him onto the table.

The doctor studied the x-rays before returning to his patient. "You're very fortunate, Mr. Richmond. No skull fractures, and there seems to be no internal bleeding. You do have a broken nose and two cracked ribs. You also have a rather severe brain concussion. I'm most concerned about the concussion. Whenever there is injury to the brain, it bears careful watching. Do you have anyone at home to care for you?"

"No," Tyler replied.

"That's too bad. I'm worried about dizziness and fainting spells. If you experience any vomiting or unconsciousness, I'll need someone to return you to the hospital immediately."

111

"I'm sorry. I live alone."

"What about those two people who brought you in?"

"Are they still here?" he inquired.

"They're in the waiting room. They're anxious to hear about your condition."

"I'd like to thank them before they leave."

"Of course. I'll bring them in."

Tyler touched the tape on his nose and ribs while waiting for George and Rebecca. His nose would never be perfectly straight again, but his ribs should heal in a few weeks. He heard the doctor talking to the farm couple in the hallway. The three of them entered after several minutes of conversation.

"I'd like to thank you both for taking care of me, and bringing me to the hospital," Tyler said.

"We're not done with you yet," George replied. "You're coming home with us, until you get back on your feet."

"That's not necessary. I'm fine." He attempted to sit up.

"You're not all right. I've explained all that. These good people insist on caring for you," the doctor informed him.

Rebecca smiled and leaned over Tyler. "You know, Mr. Richmond, the good Lord brought you to our door for His own reasons. Our work isn't finished until you get your health back."

"That's right," George agreed. "Rebecca hates to be kept from doing the good Lord's work."

Tyler smiled and looked up them. "It looks like you're stuck with me."

"You'd better wait a few days before you decide who's really stuck. I warn you, Rebecca can be a fearsome nurse."

"Good, that's settled. I need to give you a few instructions," the doctor advised. "I can't give you codeine for your pain, because of the head injury. However, Tylenol won't hurt you. Stick to a light diet for 24 hours, and no excess movement for 48 hours. Come back and see me in two weeks, no matter what. Do you have any questions?"

"No. Thanks for everything," Tyler replied.

"Well, it looks like you're in very capable hands," the doctor smiled.

George and Rebecca assisted him into a wheelchair. Rebecca patted his shoulder in a motherly fashion. He felt overwhelmed by the kindness of these two good people. It was not in his nature to lean on others for support, but he accepted this gift of aid and comfort. He needed time to heal. He winced from the pain in his head and closed his eyes. He would think about the future tomorrow.

CHAPTER 18

The sound of a barking dog filtered through the upstairs window. Rays of sunshine bathed the room in a pleasant glow. Tyler felt the warmth on his face, but hesitated before opening his eyes. He needed time to clear his head and get his bearings. The recollection of the previous night's events stilled burned in his mind. Less vivid was the memory of the events following the hospital visit and the transition from the Weaver's car to this cozy bed. He indulged himself in the comfort. He had no immediate interest in returning to reality. An old clock ticked somewhere in the bedroom. The sound of voices emanated from the kitchen below. George and Rebecca must be discussing the dilemma of having an unexpected guest. He thanked whatever fates had brought him to these good people. He covered his head with the sheet and appreciated the temporary security. Someone knocked on the door.

"Mr. Richmond, are you awake?" George called, from the hallway.

"Yes, come in," Tyler replied. His voice sounded strange to his ears.

The farmer entered carrying a tray with coffee and donuts.

"I know the doctor said to eat light, but one of Rebecca's donuts won't hurt you. I've been eating them for years and they haven't killed me yet."

"Thanks, I'm really hungry. I love coffee and donuts."

"That's a good sign. My German ancestors used to say that; a healthy body was the result of a good appetite and hard

114

work. I think it was a trick to make us work harder. Those old Germans were a cagey bunch. Do you take cream and sugar in your coffee?"

"Yes, please." He pushed himself into a sitting position. George prepared the coffee and handed it to him. "I wish I could say you look better this morning, but the truth is you look really awful."

Tyler attempted a smile, but facial movements took considerable effort. "Thanks, I believe you. I won't bother to look in the mirror."

"I don't blame you. Take my word for it, I don't think you could stand the shock." George chuckled and settled into a chair.

"In that case, I'll delay viewing the damage for a while longer."

He sipped his coffee. It tasted delicious.

George pulled his chair closer to the bed. "I know you don't feel much like talking, Mr. Richmond, but is there anyone we should call for you? We only have one telephone in the kitchen, and I don't think you could make it down the stairs."

He needed to call Molly to see if Heather had returned. He needed to inform the college he could not teach on Monday. He needed to notify the police about the beating and his missing car. He needed more time to fabricate an account of the incident. The effort of these intense deliberations increased the pain in his head. The calls could wait until he could get out of bed without falling on his face.

"You're right, but I'll use the phone later. By the way, please call me Tyler."

"Okay, Tyler." George patted his leg. "All you need is rest and some of Rebecca's soup. You'll be up in no time." He got up to leave. "Finish your coffee. We'll check on you later."

"I can't thank you enough."

"Don't worry about it. I'll send you a bill." He smiled and left the room.

Tyler took several bites of a donut and finished his coffee. The food warmed his stomach. He settled his throbbing head on the pillow and closed his eyes. There were numerous details to consider, but they would have to wait. He drifted off into oblivion – to a place without pain or responsibility. Time passed and the healing process continued. Much later, a soft knock on the bedroom door brought him back from a deep sleep. He strained his eyes to read the bedside clock. 5:10. He had slept for over eight hours.

He sat up. "Come in."

Rebecca appeared with a tray of food. She had arranged her hair in a tight bun, and wore lace bonnet. He recognized it as the same worn by the Mennonite ladies at the farmer's market. The sight of the smiling woman in her little bonnet cheered him. George and Rebecca were Mennonites. The revelation was comforting.

"I'm sorry to disturb you, Mr. Richmond, but you need to eat something. I brought you some chicken broth, a little bread, and some hot tea. The tea is made from special herbs and will help you heal."

"Please call me Tyler. You've been very good to me."

"It's our pleasure. Let me help you with the broth." She took a spoon off the tray and placed a napkin under his chin. "Would you like me to feed you?"

"No, I can manage."

She handed him the spoon and steadied the bowl while he took his first sip. The rich flavor stimulated his taste buds and passed with welcome relief to his stomach. Rebecca dipped a piece of bread in the broth and placed it gently between his bruised lips.

"You're a mystery to us, Tyler."

"I'm sorry. I haven't told you very much about myself."

"I know quite a lot, but it doesn't matter. You'd be welcomed, no matter what. For instance, you're educated and polite. I can also tell you have a good heart. The important thing is you're hurt and need our help." She dipped another piece of bread in the broth and fed it to him.

Tyler felt a pang of guilt for deceiving her. "I'm a teacher. I teach at Stonewater College."

"I knew you did something like that. I want you to try my tea. Let me help you." She lifted the cup to his lips and let him drink when he was ready.

He swallowed the hot, dark liquid. "I've only lived in Stonewater for four months, but I've learned to love the valley."

She smiled. "I've lived here all my life, and I love it more each day."

"I hope I can stay, but it's been a rough four months."

She viewed him with interest. "George and I want to help if we can."

"Thank you, but you can't get involved. They stole my car and nearly killed me for trying to help a student. I'm dealing with dangerous people."

She sighed and patted his arm. "You're safe here. Evil lives in the world, but we reject it. I pray you get well soon and return to a life of peace."

Tyler grimaced from the pain in his jaw. "I'm a peaceful man. Believe me, I'd like nothing better than to avoid trouble, but I've got some problems to solve before I can find peace."

"One thing at a time. First, you get well. I'm going to get you some ice. Your nose and eyes are still swollen." She got up to leave.

"Your tea is great medicine," he informed her. "I hope it's strong enough to cure my ugly face."

Rebecca smiled. "Your face will heal soon, Tyler. The human spirit takes a little longer. Be patient." She squeezed his hand and left the room.

He finished the broth and tea before sinking back on his pillow. The throbbing in his head had returned in force. He closed his eyes and thought about Molly's loyal support of Heather. Rebecca returned sometime later, and placed an ice pack over his eyes and forehead. The ice eased the pressure in his brain. She collected the dishes and turned off the light.

It did not take long for him to embrace the peace of sleep. Unwelcome dreams were the only intrusions during the long night.

Sounds from the farmyard woke him on Sunday morning. He heard the dog and chickens replay the refrain from the day before. The concert either celebrated the joy of being alive, or the anticipation of food. Food was the more likely cause for the ruckus.

Tyler stretched and felt an urge to empty his bladder. He eased his legs over the side of the bed. The dizziness did not seem unbearable, so he continued to move to his feet. He opened the bedroom door, and limped down the hallway to the bathroom. Once inside, he sat down and balanced himself on the toilet seat. The relief was exquisite.

The old claw-foot bathtub caught his attention. A hot bath would soothe his aching muscles, and clean his body. He turned the porcelain knobs, and waited for the tub to fill before lowering himself into the warm water. The sensation invigorated his entire being.

George knocked on the bathroom door. "Are you all right?"

"I'm fine," he replied. "Just taking a bath."

"Good for you. Call out if you need help."

George and Rebecca visited him before leaving for church. Rebecca wore a plain calico dress and her lace bonnet. George wore a black suit and crisp white shirt.

"We'll say a prayer for you," she promised.

"Thanks," Tyler replied. Her sincerity touched his heart.

"Why don't you join us for dinner after church?" George invited. "We'll be home by noon."

"I'll do that. I need to get out of this bed and move around."

"Hold on colt. Those wobbly legs aren't ready for the races. You'd better set a slower pace."

"I will," Tyler replied. "I just need to get off my back."

Rebecca patted his arm. "Drink your tea. We'll be home soon."

He waved as they left the bedroom and took the opportunity to examine his solitude. His first impulse was to call Molly. He gripped the handrail and maneuvered down the stairs. Dizziness returned as he reached for the wall phone in the kitchen. He sank down on a chair after dialing Molly's number. A female dorm resident answered the phone.

"May I speak to Molly Cross, please?"

Several minutes passed before she answered. "Hello?"

"Molly, this is Tyler."

"Tyler? Where are you? You've been missing for two days. I was afraid you might be dead."

"I know. They almost killed me, but I'm all right."

"Thank God, at least *you're* okay."

"What do you mean?"

"Heather is missing, too. She never came home Friday night."

"Oh, no. Don't tell me that."

"I panicked. Saturday morning, I called everyone who knows her. No one had seen her. On Saturday afternoon, I reported her missing to the campus police."

"Who did you talk to?"

"Officer Grubb. I also told him about you. I was afraid you might be in trouble. He's concerned about you both."

"Ben Grubb's a good man. I trust him. Tell him I'm fine, but we've got to find Heather."

"I didn't know what to tell him. I was afraid to say anything about the 'Fantasy Lounge'."

"That's where I left her. They took her back inside before I could get her out."

Molly gasped. "Are you hurt?"

"I'll heal, but the big guy gave me a rough time and stole my car."

"What can we do? I had to call Heather's parents last night. I hoped she'd gone home for the weekend. Her father freaked and is on his way to the college."

"What did you tell Grubb?"

"I wanted to talk to you first. I said she stays out late a lot, and I didn't know where she went. I could tell he didn't believe me, but he didn't press the issue. He asked me not to talk to the sheriff because he wanted to ask some questions on campus first."

Tyler evaluated the crisis. "Then the dean must know all about this."

"The whole campus knows."

"Listen, Molly, I've got to get back. I don't have a car, but I'll call you when I get to my apartment."

"Do you want me to come get you?"

"No, I can get a ride."

"Hurry back. The police keep asking questions, and I need your advice."

"Just keep the lid on. I think Heather got scared and went into hiding. With any luck, she'll come back when she thinks it's safe."

"I hope you're right."

"Me, too. I'll call you when I get back."

"Hurry, please. I need your help."

"It won't be long. Stay calm and things will work out. Goodbye."

He waited for the line to go dead before hanging up the telephone. The clock methodically ticked off the minutes. The news of Heather's disappearance sent shock waves to his brain. He had to find her. He would tear the 'Fantasy Lounge' apart and expose the whole operation to bring her back. He rose to his feet and nearly passed out.

CHAPTER 19

Mayor Bob Andrews could not come to terms with his distress. There was no one more precious to him than his daughter. Molly's phone call was the beginning of the nightmare. Heather would not just disappear. Something had to be responsible for her behavior. Bob refused to consider all possibilities. Molly made an effort to sound calm over the phone, but she could not disguise her fear. Bob attempted to glean what he could from her.

"I'm driving down to the college in the morning. I've got to find Heather. Will you help me?"

"Of course I will. I just don't know where to look."

"We'll look everywhere. Has anyone notified the authorities?"

"Yes, I reported her missing to the campus police."

"Good. If she turns up tonight, have her call me. It doesn't matter what time it is."

"I will – just as soon as she comes in."

Bob arrived in Stonewater Sunday morning and headed straight to the dorm. Desperate hope drove him forward. He refused to dwell on negative thoughts, but an inner voice warned him to prepare for the worst. He ran up the front steps and stormed into the lobby. It was 8 a.m. He dialed the number of the hallway phone. Molly answered after three rings and arrived downstairs two minutes later.

Bob's eyes pleaded for a miracle. "Is there any word?"

"No. She didn't come home last night."

"Oh God, where do we start?"

Molly collapsed on a lobby chair. "I don't know. I guess we can begin with the campus police. They might have some information."

"Let's go. I've got to do something."

He pulled Molly out of the chair. They drove to the campus police office. Ben Grubb had just checked in for duty when Mayor Andrews burst into the office. Ben did his best to calm him. He assured him it was not unusual for students to disappear for a few days.

"Sometimes they sneak off to other colleges for weekend parties or go to rock concerts. We've never had a student missing for very long."

"Heather wouldn't do that," Molly insisted.

Bob turned away with misery on his face. She regretted having spoken so abruptly.

"Did she have a boyfriend, or someone special out of town?" Ben inquired.

Bob shook his head, and deferred the question to Molly.

"No, I don't think so," she replied.

"That's all right. We'll figure this out."

Bob paced the floor. "Have you reported her missing to the sheriff?"

"No, not yet."

"Why the hell not?" he exploded. "She's been missing for almost 48 hours."

Ben took a deep breath. "The sheriff's office won't do much right away. They're used to students pulling pranks and disappearing."

"Pranks? This is my daughter we're talking about. Heather wouldn't just disappear."

Ben leveled his eyes on the frantic man. "It hasn't been 48 hours. If she's not back by tonight, we'll begin a full-scale search."

"I'm not waiting until tonight. I'm going to the sheriff right now."

122

"Suit yourself," the campus cop shrugged. "They may not be ready to cooperate."

"They will if I offer a reward of $10,000."

Bob turned away and left the cop shaking his head. He drove back to the dorm, and dropped Molly off to wait by the phone. After that, he headed to the sheriff's office.

Contrary to Ben's opinion, the sheriff's office took a keen interest in Heather's disappearance. The deputy on duty knew the sheriff wanted to exercise more law enforcement authority over the college. This was an election year and the sheriff could gain political advantage by demonstrating protection of the students. Also, a show of force might attract media attention. The deputy gave Bob directions to the local newspaper office and then he called the sheriff.

The *Stonewater Times* had not run a good story on the college in years. They covered the usual academic and athletic news, but no major media event had surfaced. An occasional obituary notice punctuated farm news, livestock prices, and weather reports. Church events filled the Saturday pages, but college news accounted for little space. The editor was desperate for anything of regional significance to produce headlines.

The skinny kid in the news office claimed to be a reporter. The fact he had acne and chewed bubble gum did little to reassure Bob. Unfortunately, no one else was available. The kid looked bored until Bob mentioned the reward. The reporter cleared his desk of assorted debris and grabbed a notebook. Bob spent thirty minutes relating all the facts in the case. In addition, he supplied background data on her family life and academic accomplishments. He fought back tears as he recalled tender moments from the past. The kid requested a photograph of her, and Bob supplied one from his wallet. The young man popped his gum and exhaled.

"Wow. This is a great story."

"I don't care about giving you a great story. I want my daughter back."

"Of course. Sure, sure. We'll run this on the front page. The rest of the staff will be in this afternoon to work on the Monday edition."

"Are you sure the story will be on the front page?"

The kid displayed his crooked teeth. "Mister, I've been here all weekend. Believe me, your story is the only one we've got."

Bob nodded, and thanked the young man. He returned to Molly's dorm. There had still been no word from Heather.

"What next?" Molly asked.

Bob rubbed his eyes, feeling the effects of emotional fatigue. "I need to talk to someone in charge around here. Who do I call?"

"The dean, I guess, but he's not in his office today."

"I don't care, I'll call him at home. I need more firepower to find Heather."

The college operator did not want to release Dean Henderson's unlisted phone number. Bob swore and yelled he had an emergency. The flustered woman agreed to have the dean return his call, if she could reach him. The dorm phone rang five minutes later.

"This is Dean Henderson. How may I help you?"

Bob rattled off the details of Heather's disappearance. He insisted the dean take immediate action.

"Have you notified our campus police?" the dean inquired.

"Yes, I have."

"In that case, I'm confident she'll be located."

"It's been almost two days. I'm not waiting any longer. I've also notified the sheriff's office, and the local newspaper. Are you going to help me or not?"

The dean gasped. "You what? That was very unwise, Mr. Andrews. We'll have panic on our hands."

"I don't care about your panic. I want my daughter back. I'll do whatever it takes."

"I see. Please give me an opportunity to make some inquiries before you make any more statements to the authorities. A general panic will not help us find your daughter. I'll call back shortly." The dean hung up.

Bob cursed the college administrator and slammed his fist against the wall. He refused to wait for some paranoid bureaucrat to take action.

"I can't hang around here. I've got to do something." Molly watched as he paced the hallway. Suddenly, he turned to her.

"I just remembered that Heather told me she worked nights at the Stonewater Inn. Maybe they might know something. I'm going over there. Would you wait here by the phone?"

Molly nodded as Mayor Andrews took off down the hall. She needed to talk to Tyler Richmond. Tears began to flow freely down her cheeks. She had never felt more alone in her entire life.

CHAPTER 20

Tyler limped down the stairs after George and Rebecca returned from church. He fought off his discomfort and attempted to clear his head. Rebecca looked up as he entered the kitchen.

"Where's George? I need to speak with him."

Rebecca observed the distraught look on his face. "He's in the barn. It looks like you've had some bad news."

"Very bad. I'm sorry, but I need to go home right away."

"You're not well enough. It's out of the question. You could fall and kill yourself. You need to stay here for a few more days."

He smiled at her motherly advice. "I wish I could, but I'm needed in Stonewater."

"You won't be good to anyone if you're dead."

"I won't die," he promised. "If you give me some of your tea, I'll drink a pot every day."

"I can't stop you, but I hope George can talk some sense into you. He'll be back soon."

"I can't wait. I'll go find him." He moved down the porch steps, and limped toward the barn.

Rebecca called out after him. "You'd better be careful."

He smiled, and waved back to her. Tyler found George opening a bag of grain. The farmer looked up in surprise.

"What are you doing out of bed?"

"I need to go back to Stonewater. Can you give me a ride?"

"You're not ready to travel. What's the rush?"

"I just received some bad news. One of my students is missing. She may be in danger. I've got to get back."

George scrutinized Tyler, and gestured for him to sit down on the grain bags. "Is this the same girl you told me about – the one you tried to help?"

"Yes. Now, she's missing. I can't stay here if she's still in trouble."

"I understand," George nodded. "But if I'm not mistaken, you nearly got killed helping her last time."

The pain of the memory crossed Tyler's face. "That's true, but I'll keep my distance this time."

" I wish we could do more to help. Rebecca and I have grown fond of you."

"I feel the same way, but I can't get you involved in this."

"Sometimes it helps to share your troubles with others."

"I don't want you involved in the investigation. The sheriff might come out here asking questions. The less you know the better."

"If that's the way you want it – I won't ask any more questions."

"Thanks. I promise to tell you the whole story after this is all over."

"Okay, I'll take you back on three conditions. First, you let us call every day to check on your progress. Second, you call us if you need anything. Third, you come back to visit after you feel better. I might even put you to work. There's nothing like a little farm work to clear your head."

"That sounds like your German ancestors talking," Tyler grinned. "I accept your conditions."

"Good. Let's go."

Rebecca insisted on packing a bag with sandwiches and homemade tea for him. He listened to her medical instructions and agreed to follow them. She dabbed tears from her eyes when it came time for the final goodbye, but seemed cheered when he promised to return. She waved as the car pulled away from the house.

Tyler leaned back and looked at George. "You know, I've been dying to ask you something."

"Like what?"

"I thought Mennonites drove buggies. How come you own a car?"

George looked amused. "Some of us do – the Old Order people. I still have a buggy in the barn. It belonged to my father. Many of us changed with the times, but we still hold onto our faith. We're against war and we follow the path of peace. Jesus taught us to love our fellow man and to forgive those who do us harm. We'll never change our basic beliefs."

"I've never met anyone like you before."

"We're not so different, but modern life is too complicated. We prefer to live off the land and stick to basics – our religion, our families, and our farms. That's it – not much else to understand."

"It's hard to believe life can be so simple."

"You should try it," George laughed. "You'd make a good Mennonite."

"I don't think I'd fit in. I'm not ready to forgive my enemies."

"Give it time. People can change."

George left him at his front door and wished him well. He made him promise to take his medicine and stay out of trouble. Tyler entered his apartment and found everything exactly as he had left it. It felt good to return to familiar territory. He collapsed on the couch and closed his eyes. It was time to call Dean Henderson. He dialed the college operator. She patched him through to the dean's home after he identified himself.

"This is Dean Henderson."

"Sir, this is Tyler Richmond. I'm sorry to report I won't be able to teach this week. I've had an accident and I'm badly injured."

"What happened?" The dean sounded skeptical.

He took a deep breath. "I was hiking in the woods and was attacked by strangers. They beat me and stole my car. I have a broken nose, a concussion, and cracked ribs."

"Did you report this attack to the police?"

"Not yet. It's taken a while for me to heal and regain my strength."

"I see," the dean paused. Tyler heard him emit a deep sigh on the other end of the phone. "It will be necessary for you to make a police report, but I'm concerned about publicity. Some of our students and their parents might not react too well to an attack on a member of our faculty. It would cause undue concern in some quarters."

Tyler considered the meaning behind the dean's statement. "I understand. I have no intention of involving the press. I just want to get my car back and return to work."

"That's fine. I'll have Ms. Plum cover your classes. I expect to see you next week, and I would like to have a copy of the police report."

"Yes sir. I'll bring you a copy."

"Good. Some things are best kept out of the public arena. I hope you agree with me."

"Absolutely."

"In that case, I'll see you next week. Goodbye, Mr. Richmond."

Tyler marveled at the conversation that had just taken place. There had been no gestures of sympathy or concern. The old man had also neglected to mention anything about Heather's disappearance. The entire focus had been on damage control. Both incidents could end up being an embarrassment to the college. The dean would not let that happen. Tyler remembered his promise to call Molly. He sat up and dialed her number.

"Molly, I'm home."

"I'll be right over." She hung up before he had a chance to reply.

CHAPTER 21

Molly was not prepared for the shock of seeing Tyler's injuries. His nose looked crooked and bulged under the tape. Both eyes were black and almost closed. There were bruises on his face and his lips had swollen to grotesque proportions. She found it inconceivable that he could greet her with a smile.

"I had no idea," she gasped.

"It takes some getting used to. I avoid looking in mirrors. Come on in."

She removed her coat and threw it on the couch. Under different circumstances, he would have been amused by her boldness.

"I can't believe what they did to you."

"It's real enough. I hope Heather got away in better shape. Is there any more news?"

"Not really. I told Officer Grubb you were safe. I didn't say anything about the beating, but he knew you'd had some trouble. He's coming to see you."

"I wonder if the dean has talked to him?"

"I don't know. He just wants to pay you a visit."

"That's okay. I want to talk to him, too. I think we can trust him."

Molly looked nervous. "Are you positive? How much are you going to say to him?"

"I'm not sure. I'll see how it goes." He rubbed his forehead. "You've got to think. Where would Heather run if she was in trouble?"

She grabbed her curly red hair and groaned. "That's all I've been thinking about. I've racked my brain trying to figure this thing out. I was her only real friend, but she still refused to confide in me. There's no one else. Someone must have kidnapped her."

He shook his head. "I know you're probably right, but she wasn't kidnapped for money. Everything points to the goons at the redneck joint, or one of her customers. Heather stood out like an irresistible target to someone with a sick mind."

Tears welled up in Molly's eyes and spilled down her cheeks. "Why didn't I stop her?"

He took hold of the distraught girl's hand. "You couldn't. Heather chose to go. She must have known the risks, but she kept going back. The frustrating part is we don't know why."

"I could have stopped her," she insisted. "I should have told her parents."

"You were doing your best to spare them. Most friends would have done the same thing."

"I know, I know," Molly moaned. "I still feel responsible."

He faced her with all the composure he could muster. "It is not your fault. We can't change what's happened, but you've got to believe she's coming back. They let me go. I'm sure they'll release her, too."

"Oh, I hope you're right."

"You need to go back to the dorm. You'd be the first person Heather would call if she needed help."

Molly retrieved her coat. "Okay, but I'm going to check back later. Do you need any food, or anything?"

"I'm fine. I'm going to call the sheriff and report my car stolen. If they can't find it, I've got to call the insurance agency."

"Good luck. I hope you feel better."

"I'm fine. Call me later."

She nodded and left the apartment.

Tyler sighed and went to his bathroom for some aspirin. The excitement had caused his head to start pounding. He swallowed two tablets and returned to the living room. He picked up the phone book and thumbed through the pages. The doorbell rang before he had a chance to dial the number. He opened the door and found Officer Ben Grubb staring at him.

"You look like shit. What happened?"

"It's a long story. Come on in. I'd planned to call you, anyway."

Ben followed him inside and examined the damaged face.

"Damn, you look like you've been stomped by an elephant. Hurts like hell, doesn't it?"

"Yes, Ben, it hurts."

"I thought so. Want to tell me about it?"

Tyler sat down on the couch. Ben sat down on a chair facing him.

"I was just about to call the sheriff to report my car stolen when you rang the bell."

"Your car was stolen, too? We do have a lot to talk about. By the way, wasn't that the Cross girl I just saw leaving?"

He regarded the campus cop with caution. "You know it was. You've been questioning her for two days."

Ben grinned and slapped his leg. "You're right. But you know, Doc, this doesn't add up. Here you are, looking like you've been attacked by a horny rhino. Your car's been stolen, and the roommate of a missing student just left your apartment. If I'm right, you had your 'accident' about the same time Heather disappeared."

"You're one hell of a cop," Tyler acknowledged.

Ben leaned forward. "You've got to admit we need to tie up some loose ends."

"How did you know I'd been in trouble?"

"The dean called me this morning. He asked me to look into it."

"I didn't explain very much to the dean. I'm trying to keep things from blowing out of control." He studied the man across from him. "Do you have to report everything I tell you?"

"Hell, no. I don't tell that old fart any more than I have to. I'm only concerned about bringing a young girl home."

"Me, too," Tyler agreed.

"I take it you know the girl."

"Yes. Her roommate is a student of mine. Molly got me involved in this and I've been trying to help her."

"Tell me about it." Ben took out a notepad.

Tyler told him the entire story from the beginning to end. He explained how he had first been introduced to Heather, and how Molly had followed her to the 'Fantasy Lounge'.

Ben looked up. "I've heard about that place. The locals have been trying to close it for a year."

Tyler went on to recount how he had assumed a disguise, and visited the lounge Friday night. "You know, I noticed a funny thing. Even though the girls wore skimpy costumes and cheap make-up, most of them seemed too intelligent to be in that dump. Heather hustled drinks right along with them."

The campus cop frowned and continued taking notes.

Tyler described Heather's confrontation with Ronnie, and how he had attempted to convince her to get away from danger. "I couldn't understand it. She seemed tied to the place and was afraid to leave." Tyler winced as he recalled his run-in with Tiny and the meeting with Carl Russo. "Those two guys looked like gangsters. The big one gave me these decorations." He pointed to his face.

Tyler told Ben about leaving Heather in Carl's office, the long drive into the woods, and details about the beating. "I've been recovering for the last two days with a couple in the country. I came back as soon as I heard about Heather's disappearance."

"Who'd you stay with?" Ben inquired.

He hesitated. "I'd rather not bring them into this. They don't know anything about Heather."

Ben nodded. "That's okay with me, Doc. I'm just trying to cover all the bases."

"That's it. I've told you everything. What do we do now?"

Ben stretched and got out of his chair. "You stay out of sight. I'm going to check out the joint where Heather worked."

"I've got to call the sheriff to report my stolen car."

"Yeah, I guess you do. Keep things simple. I don't want them to tie you in with the Andrews girl – yet. If we get her back, your name might never have to come up."

"All right. I'll use the same story I told the dean."

"Good." Ben put on his coat and turned to leave. "By the way, Doc. You did a good thing. It's not your fault she's missing."

"Thanks. I wish I'd done better."

"Don't worry about it. I'll do my best to track her down. Stay out of sight and don't talk to anyone. I'll be in touch."

"Thanks again."

They shook hands and the campus cop left the apartment. Tyler felt relieved to have shared his story with someone he could trust. He had faith the big man would keep the real facts under wraps while attempting to do his utmost to find the missing student. He returned to the telephone and dialed the sheriff's department. He explained about his stolen car. The officer listened, and advised him there might be a delay before someone could take his statement. Tyler hung up and touched his sore nose. He went into the kitchen to prepare an ice pack and make a cup of coffee. The ice relieved the ache and the coffee helped him to relax. The doorbell rang one hour later.

Tyler was surprised to find a tall woman with auburn hair and pale green eyes in his doorway. She appeared to be in her late twenties, and was fashionably dressed in a white sweater and gray wool skirt. She had the body of an athlete, and carried herself with poise and confidence. The attractive woman smiled as she reached into her purse. Her sparkling smile and natural good looks caused his blood pressure to jump a notch. The smile faded as she assessed his damaged face.

"Good afternoon. I'm Deputy Diane O'Malley." She displayed her badge. "Are you Mr. Richmond?"

"Yes. Please, come in." He ushered her to the chair previously occupied by Ben Grubb. "Can I get you some coffee?"

"No thanks. I've already had my quota. Sorry, if I surprised you. All the other deputies are on assignment. I'm the new kid on the force, so they sent me to investigate your missing car. I hope you don't mind?"

"Not at all. If I looked surprised, it was probably because I was expecting someone in uniform."

The woman smiled. "I do own a uniform, but don't wear it often. I'm a member of the Special Investigations Team. None of us wear uniforms. What happened to your face?"

He recounted the same story he had used on the dean. Deputy O'Malley took notes, and looked up from time to time to ask a question.

"How many men beat you?"

"I'm not sure. They hit me from behind."

She regarded him curiously. "That's strange. Most car thieves avoid violence. You look like you were beaten purposely."

The battered man squirmed in his chair. "I don't know anything about that," he replied. "I've told you all I can."

She searched his eyes. "Are you sure? It sounds like you might have left something out."

Tyler hesitated. "That's it. That's all I can remember. Everything happened so fast."

"It's not unusual for victims to leave out important details about a crime. I'm sure you're not omitting anything on purpose." Her smile burned into his conscience.

"Of course not."

"If you think of any additional information you will call me, won't you?" She handed him her business card.

"Absolutely."

"Thank you. I also need to have your occupation for my records."

"I teach at Stonewater College."

She looked up from her notepad. "Then, you must know about the missing student."

"I heard about it."

"Do you know her?"

"She wasn't in any of my classes," he hedged. "I hope you find her soon."

"Me, too. You know, Mr. Richmond, we might already have your car in the impound lot. I'll check there first."

"Thanks."

"I do wish you'd called sooner. It's important for us to get on a case as early as possible."

"I'm sorry, but I was in rough shape for a few days."

"I understand. I'll do whatever I can."

She put away her notebook and stood up to leave. Tyler's heart quickened as he observed the movement of her body. She wore no wedding ring. He prayed no Mr. O'Malley waited for her at home. The captivating woman had ignited an emotional response in him, despite the pain of his injuries.

"Thanks for coming over."

"That's what I get paid for." Her face expressed no deeper meaning. "I'll call you if I make any progress, or I might need to ask you a few more questions."

"That's fine. I'll be here. I don't expect to travel anywhere for the next few days."

"I don't blame you. It was nice meeting you, Mr. Richmond. I hope you're feeling better soon."

She extended her hand and he clasped it. The touch of her skin was magnetic. He relinquished the contact reluctantly and escorted her to the door. She departed after one last sympathetic smile.

Tyler retrieved his ice pack and settled down on the couch. He had taken the necessary steps to propel the investigation forward. Ben Grubb was on the right track to find Heather, and Deputy O'Malley had the details to locate his car. He remained hopeful for a positive outcome. After all, his injuries would heal soon, and he could always replace the Toyota. Heather's safe return was the only thing of real importance.

CHAPTER 22

The call came late Monday afternoon. Tyler answered on the third ring. Ben Grubb was on the line.

"They found her." An agonizing silence followed.

"Where? Where is she?"

The campus cop conveyed the dreaded news. "She's dead."

"No." Tyler almost dropped the receiver. "How? Where?"

"Some hikers found her by a lake this morning. She's been dead for a few days."

"How? How did it happen?"

"I don't know the details. We won't know anything for sure until they do an autopsy."

Tyler cleared his throat. There had to be more information. Heather Andrews was dead. Nothing could make the devastating news more palatable.

"Does her father know?"

"Yeah. He's still in shock. They had to give him a sedative."

"How about Molly? Has she been told?"

"I don't think so. I thought you'd want to break the news to her."

"I'll call her after you hang up." He whispered into the mouthpiece. "I think I know who did it, Ben."

"I know you do. It's time to set the record straight. It's too late to protect Heather. We've got to find a murderer."

"You can pick them up at the 'Fantasy Lounge'."

"No one's there. I spoke to a bartender named Claudia. She said the manager and the big guy blew town. They left her behind to lock up. Those two assholes must be out of the state by now."

"What can we do?"

"I don't know. We've got a hell of a mess on our hands. The dean is ducking for cover, and refuses to meet with reporters. The climate is pretty ugly, but you need to talk to the cops. The goons who killed her are getting farther away by the minute. I think you should tell the whole story to the sheriff."

"You're right. I spoke to a deputy yesterday. I'll call her back in a few minutes."

"Okay, but do me a favor. Keep me posted on everything that happens."

"Sure, I will. Thanks for everything. I'm glad you were the one to tell me."

"That's okay. Stay in touch." Ben hung up the phone.

Tyler sat frozen and stared off into space. The impact of Heather's death numbed him to the core. There must have been something he could have done. Maybe he should have moved sooner to rescue her. Maybe he could have called for help. Guilt and regret plagued him and drove him into melancholy. He made a silent oath to help find her killers.

His hand stalled over the phone. He was reluctant to call Molly. Unfortunately, no one else knew her well enough to assume the responsibility. He steeled himself to take on the formidable task. He picked up the receiver and dialed the number.

"Molly, this is Tyler."

"What's the news? Have you heard anything?"

He swallowed hard. "They found her. Ben Grubb just called me. They found her in the country by a lake. She's...She's dead."

He waited for a reaction. There was none.

"Molly? Molly, did you hear what I said?"

The tortured silence seemed to last an eternity. Tyler listened without further comment. Molly needed time to absorb the fatal information. A choking sob exploded over the telephone line.

"I knew it. She'd been gone too long. They killed her, didn't they?"

"It looks that way. Ben couldn't say how she died."

"Why? Why? She didn't do anything."

Tyler took a deep breath. No response could explain the tragedy. "No one knows...yet."

She fired questions at him. He had no answers and could only reply in frustration. "There's nothing else I can tell you. We'll have to wait for the autopsy results."

"I've got to do something. I want them to pay."

"They'll pay. We know who they are. I'm going to call the sheriff. We've got to tell the whole story. It's the only way we're going to find the killers."

"I know. But I feel terrible for her family."

"It's the only way. Are you with me?"

"You know I am."

"Good. I'll call you right back after I get done talking to the sheriff. Are you all right?"

"Yes, but please call soon. I feel so useless here."

He promised he would and hung up the phone.

Tyler searched for the business card containing Deputy O'Malley's telephone number. She seemed like the logical point of contact. He needed a sympathetic ally. If Heather's secret life had to be exposed, he counted on Deputy O'Malley to exhibit understanding and discretion. His instincts told him she should be the perfect choice. He dialed the number and waited for her to come to the phone. His heart beat rapidly as he considered his strategy. The revelations about Heather's weekend activities would have an impact on the investigation into her death. Unfortunately, he could not avoid hurting the people she loved. He had to tell the truth at all costs.

"This is Deputy O'Malley." Her voice sounded crisp and professional.

"Hi, it's Tyler Richmond. I need to talk to you about Heather Andrews. I have some information about the case."

"What a coincidence. I was just about to call you. We found your car."

"That's great. When can we talk?"

"Are you at home?"

"Yes."

"Stay where you are. I'll be over in a few minutes. I need you to come to the office to make a statement and claim your car. Do you feel up to it?"

"Sure, I'll be ready when you get here."

He went into the bedroom to change. He managed to move without much pain, but experienced a twinge when he bent over to tie his shoes. The signs of the beating were still evident, but the swelling had subsided and his vision had cleared. He finished dressing and waited. The doorbell rang twenty minutes later. The female investigator had a male deputy standing beside her in full uniform. Tyler felt uneasy. Neither of them looked particularly friendly.

Deputy O'Malley spoke first. "Are you ready to go, Mr. Richmond?"

"Yes, thank you."

They escorted him to the patrol car. The male deputy opened the rear door for him, and he slid onto the back seat. A screened partition separated him from the two deputies in the front seat. He wondered how many criminals had occupied this same spot.

"This is Deputy Jake Harris. He's on the team investigating the Andrews' murder. He's anxious to talk to you."

Deputy Harris glanced over his shoulder without saying a word. He appeared to be in his mid-thirties, and had the look of a prizefighter. Hard muscle stretched the fabric of his shirt. His face appeared to have experienced some rough times. He had either been in contact sports, or had suffered an accident. His eyes conveyed no humor and he wasted no effort on social conventions. This was a hunter in search of prey.

Tyler leaned forward. "You said murder. Do you know that she was murdered?"

140

"It looks that way. We'll discuss it in the office," Deputy O'Malley replied, coolly. The rest of the ride took place in silence.

After they arrived at the sheriff's office, the woman led the way into the building. Tyler and Deputy Harris followed on her heels. The desk clerk looked up with interest as they passed. The three of them stopped in front of a room marked *Interviews*. Deputy O'Malley ushered Tyler inside, while Deputy Harris closed the door behind them.

"Take a seat, Mr. Richmond."

He sat on a straight-backed chair next to a small wooden table. The stark environment and the cold stares from both deputies caused him distress.

"Is there a problem?"

Deputy O'Malley spoke first. "We found your car today. Do you know where?"

"How could I? It was stolen after I was beaten."

He watched as both deputies looked at each other.

"We found your vehicle near the murder site."

"Oh, no." He slumped in the chair. The impact of the revelation caused his heart to pound at breakneck speed.

"That's not all. We found Ms. Andrews' fingerprints inside your car. How do you explain that?"

"I've already told you. I don't know what happened to my car after it was stolen."

"Mr. Richmond, you're not required to answer our questions." She read him his rights. "Would you like to have a lawyer present?"

Tyler sat up straight. "What's going on? I don't need a lawyer."

She reached into her purse, and pulled out a small tape recorder. "May I record your statement?"

"Please do. It's a long story."

He began the account with his arrival in Stonewater and the events leading up to Heather's death. He described his relationship with Molly and the first meeting with Heather.

He spoke frankly about the experience in the 'Fantasy Lounge'. He omitted nothing and included Ronnie's threat. He ended by relating the graphic details of the beating, and his recovery at the Weavers' farm.

Deputy O'Malley regarded him with interest. "That's quite a story. Can you prove any of it?"

"Talk to Molly, I mean Miss Cross. I can lead you to the 'Fantasy Lounge', and to the spot where I was beaten. If necessary, I can take you to the Weavers' farm."

"I expect we'll do all that."

"Great, and you'll find out I tried to rescue Heather, not kill her."

"Are you willing to take a lie detector test?" Deputy Harris interjected.

"Whatever it takes, but you need to chase the real killers."

"It's necessary for us to follow up on all leads," Deputy O'Malley replied.

"I appreciate that, but you're looking in the wrong direction."

"We'll be the ones to decide that," Deputy Harris snapped.

They shot more questions at him to clarify the details of his story and released him two hours later. Deputy O'Malley drove him home, and advised him not to leave the area. He not only promised to stay in Stonewater, he offered to assist the investigation in any way possible. She smiled for the first time that day, and thanked him for his cooperation.

The next day the *Stonewater Times* ran the following headline:

LOCAL PROFESSOR QUESTIONED IN STUDENT DEATH

CHAPTER 23

Dean Henderson wasted no time summoning Tyler to his office. The scandal was beginning to take a toll on the old man's health. Even in the best of times, he suffered from a variety of maladies. High blood pressure, indigestion, migraine headaches, arthritis, and constipation were all part of his daily torment. It took every ounce of his endurance to project minimal levels of civility. The stress caused by this latest catastrophe nearly shattered his remaining equanimity. Tyler Richmond had good reason to feel anxiety. Dean Henderson glared at him with icy blue disgust.

"I'll get right to the point. Your arrest yesterday caused this institution great embarrassment. We are now facing one of the greatest scandals in the history of this college."

"You are misinformed. I was not arrested. I was brought in for questioning."

"The newspaper makes it look like an arrest. According to the reporter who wrote the story, you are the prime suspect."

"They questioned me because my car was found near the murder site. Whoever stole it must have driven it there. If you recall, I've already explained how my car was stolen."

"I find that difficult to accept. I don't believe in coincidence. I only accept hard facts. You have no facts on your side, only an implausible alibi. In short, Mr. Richmond, your story lacks credibility. In my mind, you are only worthy of contempt."

"I've told you the truth, and I've agreed to assist the sheriff in finding the murderers."

"Nonsense. It's all a smoke screen. You are involved in this case all right. I don't know how yet, but the stench of guilt is all around you."

Tyler had to control an urge to wrap his hands around the dean's scrawny neck. The old man had convicted him without the benefit of any evidence. He struggled to swallow his hatred for this self-appointed judge, who seemed ready to banish him from the college. The dean's acrimony had replaced sound reasoning, and no defense in the world could fend off this relentless assault. Nothing remained, except punishment for crimes he had not committed.

"You don't have the slightest intention of listening to anything I have to say, do you?"

"I want you out of here today. I want you off this campus. I want you out of this state." The dean's face turned bright red and his eyes bulged.

Tyler released his emotions. "What are you afraid of? You're losing control, aren't you? That's what it is. You might lose your job, and there'd be nothing left. You're at the end and you know it."

"Get out of here," the old man rasped. "I never want to see your guilty face again."

"I'm afraid you will. You see, I'm not guilty and I'm a damn good teacher. I'll be back."

"Never. Get out of my college!"

"Your college? I think the trustees might disagree with you about that." He turned and strode out of the office.

Tyler entertained no thoughts of leaving Stonewater. He was too entrenched in the murder investigation to consider that possibility. However, he had to neutralize the threat from Dean Henderson. He devised a plan to swiftly counteract the judgment against him. He wrote a letter to the college president and the Board of Trustees pleading his case.

The president of Stonewater College, Roger Colson, had deep roots in Virginia society, but spent very little time in day-to-day administration. Technically, he could overrule any of the dean's decisions, but rarely exercised the privilege.

In his letter, Tyler omitted any personal condemnation of the dean, but claimed his dismissal was totally unwarranted. He requested immediate reinstatement to the faculty. The next step required support from his fellow teachers. He obtained endorsements from Barry, Sheila, Ms. Plum, and several others. They promised to write letters to the trustees on his behalf. He would have to wait for the decision of the board in order to get his life back.

Deputy O'Malley called him later in the day and requested permission to come to his apartment. She arrived fifteen minutes later without Deputy Harris. Tyler met her at the door, but she brushed past him.

"We need to get a few things straight."

"Won't you have a seat?"

She shook her head and paced the floor. "You lied to me. I want to know why."

He rubbed his forehead. "I had to. I hoped Heather might still be alive. I wanted to protect her."

"Protect her? That lie of yours cost us valuable time. Why didn't you tell me you left her behind at the 'Fantasy Lounge'? We could've gotten a head start on her killers."

"I'm sorry, but she was a nice girl in a bad situation. I felt responsible for her reputation. I had no idea they'd kill her."

"Very noble, I'm sure. Don't you know there's a penalty for giving us false information?"

"I said I'm sorry. I hope you understand."

Diane stared at him. She almost seemed amused by his response.

"You're a piece of work – a real knight in shining armor. What am I going to do with you?"

"You said you were going after her killers. Does that mean that I'm not a suspect?"

She gestured for him to get to his feet. "Come over here and roll up your sleeves."

He followed her instructions. She inspected both his arms,

and the area around his neck and face.

"I see lots of bruises, but no scratches. During the autopsy, they found human skin under her nails. She scratched her assailant. You're clean, but I'd like to do a tissue match – just to be sure."

"No problem – whatever it takes. I need to get the newspapers off my back. You believe me, don't you?"

"I believe you didn't kill her, but you're right in the middle of this whole thing. There are still lots of questions to answer."

"I know. How did she die? Do you know yet?"

She hesitated. "We haven't released it yet, but she was strangled. There were some other bruises on her body, but nothing serious. It'll take a while to get back all the results."

"Is there anything else?"

She regarded him curiously. "Do you mean was she raped?"

He nodded miserably.

"No, she was murdered for another reason."

"I thought the guy in the bar could have done it – Ronnie."

"We're checking him out, but it looks like the thugs from the lounge did the crime. We've called in the FBI. We know the suspects have already left the state."

"I'm sorry if I delayed your investigation. I really want you to catch those guys."

"We'll get them, but in the meantime, I'd like your help. We need to re-trace your steps. I want you to show me everywhere you went that night."

"Sure, I think I can show you where I got the beating, and I can introduce you to the Weavers."

"That'll help. Is there anything else you can tell me?"

"Have you talked to the bartender? Maybe she can give you a lead on the other girls. I can describe several of them, but they all had fake names. One girl was called Amber. Some of them may be college girls, like Heather. If so, they're all running scared."

Diane nodded. "I think you're right, but let's take this thing one step at a time. I'll pick you up in the morning for our little trip to the country. I'll need to bring Deputy Harris with me. This visit was off the record."

"Thanks for trusting me. I want to help out in any way I can."

"You already have, but keep this to yourself. No one else knows about the cause of death."

"I promise, and I'll be waiting for you in the morning."

Tyler shook her hand. His skin tingled from her touch. He sighed and closed the door.

After her departure, he attempted to reconstruct Heather's final hours. Tiny undoubtedly drove back to the 'Fantasy Lounge' after giving him the beating. Carl most likely gave him the order to take Heather away. Tiny wouldn't have murdered her without orders from the boss, or he could have killed her by accident. At any rate, the helpless girl probably died at Tiny's hands. The image of her final moments caused him great pain. The cruelty of the act defied understanding.

Tyler remembered his promise to call Molly. She sounded out of breath when she answered the phone.

"I can't believe what they put in the paper. It makes you look like a murder suspect."

"The dean's already pointed that out to me."

"What happened?"

"He fired me," he replied, in a subdued tone. "At least, he wants to. I've already appealed to the Board of Trustees."

"That's bullshit! I'll start a protest. You're a hero, not a villain. We've got to make them understand."

"I've already started the appeal process. I don't want you to get involved. Several faculty members have already agreed to go to bat for me."

"The trustees need to hear from the students, too. You're a great teacher. Lots of other kids agree with me, and we'll stick up for you."

"Thanks, but this is my fight. You've got enough to worry

about. Let me handle this one."

"Not a chance. If there's anything I can do, I'm going to do it. You should know that about me." She paused and took a breath. "What's happening with the sheriff?"

He smiled. No one could argue with Molly when she was fighting for justice. "It was tense at the beginning, but now I think they believe my story. The FBI is looking for the real suspects."

"Did they say how she died?"

He remembered his promise to Diane. "They suspect murder, but haven't released the cause of death. Have they talked to you?"

"They sure have. I told them the truth about the 'Fantasy Lounge', and how I got you involved."

"Good, they're on the right track. I'm going out tomorrow to show them where I got beaten, and I'll take them to the Weavers' farm. I hate to get those good folks involved."

"I know. This whole thing's a mess. By the way, Mr. Andrews called me. Heather's funeral is Saturday in Bellville. Will you go with me? We can be back here Saturday night. I don't want to drive up there alone."

"I'll be glad to, but we'll have to take your car. Mine's still being held by the sheriff."

"No problem. I don't mind driving. I just need some company."

"All right, you've got me. I'd like to meet Heather's family, and extend my sympathy."

"Her father wants to meet you, too. I told him about everything you did to help her."

He shook his head sadly. "He won't want to hear what I have to say about Heather."

"He knows you tried. He's desperate to understand what happened."

"Me, too. I'll call you tomorrow."

"Okay. I'm sorry about your trouble with the dean. I know we can win this thing."

"I hope so. Get some rest, Molly. We'll see what happens tomorrow."

Tyler got up and grabbed a beer from the refrigerator. He considered what to say to Heather's father. He would have to destroy the man's illusions about his beautiful daughter. The facts defied understanding, but he would share the most pertinent fact of all – she hated working at the 'Fantasy Lounge'. Fear held her there as a hostage. Her final words in the parking lot still rang in his ears.

"I can't leave. You have no idea what this is about. Why did you have to find me?"

CHAPTER 24

The first snowflakes of the season fell on the valley. They danced with the wind during their descent and settled peacefully onto the earth. The thin white carpet sparkled in the early morning light. Later, the sun melted the fragile blanket and brown landscape pushed through the pristine splendor. The snow softened the impurities on the ground, but the relentless thaw brought back the stark scenery. Naked trees and barren earth were once again exposed without adornment.

Tyler observed the snow flurry from his apartment window. His mind focused on the swirling flakes and he felt a hypnotic attachment to the display. The feathery motion instilled a feeling of peace and relieved his distress. Reality would return once he left the window, but he felt content for the moment.

Eventually, he went into the bathroom to shave. He had neglected the chore for several days, and it was time to attack the stubble. He inspected his damaged face in the mirror. The swelling around his eyes had almost disappeared, and a yellowish tinge had taken the place of the purple circles. His nose had still not recovered, but it seemed less unsightly. All in all, his bruised parts were healing.

Diane O'Malley arrived after breakfast, accompanied by Deputy Harris. Jake seemed less sullen this time, but he still kept a wary eye on Tyler. Diane spoke for them both.

"I'd like to thank you for agreeing to assist us with the investigation, Mr. Richmond."

Her face appeared blank and impersonal, but Tyler noticed a twinkle in her eyes. He acknowledged the look with a subtle smile. The twinkle vanished.

"You're welcome. I want to do all I can to help you with the case."

Deputy Harris inserted himself into the conversation. "We need to know everything that happened that night, and inspect everywhere you went."

"I started here in the apartment and drove straight to the 'Fantasy Lounge' in disguise. Molly helped me put on the make-up."

"We already know all that. Let's drive out to the fantasy joint and take it from there."

Tyler followed the two deputies to the parking lot, and got into the back seat of the patrol car. He still felt uncomfortable behind the steel mesh screen, but the mood had improved since the trip to the sheriff's office.

Diane chatted easily, and asked a variety of questions. "I know you wanted to rescue Heather, but what was your plan to get her away from the 'Fantasy Lounge'?"

"I had no plan. I didn't know what to expect. Molly told me Heather worked in the place, and that was all. I had to find out if she was in danger before I did anything."

"It was kinda dumb of you to walk into a situation like that alone," Jake snapped..

"I guess it was. I thought the disguise would cover me. I only planned to look around."

"You're lucky they didn't kill you, too."

Diane spoke up. "We need to know everything you saw, and a description of all the staff. Even the slightest detail could be a great help to us."

They arrived at the lounge twenty minutes later. Someone had bolted the front door shut, and attached a red plastic sign announcing the place was closed. The three of them got out of the car, and the deputies followed Tyler around. He stopped at the far end of the lot.

"This is where I parked my car. Heather's was parked over here. By the way, whatever happened to her car?"

"We found it abandoned three miles south of here. They drove it into the woods."

"You said my car was left at the murder scene, and hers was found three miles from here. Tiny and his boss must have hurried to cover their tracks."

"They took off right after the murder. They emptied the safe and told the bartender to lock up. That was it. The 'Fantasy Lounge' went out of business."

"It doesn't make sense. Why would they commit murder if business was so good? The place was packed the night I was here."

"We're not dealing with rocket scientists. These are low-life scum without many smarts. Who knows, they might have killed Heather by accident. That's all part of the puzzle. Tell me again, what happened in the parking lot?" Diane insisted.

He described his urgent attempt to get Heather to leave with him. He told Diane about Heather's fear of being followed, and how she refused to run away. He tried to remember her exact words. Deputy Harris took notes as Tyler recalled the episode.

"She said something like, 'I can't leave. They'll follow me.' She made it clear she was more afraid of the owners than the customers. She also said, 'You have no idea what this is about, do you?' She looked trapped and scared to death."

"What happened next?"

"Tiny dragged us inside. He'd seen me pass the note to Heather and was suspicious. He took us into the boss's office."

"Is that the first time you met Carl Russo?"

"First and only time. He ordered the big guy to slap me around, and my disguise came off. After that, we were sunk."

Deputy Harris jumped in. "Is that the last time you saw Heather alive?"

"Yes. Carl kept her behind in the office as Tiny dragged me to my car. He locked me in the trunk."

"Did Carl indicate, in any way, that he might be planning to harm Heather?" Diane inquired.

"No. He said they were just going to talk."

Diane's final question caused Tyler's heart to sink.

"Why do you think Heather was working in a place like this?"

"You mean Heather, and the others. She wasn't the only one trapped in this dump. That's all I've been thinking about. I don't have a clue. We need to find the other girls."

"We'll find them. Do you think you can take us to the exact spot where you were beaten?"

"I think so. It's right across the road from the Weaver's farm."

They climbed back into the patrol car, and Tyler indicated the direction for Deputy Harris. He closed his eyes, and tried to recall sensations from that horrible night. The exercise brought back painful memories. This route had carried him to the brutal appointment with Tiny. A short time later, they arrived at the entrance to the Weaver's farm. Diane remarked about the rural charm of the place. Once they passed the farm, Tyler strained his eyes for the dirt road into the woods. After considerable effort, he directed the Deputy Harris to pull off the county road.

"There must be hundreds of horse trails like this. How do you know this is the right one?" Harris growled.

"I'm not one hundred percent sure, but the angle looks right."

"This road will play hell on the car," Jake grumbled, as they bounced over the rocks and ruts.

The bumps in the road conveyed a familiar memory to Tyler. This had to be the same route. The journey ended after they entered a clearing in the woods. They all left the car. The deputies watched as Tyler surveyed the area. The early morning snow had melted, leaving the bare ground exposed.

"Look over here," Tyler shouted. "There's my broken flashlight."

"Don't touch anything," Jake yelled out. "That's evidence."

He opened the trunk of the car and returned with a brief-case and rubber gloves. He opened the case next to Tyler and removed some plastic bags. He collected all the plastic shards and deposited them in the bags.

"Look, this large piece has blood and hair on it."

"I hit him pretty hard. I remember a lot of blood on his face."

"We'll be able to have the lab identify them for us," Diane advised. "It'll be interesting to see if these samples match the ones at the crime scene."

Tyler remembered the tissue found under Heather's nails. "It's hard to be sure, but I think I landed on the ground over there. My blood should be on the leaves."

"Stay put," Harris ordered. "I'll check it out."

He moved to an area where the leaves had been disturbed. He squatted and sifted through the ground cover with his fingers.

"This might be something. I'll take back some samples." He deposited a handful of leaves in one of the plastic bags.

"Is there anything else?" Diane asked.

"I don't think so, but this is definitely where he left me."

Diane patted his shoulder. "You know, the murder scene is about five miles from this location. If you were beaten and left unconscious here, there's not much chance you could have committed the murder."

He smiled and shook his head. "You must be a great detective to figure out what I've been telling you all along."

"I always wanted to believe you," she whispered. "I'm happy we have the evidence to prove it."

Deputy Harris joined them. "I think I've got everything."

"Great. Let's go meet the Weavers," Tyler suggested.

It had been less than a week since he left the Weavers' farm, but he missed their cheerful company. He wished he had called to warn them about this visit. They might feel concerned to see a sheriff's car rumbling up their gravel driveway. Now, it was too late to prevent the surprise. He would find time to explain later.

The car stopped in front of the house, and Rebecca met them at the door. She looked radiant in her white apron and lace bonnet. Her face registered alarm at seeing the two deputies, but she brightened when Tyler stepped forward. She smiled and gave him a hug.

"We've been very worried about you. Are you all right?"

"I'm fine. These deputies need to ask you some questions."

"We read about the trouble. I'm sorry about that young girl. George was afraid they might blame you for it."

"That's why we're here."

"George is in the barn. I'll call him up to the house. Come inside and have some coffee."

"Thank you, Mrs. Weaver," Diane replied. "We won't take up much of your time."

Rebecca ushered them into the living room and left to call George. Tyler and the deputies heard her ring a large dinner bell on the back porch. She returned to her guests smiling.

"I have to ring the bell pretty loud. George's hearing is getting worse all the time. He'll be here in just a minute. I'll go get us some coffee."

Diane thanked her, and turned to Tyler. "Well, there's no doubt these people know you."

"They not only know me – I owe them my life. They took me into their home without question. I would've frozen to death if I'd stayed outside much longer."

Rebecca returned with a tray of coffee just as George stomped into the living room.

"What's going on?" He spotted Tyler. "I've been worried about you."

Diane stood up. She introduced herself and Deputy Harris. "We're sorry to bother you, but we need to ask you both some questions about Mr. Richmond."

"It's no bother. This is a fine young man, and we want to do all we can to help him."

"What time did Mr. Richmond arrive here?"

"It must have been after 1 a.m. I checked the kitchen clock when we left for the hospital. It was 1:45," George replied.

Diane asked a number of questions about the incident, and the extent of Tyler's injuries.

"He told us he was trying to help that young girl, and I believe him," Rebecca insisted.

"We don't consider Mr. Richmond a suspect, Mrs. Weaver. We're just trying to tie up some loose ends."

"I'm glad to hear that. Tyler couldn't hurt anyone."

Diane smiled at him. "I agree with you, but I need to ask a few more questions."

The whole interview process took long enough for everyone to drink a cup of Rebecca's good coffee, and eat several homemade cookies. Diane thanked the Weavers for their cooperation and got up to leave. Tyler requested a few minutes to speak to the Mennonite couple in private. Diane said they would wait for him in the car.

"I'm sorry I didn't warn you about this visit."

"I told you we wanted to help. I was worried after I read the paper," George replied.

"They know who did it. I'll come back here as soon as I can, and tell you the whole story."

"You need to bring that pretty deputy back with you. She's got her eye on you."

Tyler reacted with surprise. "How do you know that?"

"I saw it written all over her face, and I'm not usually wrong about these things."

"George is right," Rebecca agreed.

"It must be a gift from your German ancestors," he teased.

"It must be. Come back and see us soon."

He promised he would.

Tyler viewed Diane O'Malley with renewed interest during the return trip to Stonewater. He hoped George was right. He looked forward to spending some private moments with the attractive deputy. The investigation might hinder his plans, but he promised himself to explore the possibilities of a relationship.

CHAPTER 25

Most of the town of Bellville turned out for Heather's funeral. Long lines of mourners stretched down the sidewalk in front of the First Baptist Church. Many local businesses had closed their doors for the afternoon. Buses arrived carrying students from Stonewater College. Heather's high school teachers and former classmates paid their respects. The church sanctuary overflowed with floral arrangements and messages of sympathy. The local florist had to enlist help from several regional suppliers to meet the demand. Heather's lonely casket sat closed beneath the pulpit, draped with a blanket of yellow roses. Tyler and Molly arrived an hour before the ceremony. The hundreds of people standing in front of the church stunned them.

"I knew the crowd would be big, but not this big," she exclaimed.

Heather's parents invited Molly to join them in the front row of the church. Heather's best friend needed to sit among those who loved her most. Tyler felt uncomfortable joining the select group, but Bob nodded a tearful greeting as he took a seat. The service commenced with somber organ music.

The funeral lasted much longer than expected. Everyone wanted a private moment with the deceased girl. Following the church service, a procession of cars followed the hearse to the town cemetery. Heather Andrews was buried on a cold, overcast November afternoon. Her killers still remained at-large.

Bob Andrews approached Tyler at the cemetery, and shook his hand.

"I'm glad to meet you, Mr. Richmond. Molly told us how much you tried to help Heather. We're having a few folks over to the house afterwards. Please join us before you leave."

Tyler said he would. Friends and neighbors had dropped off casseroles, sandwiches, salads, and desserts for the grieving relatives. The Andrews family had a houseful of guests by the time they arrived. Molly's acquaintances hugged her and offered their condolences. Tyler grabbed a deviled ham sandwich and circulated. Bob approached him a short while later.

"Can we talk in the other room?"

Tyler followed him into his study. Heather's father closed the door and offered him a chair.

"Molly told us some of the details leading up to Heather's death. She said you were with her the night she was killed. Can you help me understand all this?"

Bob's face conveyed total misery. His eyes were swollen and red. His body twitched and squirmed, as if controlled by an unknown force. His grief appeared to be all–consuming.

Tyler swallowed. "I didn't know Heather, but Molly asked me to help her. I only wish I could have done more."

Tears started to flow from Mayor Andrews' eyes. Tyler waited for him to regain his composure. He covered all the details up to the night of Heather's murder, and described his final conversation with her.

"I'm convinced she hated working at the 'Fantasy Lounge'. Someone was holding her there against her will. I tried to take her away, but she was afraid to leave."

"None of this makes sense. She'd never work in a place like that."

"We think we know who killed her. We don't know why, and we don't know how she got mixed up with that bunch. Another thing that disturbs me is there were other girls in the lounge like, Heather – attractive, intelligent girls. I'll bet anything they were Stonewater students, too."

"I've got to know," Bob sobbed. "I won't rest until I find the people responsible. Heather was the most precious thing in my life. I won't let her memory get smeared by scandal."

Tyler considered his response. "You can be proud of Heather. I saw her as a brave, strong-willed young lady. She never wanted you to know about her trouble, and she did her best to survive in an ugly situation. The police are going to solve the murder, and I'll bet her reputation will be cleared once the truth is revealed."

"Thank you," Bob replied. "I know you were attacked trying to help her."

"I'll heal, and I'm in this thing until the end. The investigation might help us save others."

"I'll do anything you need. Please call me at any time."

"I will," Tyler promised.

Bob thanked him again, and returned to grieve with his family and friends.

Molly drove them back to Stonewater later that afternoon. They talked about the funeral, and the gathering at Heather's home. Tyler shared portions of his conversation with Heather's father. Molly insisted she wanted to participate in the investigation.

"The sheriff might not appreciate us getting in the way," Tyler advised. "I'm going to meet with Ben Grubb tomorrow and see if we can track down those other girls. I'm convinced they're the key to this whole thing."

He called Ben the next day and asked him to come to the apartment. The sheriff's department still held his Toyota. If they didn't release his car soon, he'd have to consider a rental. The injuries no longer hindered his mobility, and he wanted to participate in the investigation.

The campus cop arrived one hour after being called. "Looks like you're kinda stuck here."

"I need a car. There's a lot of work to do. We've got to find those missing waitresses."

"Slow down, Einstein. The sheriff's running the investigation."

"They're looking for a murderer. We know who that is.

I'm looking for something else."

Ben viewed Tyler with a mixture of amusement and respect. "You don't quit, do you? I heard the dean fired you, and you still won't give up. You're either a real dumb shit, or a remarkable human being."

"I'm neither. I didn't deserve to be fired, and I care a lot about Heather's murder. I got mixed up in this thing with her, and I'm going to see it through to the end. I can't stand by and watch someone else do all the work. If I'm not mistaken, I think you feel the same way."

Ben smiled broadly. "You're a real smart ass, Doc. I shouldn't stick my neck out for you, but I've got a real soft spot for fools who tangle with the dean. Yeah, and I care about the dead girl. I care about all the kids."

Tyler smiled in return. "I knew that. Let's get down to work. The key to finding the waitresses is the bartender."

"I've already talked to her, and the sheriff's men have grilled her, too. She musta gotten a big payoff from the bad boys, because she's developed a real bad case of amnesia. She won't admit to knowing the Andrews girl, or any of the other girls."

"That makes it tough. We need to try again. I can describe a few of the girls and I got a good look at Amber. If we ask around, maybe we can find her and the others."

"It's a long shot. We're not even sure they're on campus."

"I know, but it's a start. We might get lucky. All we need is for one of them to talk."

Ben shook his head. "All right, I'm with you. We'll give it a shot. I'm also going to check with student records. If the other girls are students, they could've dropped out of school. We might be able to track them down that way."

"Ben, you're a genius. I knew you were a great cop."

"You may not think so if I get fired, too. Give me those descriptions and I'll start asking questions."

Tyler spent the next thirty minutes attempting to recall the physical characteristics of each waitress. Ben took notes and left the apartment with a promise to call if anything developed.

Two days later, Tyler received a call from the secretary to the college president. President Colson would like to see him in his office at 2 p.m. that afternoon. Would he be available to make the appointment? He hung up the phone with feelings of optimism, and a degree of trepidation.

President Roger Colson greeted Tyler as he entered the spacious office. The room had been designed to project an image of southern elegance. The mahogany furniture, the plush carpet, the extensive book collection, the large college crest behind the desk, and the display of flags around the room were all intended to impress. Colson fit into the environment perfectly with his styled silver hair and expensive gray suit. He looked like the perfect prototype of a refined Virginia gentleman.

"I'm very pleased to meet you, Mr. Richmond. I regret we haven't had an opportunity to become acquainted." They shook hands and the president offered Tyler a seat in a French provincial chair.

"It's an honor, sir."

President Colson sighed and sat down on a matching chair. "These are very difficult times at Stonewater College. The death of Ms. Andrews has us all deeply disturbed."

Tyler nodded, but kept silent. The college president continued.

"The Board of Trustees requested that I hold this meeting with you. They received your letter petitioning for reinstatement to our faculty. There has also been strong support for you from some members of our faculty, and a number of students. You'll be pleased to hear the sheriff sent me a letter verifying you are not a suspect in the case. He also praised you for actively assisting with the investigation. In light of these developments, the trustees directed me to rescind your dismissal."

Tyler had to fight back an impulse to jump out of his

chair and shout for joy. He replied in a barely controlled voice.

"Thank you, sir. I love teaching at Stonewater, and I look forward to a long association with the college."

"Please understand Mr. Richmond, the reinstatement does not guarantee a contract extension beyond this year. You will be judged on your teaching ability and overall contributions to the college at the end of next semester."

"I understand. Dean Henderson made that point clear on a number of occasions."

President Colson reacted almost imperceptibly to the trace of bitterness in his remark. "Dean Henderson has been a valuable asset to this college for many years. We rely on his judgment in our continuing pursuit of academic excellence. Admittedly, this latest crisis has us all on edge. Your dismissal turned out to be premature. I assure you, your final evaluation will be fair and impartial."

"That's all I can ask," Tyler replied. "I'll do my best to earn your approval."

"I'm sure you will," the president smiled. "I wish I had more time to interact with our faculty, but it's just not possible. I will keep an eye on your progress, and I wish you well."

"Thank you, and please thank the trustees for me."

"I will."

They shook hands and Tyler left the office. He felt elated to have been given a new lease on his career.

Diane O'Malley stopped by his apartment the next morning. She wore blue jeans and a FBI Academy sweatshirt. He enjoyed seeing her dressed casually.

"Is this visit social, or official?" he inquired, smiling.

"Official, of course." She returned his smile. "It's my day off, but I thought you could use some good news. We're finished with your car, and you can pick it up today."

"Great, I need transportation to work. I got my job back yesterday."

She could not disguise her delight. "That's wonderful.

I'm very happy for you."

"I had great support from my friends, and it seems the sheriff wrote a letter on my behalf. I wonder who asked him to do that?"

She blushed. "Someone must have cared enough to set the record straight."

He looked into her soft, green eyes. "I'm greatly indebted to that someone. If you ever find out who it is, I'd like to thank them personally."

"I'll see what I can do," she responded.

He asked about her sweatshirt. "FBI Academy?"

"Honor graduate, and former agent."

"What happened?"

"It's a long story," she replied, vaguely.

"I'm sorry. It's none of my business."

"That's all right. It's ancient history. I made the mistake of marrying my supervisor. Our careers and our marriage were not compatible. He went on to get promoted and I got out of the FBI – and the marriage. That's why I'm here."

"Lucky for me."

"You may change your mind about that."

He took hold of her hand. "Not a chance. I have not begun to show you my gratitude."

She pulled out of his grasp. "You shouldn't get mixed up with a cop. The timing is not very good right now."

"Now that I have my job back, I have time to wait. I'd like to take you out to dinner soon – for official reasons only."

"We'll see," she replied. "Come on, I'll drive you to the impound lot to get your car. I hate to see a man left stranded and all alone."

Diane walked him through the process of signing the necessary papers to claim his car. After the attendant handed him the keys, he regarded the Toyota sadly.

"You know, I don't think I can ever drive this car again without thinking about Heather."

She nodded sympathetically. "I know what you mean."

"It's time for a new car and a new start. I have a job for at least six more months, and my personal life is looking up. Can you point me in the direction of a good used car dealership?"

She gave him directions to a reputable establishment, and waved goodbye.

The owner of the dealership greeted Tyler with a smile. He accepted the Toyota as down payment on a seven-year-old BMW 318i. The BMW had just arrived on the lot, and the dealer arranged low monthly payments. Tyler drove away, after one last look of regret at the Corolla. He felt as if he had discarded an old friend. But the BMW would carry him into the future. He hoped Diane would become a prominent part of that future.

CHAPTER 26

The professor's world had begun to unravel. It had been ten days since Heather's murder, and events were spinning out of control. Carl and Tiny were on the run. His former business associates or any of the female students could identify him. He faced the possibility of exposure and being charged as an accessory to murder. He had already taken steps to protect his identity. Carl and Tiny would not implicate him. The gangster code would not permit them to rat on a partner in crime. He contacted each one of the girls. He reminded them of the photographs and the damage they could still cause. He promised to protect their secret, if they promised to maintain their silence. However, he could not afford to keep them on campus. He told each student to transfer to another college out of state. All of the girls agreed to his terms, except Amy Flanders, who paid him a visit.

She released her anger in a venomous outburst. "You killed her. You had her murdered!"

"Calm down, Amy. That's not true. I never wanted anyone to get hurt."

"This is just a game to you, isn't it? You made us do your dirty work. But your hands aren't clean now. Heather's dead because of you."

"That's not true. I had nothing to do with her death."

"You're full of shit. You sent her there. You're responsible for all of us."

"I am responsible for you, and I don't want to see you get hurt. It's over. Go away quietly and Amber will no longer exist."

"I've got a better idea. Why don't you leave? Run away like the criminal you are."

"That's not possible. It would cause suspicion. You're just one of many students who drop out all the time. The stress of college life is tough on students."

"I can handle college life. I just can't handle you, and your sick games."

He began to pace the floor. "I don't have time for this. I told you it's all over – you're out of it. If you cause trouble, I'll release the photographs. Do you want to see them again to refresh your memory?"

"No!" she shouted. "I hope they catch you. You deserve to die as much as Tiny. I know it was Tiny. I saw him drag her out of Carl's office."

"Then, you know I had nothing to do with it."

"How do I know? You could have ordered her killed."

"I didn't," he replied.

"What's going to happen to the others?"

"All of you will leave Stonewater, but not all at once. You need to go first."

"Thanks for the honor. What am I going to tell my parents?"

"You hate Stonewater. You hate your professors – anything. Just leave quickly."

"I must be dangerous."

"You're upset. I can't afford to have you lose control."

"You're scared. I hope you stay scared until the day you die," she sneered.

"You need to worry about yourself. Keep your mouth shut, and we'll all get through this."

"I'm going, but I hope you rot in hell!" She turned, and stormed out of the apartment.

He took a deep breath after she slammed the door. The professor cursed his bad fortune. Everything had gone smoothly until Heather started trouble. Carl thought he could control the girl, and seemed pleased by her progress. What had gone wrong? Amy had caused problems, too, but Carl had managed her. Heather's murder was stupid and unnecessary. That one moment of violence now threatened his security, and placed him in jeopardy of exposure. He refused to tolerate any risks to his safety, or his position at Stonewater College.

******

The daily newspapers tracked the progress of the investigation. A nationwide search was underway for Heather's killers. All the evidence pointed toward Carl Russo and Albert (AKA Tiny) Stanski as the prime suspects. The FBI circulated photos and descriptions of the fugitives around the country. State and local newspapers featured photographs of Heather, and the 'Fantasy Lounge' duo. The national tabloids also got into the act.

> *Secret Life Of A College Girl*
> *Coed Hooker Dead From Sin*

The lurid coverage and gossip devastated Heather's family and friends. Dean Henderson refused to make any statements.

The professor followed the investigation with great interest. Carl and Tiny were the only ones accused in the case. Tyler Richmond received temporary notoriety as a suspect, but the sheriff absolved him of all complicity. He wondered why Tyler had gone to the 'Fantasy Lounge'. What was his relationship to Heather? The newspapers did not explain his role in the case, and Tyler refused to discuss the investigation. He considered questioning him, but felt it might create undue suspicion. He decided to wait for more news coverage.

The tension on campus increased with each passing day. Students feared for their safety, and verbally attacked the college administration for their lack of action. The college police broke up pockets of dissent, and had to escort aggressive reporters off campus. Angry parents clogged the phone lines with complaints and threats to withdraw their children from the college. President Colson and the trustees huddled daily to discuss public relations strategies to counteract the tragedy. Stonewater College was under siege from all sides.

The professor noted Tyler Richmond's return to his teaching duties. He watched as he moved down the hallways and around the campus. Some students and members of the faculty treated him like a folk hero. He had tangled with the dean and won a stay of execution. No one had ever accomplished such a feat, and his failed rescue of Heather further fueled the fires of speculation. Tyler refused to comment, but enough information surfaced to develop numerous variations of the story. He made only one public statement. He promised to assist authorities to find everyone responsible for Heather's death. The implication of a possible conspiracy created more discomfort for the administration, and the chief culprit.

Molly Cross's actions also caused the professor great concern. She stormed around campus trying to drum up support for Tyler and her dead roommate. She formed the *Heather Andrews Support Group* for the purpose of clearing her friend's name. She refuted the popular notion of 'a good girl gone bad' at every turn. Heather had died a victim, and she promised not to rest until she found the truth. Molly organized rallies and distributed petitions. She criticized the college administration for displaying a lack of sensitivity. Her campaign returned media focus to the college, and her allegations of college involvement fueled the fire. Molly posed a significant risk to the professor. He would not allow her to get too close.

The professor scoured his apartment for any evidence that could tie him to the case. He collected and emptied bottles of Rohypnol down the toilet. Carl had provided the substance to disable his victims and facilitate the blackmail photographs. The club owner found the drug south of the border, and maintained a steady supply of the stuff. The professor also threw away other tranquilizers and depressants. The only things remaining in his medicine cabinet were non-prescription drugs and aspirin.

Next, he gathered up all the photographs locked in his

file cabinet, and moved them to a private security box at his bank. He could not afford to keep anything on hand linking him to the crime. He burned his print bed sheets in case they could be identified in the photos. He polished all his furniture, and wiped the doorknobs clean of fingerprints. Nothing in his apartment could associate him with Heather, or any of the other girls. He breathed easier once he surveyed his sanitized surroundings. Even if someone charged him with blackmail, no evidence remained behind to support the allegation.

One more detail still required his attention. The professor's assistant in the rapes, Damon Willis, might become a liability. The professor had recruited Damon for his voracious sexual appetite. Damon possessed enough intelligence to register as a part-time student, but exhibited a severe lack of good judgment. He felt no remorse for his victims and thrilled in dominating the drugged women. It became a game of omnipotence and total control. The professor recognized Damon's mental flaws, but tolerated the deficiencies. The young man was essential to the operation. Following Heather's death, Damon called. The professor agreed to meet him at a local park.

Damon fidgeted on a park bench as he waited. He jumped to his feet as the professor approached. "I'm really glad you showed up."

"Sit down, Damon. Keep this casual."

"That's easy for you to say."

"You've got to relax. We didn't kill the girl."

"Yeah, but I'm the one who set her up." Damon ran his tongue over his chapped lips.

"No one will ever know that. The cops are only after her killers."

"What about the other girls? They might talk."

"I've already taken care of them. They won't say anything, as long as I have the photos."

"That's another thing – the photos. I'm in all those pictures. I could be identified."

"No way. I was careful not to show your face."

Damon fumbled through his pockets for a cigarette. His hands shook visibly as he managed to light one. "Yeah, but what about other things. I could still get nailed."

"No one's going to see the photographs. I've got them hidden away."

"How can I be sure of that?"

"You've got to trust me. We're safe as long as no one panics. Get on with your life and act naturally. No one will touch you."

"I'd feel safer if you burned those pictures," Damon grumbled.

"I can't. Don't you understand? It's the only insurance we've got."

"You're the one with insurance. What about my insurance? Those photographs could send me to jail."

The professor put his hand on Damon's arm in a fatherly manner. "Haven't I always protected you? If you go down, I go with you. We have to take care of each other."

"I guess so."

"Things will be fine, but don't call me again. We can't afford to be seen together. This has got to be our last meeting."

"I could use some money. I'm broke."

The professor reached into his pocket and pulled out a wad of bills. "Here, make this last. I can't give you any more."

"All right, but I'm still nervous."

"You won't have any problems if you do what I tell you. It might be best if you leave town – at least for a while."

"Maybe I'll do that. I just don't know where to go."

"I gave you enough money for a bus ticket. Pick a spot and start a new life – put all this behind you."

A momentary look of relief passed over Damon's face. "All right, I'll think about it."

"Good. I think it's for the best."

Damon crushed out his cigarette and got up. "Well, I guess this is goodbye."

The professor stood and shook his hand.   "Yes, I wish you well. Don't worry, you'll be fine."

"Thanks for the good times."

The professor smiled. "You go on ahead. I'm going to stay here a while, and enjoy the fresh air."

The professor settled back down and watched his accomplice amble away. The young man might pose the greatest risk of all. His temperamental nature could wreck their fragile alliance. He had an uneasy feeling he would see Damon Willis again.

CHAPTER 27

Ben Grubb banged his fist on his desk. "These damn reporters are driving me crazy. They're all over campus. They hang out in the hallways and the Student Union. I even had to kick one out of a dorm. The blood suckers will do anything for a story."

Tyler had made it a daily habit of stopping by the office to discuss the investigation. He enjoyed Ben's company, and appreciated the campus policeman's ability to analyze evidence. These meetings provided both men with an opportunity to exchange information and ideas.

"You're right. It's like a circus around here. It's tough getting the kids to focus on education."

Ben shook his head. "I've never seen anything like it. The administration isn't talking. No one's seen the old dean in days – makes you wonder who's in charge around here."

"I guess they feel it's better to do nothing than to say something that'll make matters worse."

"Gutless worms," Ben grumbled. "I'd feel better if someone was calling the shots from above."

"I don't think Stonewater's faced a crisis like this since the Civil War. No one knows how to deal with it."

"They'd better do something fast. I checked with student records, and kids are dropping out like flies. We lost twenty just last week."

Tyler leaned back in one of Ben's chairs. "That makes our job tougher trying to find all the waitresses."

"Yeah, but a bunch of the dropouts are male, and some of the women are not too pretty. We're just looking for attractive ones, right? That should narrow it down."

"What about photographs? Do you have any pictures to show me?"

"Not yet. I wanted to pull the files on all the dropouts, but the registrar is giving me lots of static. He hates releasing privileged information. I've got photos of all our students from their ID cards, but I can't get the names of the ones who left campus."

"Keep trying. I'll ask around. Molly will help, too. She wants to be in the middle of the investigation. If any of the lounge girls lived in the dorm, they must have had roommates like Molly. We might get someone to talk."

"Maybe. I've noticed that Molly of yours is good at stirring things up."

"She's on a mission to rescue Heather's reputation."

"That mission has caused a lot of complaints. Some folks are a might touchy about rallies and petitions."

"She does draw a crowd. I'll try to get her to back off a bit."

"Don't worry, Doc. I don't mind. Maybe it's good that she's shaking the bushes. She might just flush out a snake."

"I'm glad you feel that way," Tyler smiled. "I've asked her to print up flyers requesting information about Heather, or anyone else involved in the 'Fantasy Lounge'. I figured students are more likely to approach her than one of us. She's putting them up around campus."

"You're a sneaky bastard," Ben chuckled. "What does your pretty sheriff friend think about you messing with her investigation?"

"We're not friends. The relationship is strictly professional," he protested.

"Right...and my Aunt Fanny's a disco queen. You've got it so bad, you'd get yourself locked up in jail just to peep at her through the bars."

"You've got a great imagination. I thought you professionals only dealt with facts."

"I know the facts, all right. Make sure I get a front row invitation to the wedding."

"You're a very unstable character. Let's just stick to catching the bad guys."

"We'll catch 'em. I just want to see you live happily ever after."

Tyler stood and shook his head. In reality, he liked the playful banter and teasing about Diane. He hoped Ben's insights about a potential relationship were accurate.

"I'm doing fine. If I get a contract next year, we'll have lots of time to discuss my love life."

"You'll be back. If they fire you, Molly will blow up the administration building."

"She might just do that. That reminds me, I need to go find her."

"Sure. Let me know if she digs up anything."

Tyler began studying student faces as he walked around campus. He searched for signs of recognition, and attempted to place pretty female faces into the smoky atmosphere of the 'Fantasy Lounge'. So far, none of them fit. They must be here. He knew most of the waitresses had come from the student body. Fear had forced most of them into hiding, but they could not disappear without someone taking notice. The investigation might lead elsewhere, but the trail began here.

He found Molly in the Student Union putting up flyers. Each flyer contained a photo of Heather, and a plea for information about the 'Fantasy Lounge'. Bob Andrews had paid for the printing and offered Molly anything she needed to help locate witnesses. She waved when she saw Tyler.

"What do you think? We had one thousand printed. By the time I'm done, they'll be in every building and every room on campus."

He read the printed message beneath Heather's photograph.

STONEWATER STUDENTS DEMAND JUSTICE!

Anyone having information about Heather Andrews' murder, or the 'Fantasy Lounge', should contact Molly Cross at 434-1390 or write to P.O. Box 1780. We need your help to solve Heather's murder, and to protect other students who might be victims of the conspiracy. PLEASE call now!

"It looks good. Keep driving home that point about a conspiracy, and someone might just crack. Too many people know what happened to keep this thing under wraps."

"What do you think we'll find out?"

"I'm not sure. It depends on who comes forward. Once we know how Heather got involved in the 'Fantasy Lounge', the rest of the pieces should fall into place."

"It can't happen soon enough for me."

"It will, but the administration won't be too pleased with these." He held up a flyer. "They all want the controversy to go away quietly. This keeps the scandal too close to home."

"The college's involved whether they admit it or not. I'm positive this whole thing started after Heather went to that dinner party. She said it was an important college function. That's all I know. She never said another word about it."

"All the signs seem to point that way," Tyler sighed. "I wish she'd said more, or left a diary."

"I couldn't find a thing. I searched our room and went through all her clothes, before the sheriff grabbed everything. If she left something behind, it wasn't in the room."

"Any ideas where she might have hidden something?"

She groaned. "I've racked my brain thinking of possibilities. Heather got real secretive towards the end."

"I know it's a long shot. Heather tried to handle things herself and didn't expect to die. It's highly possible she didn't leave any clues behind."

"You're probably right, but I'll keep thinking and looking."

"Good. Call me if these flyers dig anyone up."

Molly promised she would, and returned to her task.

Ben Grubb called Tyler at home later in the afternoon. "I just got word from the sheriff's office. The feds caught the two bums from the lounge trying to sneak into Canada. The dumb shits were trying to cross over at Niagara Falls. They were both carrying fake passports and airline tickets to South America."

Tyler released his breath. "Are they sure they have Carl and Tiny?"

"It's them, but they're not talking. So far, they haven't admitted a thing."

"So, what happens now?"

"They'll hold them up in New York until extradition. Once the papers are signed, they'll bring them back here for trial."

"How long will that take?"

"Could be a week or two – maybe longer if they fight extradition."

"I'm glad they're behind bars."

"That's the first reason I called. The other is, I decided not to wait for the registrar to give me student information. I started pulling photographs from our ID card files. I set aside the ones of pretty girls. I have about 300 pictures for you to look at. Can you come in and take a look?"

Tyler agreed to come right over. Ben had a stack of photographs lined up in alphabetical order on his desk.

"Sit down here. I don't know if any of these girls have left college, but if you spot a familiar face we can find out."

Ben had done a good job of selecting candidates. All of the color photos contained images of attractive female students looking their best for the photographer. None of the 'Fantasy Lounge' waitresses displayed this polished look in their undercover jobs. He screened each picture. He pulled several possibilities from the pile, but could identify no one with certainty. Thirty minutes later, Amber smiled up at him from the ID photo.

"That's her. I'm positive. She called herself Amber. She

rubbed her body all over me."

"H-mmm," Ben smirked. "It's hard to forget an experience like that."

"Amy Flanders. She lives in Custer Hall. Let's go talk to her."

"Hold on, Sherlock. She might not be there. I'll call first."

Ben picked up the telephone and dialed Amy's dorm. He spoke with someone, took several notes, and hung up the phone.

"She's gone – checked out of school last week."

"Where? Where did she go?"

"Home, I guess. I got her home address in Winchester. The roommate wouldn't give me many details."

"What now? Do we go talk to her?"

Ben shook his head. "I can't. She's not a student here anymore. I could get fired for going too far off base."

Tyler jumped to his feet. "Hell, I'll do it. I've already been fired once."

"You're a live one, Doc," he chuckled. "I like your spirit. You go talk to Miss Amber and I'll follow up with her roommate. She might know more about this thing than Molly. How about those other girls? Any of them look familiar?"

He shuffled through the photographs, attempting to make a connection. He handed the photos back to the campus cop.

"I'm not sure. These are possibles, but I didn't get real close to any of the other girls. I spent most of the time looking for Heather."

"I'll check them out while you're gone. It's less than two hours to Winchester. You can go up and back in half a day."

"I'll leave first thing in the morning."

"Be real gentle with her," Ben advised. "She's scared and desperate. If you come on too strong, she might take off for good."

"I'll go easy," he promised. "I think I'll invite Diane...Deputy O'Malley to go along. Amy might be more inclined to trust a woman."

"I'm sure Deputy Diane will jump at the chance. I just

hope you two can find your way back home."

"We'll come straight back to Stonewater, and I'll call you right away," he insisted.

"Hey, I'm a romantic. If you're a little late, I'll understand."

"I won't be late. Good luck with the roommate and the other girls. I'll see you tomorrow."

"Okay, Doc. If you're too tired, I'll come over to your place."

Tyler waved him off and left the office. Ben continued to chuckle behind him. He called Diane after he returned to his apartment. She sounded pleased he had located Amber, and agreed to go with him in the morning.

"This has to be an unofficial visit," she cautioned. "I have no jurisdiction out of the county."

"I understand, but she's a major link, and we need to talk to her."

"We'll go, but let me take the lead on the interrogation. I need you to help me prepare the questions. This could turn into a real touchy session."

Tyler agreed, and she promised to meet him at 7 a.m. The thought of seeing Amber again filled him with a mixture of anticipation and sadness. She had left college to escape her past, but he needed to dredge up the painful memories. He could not allow her to hide with so many questions left unanswered.

CHAPTER 28

Diane knocked on Tyler's door at 7 a.m. She looked radiant dressed in gray slacks, and a navy wool overcoat. Her cheeks were flushed from the early December cold, but she offered him a warm smile. He started to extend her a welcome at the doorway, but she brushed past him.

"This is crazy, you know. We don't let civilians get involved in our interrogation of witnesses."

She unbuttoned her coat and removed her plaid scarf, and handed them to him. He placed her coat over an armchair, while she wandered around his apartment inspecting the sparse furnishings.

"I never noticed before, but you don't have very much clutter in your life."

He moved toward her. "I don't need much. I never cared about owning a lot of things."

She turned away from him, and looked out the window. He took the opportunity to appraise her splendid figure. Initially, his eyes focused on the curve of her neck, but then they traveled down the length of her body. His gaze rested on the soft contour of her hips, and her firm buttocks. He felt a guilty rush of excitement as he lingered too long on her lower anatomy. Diane turned, and caught him in the act. Her smile contained no hint of rebuke.

"How about a cup of coffee before we leave?"

He attempted to regain his composure. "I don't have much to eat here. I thought we could stop somewhere for breakfast."

"I only need a cup of coffee."

He retreated into the kitchen and turned on the heat under his teakettle. He dug out a jar of freeze-dried Folgers, and found two matching mugs in the cabinet. Diane followed closely behind. She observed his preparations with amusement.

"I bet you don't do much cooking in here."

He smiled sheepishly. "You're right. I'm strictly a frozen-pizza-peanut-butter-sandwich kind of guy. I do keep my refrigerator well-stocked with beer and wine."

"Sounds like you've been a bachelor for a long time."

"All my life. I'm still searching for the perfect mate to share all this." He gestured in the direction of his frugal surroundings.

"No woman in her right mind could pass all this up," she laughed.

"No woman in her right mind would take a chance on a man with such an uncertain future," he countered.

"You'd be surprised. Some women are endowed with a strong spirit of adventure."

Her smile melted and her lovely features took on a look of sincerity. He felt a sudden urge to pull her into his arms. He wanted this woman more than any other he had ever met. The invitation in her eyes was unmistakable. The whistling kettle brought them both from the brink of physical contact. He cleared his throat and turned away from her.

"I can't remember. What do you take in your coffee?"

"Black." She placed her hand on his shoulder. "We really shouldn't do this right now. We're both stuck in this investigation. A personal relationship might create a major conflict of interest. You understand, don't you?"

"Yes." He turned and looked deeply into her soft green eyes.

She grabbed both his arms. "I want to spend time with you. You believe that, don't you?"

He forced a smile and nodded.

Diane continued, "We'll have our chance once this is over. Let's drink our coffee and go interview that girl."

"All right, but don't forget we've got a date."

"I won't."

They discussed how best to deal with Amy.

"We could call first to make sure she's home," Tyler suggested.

"Too risky. She might get suspicious and take off. It's better to surprise her at home."

They arrived in Winchester at midmorning, and stopped at a gas station for directions. The elderly station attendant pointed the way to Amy's street.

"What family you looking for? That's the high rent district."

"Flanders," Tyler replied.

"Judge Flanders?" The old man looked impressed. "His family has lived around here for over a hundred years. Yes sir, that's the right neighborhood."

Tyler thanked the man and returned to his car. "We're going to the home of Judge Flanders."

"A judge? That's all I need," she groaned. "I'm out of my jurisdiction."

"Do you want to call it off?"

"No, but I sure hope his Honor isn't at home."

They found Judge Flanders' home with little effort. They located the large two-story house on an attractive tree-lined street. A bright red cardinal chirped from one of the dogwood trees growing on the front lawn. The bird flew away as they walked up to the front door. Tyler rang the doorbell and held his breath. The door opened, and he found himself face to face with Amber from the 'Fantasy Lounge'.

"What can I do for you?" She gave no indication of recognition.

Diane pulled her badge out of her purse. "I'm from the sheriff's department. This is Mr. Richmond from Stonewater College. We're investigating the death of Heather Andrews. We're asking students from the college some routine questions. May we come inside for a few minutes?"

A look of anguish passed over Amy's face. "I don't go to

Stonewater anymore."

"We realize that," Diane replied. "We just need to ask you a few questions, and we'll be on our way."

Amy opened the door and ushered them into the living room. "I can't talk to you very long. I have to leave in a few minutes."

"We won't take long," Diane assured her. "Are your parents at home?"

"No, they're both at work."

Diane breathed a sigh of relief. Amy settled herself in a chair. Tyler and Diane sat on a couch across from her.

"How long were you a student at Stonewater?" Diane inquired.

"Three semesters. I was a sophomore."

She continued to ask a variety of innocuous questions to put the girl at ease. When she seemed sufficiently relaxed, Diane slipped into more substantial territory.

"Did you know Heather Andrews? She was a sophomore, too."

Amy flinched. "I don't think so."

"I have a photograph of her. Would you like to see it?" she offered.

"No, that's all right. I saw her picture in the newspaper."

"You never saw her around campus?"

"I'm not sure. I might have."

"Why did you leave college?"

Amy squirmed in her chair. "I didn't like the teachers."

"All of them, or just some of them?"

"Just a few, and I needed time to think about my future."

"I understand. Have you seen Mr. Richmond before? He teaches drama at Stonewater."

She studied Tyler. "I might have. I never took any of his classes."

"Do you know anything about the circumstances surrounding Heather's murder?"

Amy jumped up, and quickly looked at her watch. "I'm sorry, I really have to leave."

Diane smiled. "That's no problem. We can always come back later, when your parents are here."

Amy sank back into her chair. "No, you don't have to do that. There're only a few more questions – right?"

"Just a few," Diane assured her. "Do you know anything about Heather's murder?"

"No."

"Do you know they caught the men who killed her?"

Amy's eyes opened wide. "They did?"

"Yes. The news should be in the papers today or tomorrow."

"I haven't read the paper today."

"The suspects are Carl Russo and Albert Stanski. Albert goes by the name of Tiny. Have you ever heard those names before?"

Amy looked ready to panic. "No, I never heard of them."

"Do you know they worked at a place called the 'Fantasy Lounge'?"

"No," she replied, too quickly.

"That's strange. The story was in all the newspapers. I thought you said you read about Heather's death."

"I did. I did. I just don't remember all the details."

"Amy, I don't want to upset you, but we have reason to believe that other college students worked at the 'Fantasy Lounge'. Are you sure you never heard of the place?"

Amy looked like she might become physically ill. "I already told you, I never heard of it."

"I asked you earlier if you recognized Mr. Richmond. Do you know he visited the 'Fantasy Lounge' on the night Heather was killed?"

Amy jumped to her feet. "Listen, I'm not going to answer any more questions. I have to leave."

"Would you like us to come back later?"

"No, I wouldn't. I'm not going to answer any more questions."

Diane delivered the knockout punch. "Do you know anyone named Amber who worked at the "Fantasy Lounge'?"

"Go away," she pleaded. "I can't answer your questions."

"You can't answer my questions, or won't?"

"I can't," she sobbed.

"Do you know Mr. Richmond can identify Amber? You're Amber, aren't you, Amy?"

"Please don't do this. You have no idea how much damage you'll cause."

Diane knelt at Amy's feet and took hold of the frightened girl's hand.

"We don't want to hurt you. Please help us. Please help Heather. We need to know what happened."

"I can't – you don't understand."

"I think I do," Diane replied. "Someone's threatened you. You're afraid for your life. You're afraid you'll end up like Heather."

Amy looked down at Diane. "I'm not the only one who can get hurt."

"Who, the other girls, your parents, your father?"

"Everyone. This thing's gone too far."

"Carl and Tiny can't harm you anymore."

Amy sniffed, and wiped her eyes. "I'm not worried about them."

"Who are you worried about?"

"I can't tell you. Too many people will get hurt."

"There are more people involved besides Carl and Tiny. How many?"

"I can't say anything else. Please, don't ask me any more questions."

Diane got to her feet. "You're very brave, Amy. I can't imagine everything you've gone through. Will you answer just one more question for me?"

"What is it?"

"Did you work at the 'Fantasy Lounge' because you wanted to?"

"No way," she bristled. "I hated the place."

"Did Heather hate it, too?"

"We all did. Please don't ask me anything else."

"I won't," Diane promised. She patted Amy on the shoulder. "Listen, only one other person knows we came here today. We're not going to say anything to your parents or anyone else, but you have to promise me you'll stay put. Don't try to hide. You'll be safe if you stay at home. Take my card. If you need to talk, just call this number. Will you do that?"

Amy nodded.

"Good. I won't put you at risk, I promise."

"Thank you," she sniffed.

"I won't bother you again, unless we get a break in the case. We're going to catch the people who threatened you."

Amy shook her head. "No, you won't."

"Yes, we will. You have to believe that. Do you promise not to run away?"

"Yes. I don't have anywhere to go."

"Good. I won't come to your house again. If we need to talk, we'll go somewhere else."

Amy looked startled at the prospect, but accepted the possibility. "Okay."

Diane gave her a hug. "I'm proud of you. I'll be here if you need me."

Amy nodded, and they said goodbye. Diane and Tyler said little during the drive out of Winchester. The impact of the meeting hung over them both.

Diane broke the silence. "Judge Flanders and Mayor Andrews. What does that tell you?"

"Both important men, I guess," Tyler replied.

"Important men with a great deal to lose. Family scandal could ruin their careers. Amy and Heather were protecting their fathers."

"No wonder Amy is so afraid to tell the truth." He reached for her hand. "You're very good at your job."

"Thanks. I'm glad you were there."

"I didn't do much."

"Yes, you did. Amy knew you could identify her. That's

when she opened up."

"I don't understand why you let her off the hook."

"She was all tapped out. She's too scared to tell us anything. I need her trust. We learned a lot today. Next time, she might tell me more."

"I'm worried about her. Do you think she'll run away?"

Diane rubbed her eyes. "I don't know. She's scared. I'm certain she's being blackmailed, or worse. There's no way I could take her into custody."

"What now?"

"We keep asking questions. We gathered some good information today. Tomorrow, we'll look for more pieces of the puzzle."

Tyler turned to the lovely deputy. "Today's been a good day for us, too."

"Yes, it has," she smiled.

Diane snuggled next to him, and lowered her head on his shoulder. She left it there until they reached the outskirts of Stonewater.

CHAPTER 29

Tyler visited Ben's office in the afternoon. He found the campus cop stuffing a jelly donut into his mouth. Ben grinned and wiped a sticky glob of jelly off the side of his face.

"Damn thing's stale as hell. It's been sitting here since yesterday. I didn't have the heart to throw it away."

"I can see that," Tyler smiled.

"I notice you survived your wild adventure with Deputy Diane. Any injuries to report?"

"Nothing major. We spent all our time engaging in solid detective work."

"I bet you engaged, all right. What did you find out? Is Amy our girl?"

"No question about it."

He gave Ben the details of the interrogation, and told him how Diane had worked for a confession.

"Sounds like she knows her stuff." Ben jotted down several notes.

"I think Amy trusts her, but the girl's so scared she won't give out any names. I saw the same thing with Heather. Diane's convinced it's blackmail."

"Of course it is," Ben snorted. "Pimp tactics. You know, when some scumbag takes an innocent girl off the streets, hooks her on drugs, slaps her around, and makes her turn tricks. It looks like we've got the same thing here."

"They caught Carl and Tiny, and Amy's still scared. We know it's not those two."

"Those guys are the buyers. We've got to find the sellers. Carl and Tiny could never get on the inside."

"Inside? Do you mean on campus?"

"Sure. Can you see Carl and Tiny cruising the campus trying to recruit college girls for their sleeze bag club?"

Tyler shook his head.

"Of course not. We've got other people involved – people who blend into the college. Somehow, those girls got hooked and sold off like raw meat. If we can figure out the how, we'll catch the who."

"It had to start with that secret dinner party. Molly keeps insisting Heather's personality changed immediately after that party," Tyler added.

"Yeah, I got the same thing from Janet Weston—Amy's roommate. I talked to her this morning. She's real scared and wouldn't say much. She did admit that her roommate worked late on weekends, and she told me Amy went to a mysterious college dinner. Get this – that dinner was on a Wednesday night. You told me Heather went to hers on Friday."

"That's right. I'll have to confirm it with Molly, but I'm sure she said it was Friday night."

"Same dinner party, different nights."

"What do you think it means? Could Carl have sent out the invitations?"

"No way. Those girls expected to attend a formal college function. As far as I can tell, no written invitations were sent out and the girls were told to keep it a secret. They were invited by someone they trusted."

Tyler's jaw tightened. "Whoever it was must be on the faculty, or administration."

"Not necessarily, another student could have made the contact. The key is it had to be someone they trusted."

"The same person knew all the girls?"

"It looks that way, or a couple of them could've worked together."

"Any luck tracking down the other waitresses?" Tyler asked.

"Not much. I'm still checking it out. At least two of the girls you picked have dropped out of school. I'm still looking for the others."

"Good luck. I've got to go call Molly. She left a message on my machine."

"Be sure and give that deputy a hug for me," Ben chuckled.

"You solve this case and she'll hug you herself."

"I'll just do that. Why should you have all the luck?" He returned to his jelly donut.

Tyler called Molly as soon as he returned to his apartment. She answered the phone highly agitated.

"What's up?" he inquired.

"I got pulled into the dean's office today. He called me a troublemaker and threatened to kick me out of school, if I didn't take down the flyers. He said I had no right to involve the college in Heather's death."

"What did you say?"

"I told him the college was already involved, whether he liked it or not. Heather wasn't the only student who worked at the 'Fantasy Lounge'."

"You didn't tell him that."

"I sure did. He accused me of lying and trying to incite panic. He told me not to spread my lies anywhere else, or I'd be expelled."

"Did you argue with him?"

"I told him if he kicked me out of school, I'd drag him into court for violating my right to free speech."

"Oh, Molly," he groaned.

"What was I supposed to do? He had me in a corner."

"I can't afford to have you in trouble right now. I need your help to solve this thing."

"He threatened me. You'd have done the same thing."

"Probably," he sighed. "How did the meeting end?"

"He ordered me to take down the flyers and keep my mouth shut. I stormed out of his office. That was it. What should I do now?"

"Take down the flyers. Everyone's seen them by now, and you've passed out hundreds of others. Stay out of trouble for a while. I've got an important job for you to do."

Tyler explained some of the details from the meeting with Amy. He omitted her location, and some of the more sensitive information. He asked Molly to contact Janet Weston. Hopefully, she could gain Janet's trust and learn some secrets about her roommate. After that, they could compare notes.

Molly brightened. "I'll do it."

"Good, but stay out of trouble and take down those flyers. We can't afford any more visits to the dean's office."

"I'll be good," she promised, and hung up the phone.

Tyler smiled. He admired Molly's spirit and the way she stood up to the dean. Lately, the old boy had received so much grief he was a prime candidate for a stroke. The case had gotten so big it exceeded the control of Dean Henderson. Only a fool would attempt to stuff all the horrible facts back into Pandora's box. He wandered into the kitchen to heat up a piece of pizza.

Barry Zucker knocked on Tyler's door several hours later. He wore a crooked smile, and carried two bottles of imported beer.

"You don't always have to bring beer," Tyler chided him.

"Alas, I'm the bearer of sad tidings, and you only keep the cheap stuff in your moldy little ice box. Here, indulge yourself with the nectar of kings."

"Thanks. Come on in."

Barry settled himself in a chair, while Tyler opened the beer bottles in the kitchen. He returned with the beer and two frosted glasses.

"So, what's all this sad news?"

"Dr. Lawson is suffering from a broken heart. She feels you trifled with her affections, and left her out in the cold."

"Did she tell you that?"

"Of course not," Barry laughed. "I just hate to see two lonely people get disconnected."

"It didn't work out. There have been a lot of distractions lately. I'm fighting to keep my head above water."

"I've noticed. You've become something of a folk hero at the old Bible College. You tilted your sword against injustice, and survived an encounter with the dean of this small kingdom. Not bad for a lowly squire."

"It's not over yet. I could still go down the tubes. I do appreciate your support with the president and trustees."

"My pleasure. I consider you within my special circle of friends. Besides, I've got so much tenure it would take an act of Congress to fire me. There wasn't much risk involved."

"You're too modest, but thanks anyway."

Tyler took a long drink of his amber brew. "Can I ask you a question? I need your help with a problem."

"Anything. I'm yours to command."

"Nothing like that. It's related to psychology."

"Oh, no," Barry moaned, dramatically. "I can never get away from the office. What is it?"

"I have reason to believe someone at the college, or near the college is blackmailing some of our female students. Heather Andrews was one of them, and there might be others. What would motivate a person to do that?"

"Ah, a classic example of human manipulation. We all try to manipulate one another on some level. I bring you imported beer to encourage friendship. This is not true manipulation, but I have a need to claim you as a friend. If you reciprocate with friendship, I am fulfilled. I've written several papers on this, and regularly bore my students with lectures on the subject."

"What about criminal manipulation?"

"Now, it gets interesting. I use an example called 'behavior justification'. Good is on one side of the scale, evil on the other. Most of us live somewhere in between. Occasionally, we stray onto the wrong side, but being good people we bounce back. If we commit an illegal act, we have to balance the scale through moral justification. Are you with me, so far?"

"I guess so," Tyler replied.

"I'll keep it short. Basically, some people are weak and long to indulge in temptation without feeling guilt. They make excuses to justify their actions. This is where we get into denial. Alcoholics think one more drink won't hurt, and drug addicts believe one more hit won't do any harm. At the extreme, rapists accuse their prey of asking for it, and murderers consider their victims not fit to live. Victims in both cases must be dehumanized. These acts are committed without guilt, because they can be justified in the mind of the criminal. This fact was true with Ted Bundy, Jack the Ripper, and the other mass murderers."

"I understand, but what causes an otherwise ordinary person to step over the line?"

"A lot of things – excitement, adventure, power, or personal gratification. Criminals commit violence because they feel deprived of money, sex, or power. The unstable individual craves power, and only feels excitement when he has a victim at his mercy. Each criminal act gives him a sense of fulfillment, without guilt. This is all possible because they've justified their behavior."

"Do you think we're dealing with that here?"

"I don't have enough information to make that call. I only gave you a text book definition of a psychological disorder."

"Ben Grubb labels it 'pimp tactics'. He explained Ben's definition of the term.

"Interesting. I'll have to ask old Ben to lecture at one of my classes."

"I'm sure he'd turn you down. Most of his degrees were earned outside the classroom."

"I'd still like to discuss it with him. Do you have any more questions?"

"No, I can't think of anything else."

Barry got up to leave. "Listen, I'm not sure if there's an unstable personality at work here. If there is, be careful. Remember what I said about the criminal mind. If threatened, he'll protect himself at all costs. He'll kill without any remorse in order to survive."

"Thanks for the cheerful advice."

"No problem," Barry smiled. "I want to keep all my friends in one piece. Don't forget, if you get lonely I know a beautiful biology professor who'd welcome your call."

"I don't think I'll get lonely. If I do, I'll call you first."

"Thanks for the compliment, but I do have my limitations."

Tyler considered the warning long after his friend's departure. The idea of facing a psychopath made his blood run cold. But someone was out there still creating fear.

CHAPTER 30

The professor noted the growing tension on campus. The Cross girl had made her presence felt by plastering flyers on every bulletin board. Heather's picture was a constant reminder of incompetence and unnecessary waste. The girl did not have to die, and her demise had unleashed cries of indignation and a storm of controversy. Heather's loss, and the resulting investigation had also ruined a profitable business scheme. The 'Fantasy Lounge' would still be open for business except for Tiny's stupidity. Unfortunately, the big man could never control his impulse to brutalize helpless women.

The professor sighed and considered some of the positive aspects of the situation. Carl and Tiny were locked away in jail. He also took some satisfaction from his ability to control public opinion about Heather. After the newspapers latched onto the story about her weekend activities, he mailed an anonymous letter and a Polaroid of her dancing nude to a national tabloid. They jumped on it and ran the picture on the front page. Heather's reputation suffered and the focus of the investigation moved away from the college.

Molly Cross's campaign to resurrect Heather's image presented a new challenge. Her wild claims about a conspiracy had reached a small audience. New questions surfaced about corruption and the focus began to turn back toward the campus. The nosy college cop, Ben Grubb, had a hand in these events, but the chief culprits were Tyler Richmond and Molly Cross. The professor waged an aggressive campaign to neutralize their efforts. He used his influence with the dean to condemn their actions, and suggest they both receive severe sanctions. He advised the dean not to let this disloyalty to the college go unchecked. Heather Andrews had acted like a whore and the college had no responsibility for her death. The dean agreed, and called Molly into his office. Tyler Richmond would pay for his interference soon enough.

The professor had everything under control. Damon Willis had left town with money in his pocket. He had no reason to return to the scene of his crimes. Amy lived with her parents in Winchester. The other girls had either left college or were making plans to transfer. Admittedly, Tyler and the campus cop kept asking questions, but their investigation would go nowhere. If he could silence the Cross girl, the other zealots would become discouraged. He ruled out murder for the time being. Molly's death, so soon after Heather's murder, would have devastating repercussions. He would let Dean Henderson handle Molly Cross.

The professor smiled and greeted some of his students as he walked down the hallway to his office. He felt congenial and pleased with himself. After dropping his briefcase on the desk, he picked up his messages. Nothing of interest caught his attention, except a long distance phone call from a Mr. Burton Saks. Mr. Saks wanted to talk to him about a guest lecture series. He had never heard of Mr. Saks, and wondered what he wanted to propose. He placed the message on top of the pile and reached for his calendar. One of his female students knocked on the door as he started to check his schedule.

"Excuse me, sir. Can I talk to you for a minute?"

"I'm not taking appointments right now. I'll be happy to put you on the schedule for later this afternoon."

"I'm sorry to bother you, but it's not about class. I need to talk about a personal matter."

He tried to remember her name, but it eluded him. Normally, he would have brushed her off, but he decided to tolerate the interruption. He felt too good to offend anyone.

"I'm sorry Miss…"

"Weston. I'm Janet Weston."

"That's right. Sit down, Janet. I'm sure I can spare a few minutes. What can I do for you?"

Janet wore thick glasses and looked mousy. She was the type of student no one would notice in a classroom. She fidgeted with her stringy hair.

"I'm sorry, but I don't know who else to talk to."

"What's the problem?"

"I've been upset, ever since Heather Andrews' murder."

"Heather's death was a shock to all of us," he assured her.

"It's not just that. My roommate started acting crazy before Heather's death. She disappeared every weekend. Someone told me she was mixed up in the same stuff as Heather."

"Who's your roommate?"

"Amy Flanders – at least she was. She dropped out of school after Heather got murdered."

The professor leaned forward. "Who told you about all this?"

"Another student, Molly Cross. She came to my room last night and asked me a bunch of questions. She was Heather's roommate."

His mind raced. Molly had not been stopped. She continued to stir up trouble, in spite of the dean's warning. His good mood vanished, but he forced a patronizing smile.

"What kind of questions did she ask you?"

"Stuff about a secret college party and Amy's weekend activities."

"Secret party? What do you mean?"

"Amy got this invitation to a college dinner party during the first week of school. I guess it was a big secret, because she never told me anything about it."

"Did that bother you?"

"Not really. Amy had a much better social life than I did. I never went out much."

"Why did…Molly, think the party was so important?"

"She said Heather's attitude changed for the worse after the party. The more I thought about it, I guess Amy's did too."

"What else did Molly say?"

"Not much, except Amy and Heather were involved in the same thing. She thinks someone forced them to work at that bar. She told me not to talk to anyone about it."

"Why did you come to me?"

"I trust you," she blushed. "You're really nice to us in class, and I need advice."

"Thank you, but what advice can I give you?"

"I'm worried about Amy. She's still my friend, even though she dropped out of school. Should I call and tell her what's going on? I didn't tell you before, but Officer Grubb came to see me before Molly did. He asked the same questions. I'm afraid she might be in danger."

The professor felt a knot of tension grip his stomach. He barely managed to maintain a pleasant façade. "I think you should let the authorities handle it. I'm sure they'll protect Amy."

"I guess you're right, but I wish I'd done something sooner. I knew Amy was in trouble before she left school. Heather's roommate feels the same way."

"Don't blame yourself. You did all you could. Let it go. I'm sure everything will be all right."

"Thanks," she sniffed, and got up to leave.

"Listen, Janet, feel free to come see me at any time. I hate to see any of my students burdened with problems."

"I will," she promised, and left the office.

The professor seethed with anger. He could not tolerate Molly's interference any longer. He considered reporting her to the dean, but dismissed the notion. If Molly got kicked out of college, the problem would not go away. If anything, she would press the attack with a vengeance. She might even gain more sympathy for her cause. He needed to control her by fear, just like the others.

He packed away his calendar and shut his briefcase. The Molly problem would require careful planning. He glanced back at his messages, and decided to call the mysterious Mr.

Saks. He could not stop handling routine administrative matters. He dialed the number.

"Hello." The voice sounded sleepy, and familiar.

"Is this Mr. Burton Saks?"

"No, it's me, Damon."

"Are you crazy?" The professor exploded. "Why did you call me here?"

"Calm down. No one knew it was me. I disguised my voice."

"You're an idiot. What do you want? Make it fast."

"It's not working out. I'm broke and I can't find a job. I need a loan to tide me over."

"How much?"

"Five hundred should do it."

"Where are you?"

"Daytona Beach."

"There must be lots of jobs down there. It's a major tourist spot."

"Oh, sure – minimum wage stuff. I want to make some real money."

"I can't help you. Don't forget, our little enterprise went out of business."

"I know. I just need a loan. I'll pay you back."

The professor hated wasting time with this fool. Damon refused to go away. Every time he got himself in a bind, he came running back.

'No more!' the professor wanted to scream into the phone. He had enough trouble with Tyler Richmond and the Cross girl without any more distractions from Damon. The old relationship needed a permanent termination. He forced himself to respond calmly.

"There is no money. I gave you all I had before you left town."

"I don't need much. Help me out one more time, and I won't bother you ever again."

The professor almost slammed down the phone, but his

mind returned to the Molly problem. He could not approach the girl, but a complete stranger could handle her for him.

"Listen, I just thought of something. I need your help with a problem. If you come back and take care of it for me, I'll find some money to pay you."

"How much?" Damon's tone brightened.

"One-thousand dollars."

"What is it?"

"Not over the phone, but it's a job well-suited for you. Call me at home when you get into town. We'll meet at our usual location."

"All right, I'll be there tomorrow. I think I've got enough for a bus ticket."

"Good. Call me at home next time." He hung up the phone.

The professor hated bringing Damon back into the picture, but felt he had no choice. Nothing would stop Molly Cross from stirring up trouble, unless she had a reason. Damon would make certain she found a reason. More than anything else, the professor needed to feel safe and secure once again.

CHAPTER 31

Molly hated caving into Dean Henderson's demands. She muttered profanities while removing the flyers from bulletin boards. The old bastard seemed determined to undermine her attempts to uncover a conspiracy. He considered himself the protector of the ivy halls, and would tolerate no challenges from outside the gates, or within. Stonewater College had no right to cover up the truth. Evil lived close by and no amount of protestation by the dean would make it go away. She completed the chore before dinner and placed the flyers in a large folder. They might come in handy someday. She felt hungry and considered going to the dining hall, but decided to call Tyler instead. He might have some new information, and she needed to tell him about removing the flyers.

Memories of Heather returned as Molly climbed the dormitory stairs. She missed her friend, and the companionship of a roommate. No one was eager to fill Heather's empty bed. It would remain empty until the college assigned a newcomer to the space. Molly resented the unexpected privacy. She needed to share her life with a kindred spirit. Heather had met that need until the 'Fantasy Lounge' intervened. Recollections of the place caused her to seethe with anger.

Molly slipped the key into her lock and opened the door. She did not plan to spend much time in the room. After she dropped off the flyers, she would call Tyler at home. She closed the door and groped for the light switch. Before she could turn on the light, a strong hand clamped down over her mouth. Her heart jumped in panic. She attempted to scream, but the pressure increased on her mouth and nose.

"Don't you dare scream," a rough voice hissed. "If you make a sound, you're dead. Do you understand?"

She nodded as her mind fought for ways to escape. She wanted to kick and bite, but the hand held her fast. If she moved, the attacker might kill her. She prayed that someone would hear a noise and call for help. She felt consumed by fear. How could this happen in her dorm room? The hand moved, and the assailant stuffed rags in her mouth. He wrapped duct tape over her mouth and eyes. Once he had her immobilized, he slammed his fist into her stomach. Molly collapsed on the floor in terrible pain –unable to breathe.

The intruder dragged her across the floor and muscled her onto the bed. The gag blocked her mouth. She struggled to get air into her heaving lungs through her nose. The effort did not produce enough oxygen. She felt like she would suffocate. During the desperate fight for air, the attacker tied her to the bedposts. The realization of the danger caused her to shake uncontrollably.

"You're not much to look at, but we'll have to make do. Are you ready for your lesson?"

Molly flung her head from side to side. The gesture did nothing to deter the beast. He pummeled her with his fists until her resistance ended. After she quieted, he cut the clothes away from her body. The nightmare continued. She suffered through the indignity in deep torment. Eventually, the abuse stopped, and he lifted himself from her writhing body.

"Are you afraid? Do you hurt?"

She nodded her head painfully.

"Good. Here's the thing – stop looking for trouble. No more questions about the Andrews girl. If you don't stop, I'll come back here and do this again. Do you want that?"

She shook her head angrily.

"Okay, I think you understand. Keep your mouth shut, and you'll never see me again. If you don't, I'll know. I'm watching you. Don't ever forget that."

He got off the bed and quietly slipped out of the room.

Molly pulled helplessly on the ropes, and attempted to scream through the tape covering her mouth. The scream sounded like a garbled groan. She continued the noise until a curious dorm resident poked her head into the room. The stunned co-ed released Molly and called the campus police.

Ben called Tyler later that night. "Molly's been attacked."

"How? Where?"

"The bastard got into her room and tied her to the bed. He beat her pretty bad."

"How bad? How did he get into the room?" Tyler struggled to make sense of the news.

"We took her to the hospital, but nothing looks broken. It could have been a lot worse."

"How did he get into the room?" he repeated.

"I don't know. Men are allowed to visit until 7 p.m. This happened about five. Someone reported seeing a maintenance man on the stairs. We're checking it out now."

"I've got to go to the hospital. Will they let me see her?"

"Not tonight. They gave her a sleeping pill. You'd better wait until morning."

"Did she tell you anything?"

"Not much. She's in shock. She never saw the guy. The room was dark and he covered her eyes with tape."

"I knew she was in danger. I should have protected her."

"Don't start that crap. There's already enough guilt flying around. Get some sleep and go see her tomorrow. We'll find the guy who did it."

"All right. Thanks, Ben. I'll see you tomorrow."

Tyler paced the floor in anger. He resisted an urge to run to the hospital. He still felt responsible for the attack, and needed reassurance Molly would recover. He grabbed the phone and called Diane. She knew about the assault, and promised him that the sheriff had given the case top priority. She advised him to get some rest and let the department handle the investigation. They both knew he would not. She agreed to meet him at the hospital in the morning. He reluctantly said goodnight.

Tyler rushed to the hospital at eight o'clock the next morning. He had spent a restless night visualizing Molly being brutalized. Diane was waiting in the lobby. She smiled and guided him to a sofa. They sat down, and she took hold of his hand.

"Before we go upstairs, I need to tell you some things."

He nodded and waited.

"Molly's not too badly hurt. In fact, I think she'll leave the hospital today. Her bruises will heal, but she's terrified of returning to her room."

"I don't blame her."

"She's going to need counseling." She looked into his eyes. "There's something else you need to know ...the bastard raped her."

"Oh, no. Ben didn't say anything about that."

"I wanted to tell you myself. Right now, she's scared, sore, and humiliated. She's so ashamed, she doesn't want to see you."

"That's crazy."

She smiled and squeezed his hand. "I know, that's why we're going up to see her in a few minutes. I just needed to prepare you first."

"Thanks. I won't let her feel any shame over this."

"It's going to take time," she cautioned. "We need to find her a place to recover. She refuses to go home to her parents, and she's not ready to go back to the dorm."

He thought quickly. "She'll stay with me. I can fix up a bed on the couch."

She shook her head. "That's really not a good idea. It would only stir up more controversy."

He nodded. "You're right, but we need to get her away from here for a while."

He considered other possibilities. "The Weavers. They'd be happy to take care of her."

Diane agreed, and Tyler left to call his friends. Rebecca said they would love to have her stay with them. She encouraged him to bring her to the farm as soon as possible.

Molly looked pitiful in the hospital bed. She had bruises on her face, and a split lip. She turned toward the wall when Tyler and Diane entered the room.

"Why did you come here?"

Tyler moved closer and sat on the bed. "I thought we were friends. What kind of friend would let you go through this alone?"

His heart sank as he observed the back of her curly, red head. The attack had broken her indomitable spirit. Molly remained silent.

"I'm not going to ask you any questions. You've been through enough already. I'm here to help you get better. We're going to protect you, Molly. This will never happen again."

There was no reply.

"We're not going to leave you by yourself. My friends, the Weavers, want you to recover at their farm. They took care of me – remember? I'll take you there. If you want, I'll take you home to your parents. It's your choice."

"My mother would drive me crazy," came the muffled reply.

"Then, how about the farm? How does that sound?"

"I want to stay here."

He touched her arm. "You can't. The doctor's going to release you today. We need to find you a quiet place to recover. The Weavers are wonderful people. They'll take good care of you."

Molly did not answer.

"You'll be safe there – I promise. I'll stay with you as much as possible."

She offered no reply.

"Molly, please, let me help you. We have to stick together. We can't let them beat us."

She sat up and turned toward him. Her eyes were full of tears, and her injured lip quivered. "I don't know what to do."

He put his arms around her. "You're going to get through today, tomorrow, and the next day. After that, we'll talk about the future. Promise me you'll concentrate on getting well."

She sobbed on his shoulder. "All right, I will."

"Will you let me take you to the Weavers?"

She hesitated. "Yes."

He stroked her hair. "Good. Get some rest. I'll come back for you later."

He lowered her head onto the pillow.

"Thank you," she whispered, and closed her eyes.

Tyler looked over at Diane. Her eyes were moist and bright. She held out her hand, and led him out of the hospital room.

Diane borrowed Molly's key, and returned to her dorm room for some clothes. She packed a small suitcase and brought it back to the hospital. Tyler waited in the hallway while Diane helped her dress. When she was ready, they checked her out of the hospital. They drove away from Stonewater into the sanctuary of the country.

Rebecca rushed outside when she heard the car approach. She helped Molly out of the back seat and patted her hand.

"You poor thing. I'm so glad Tyler brought you to us. Come inside and I'll put you to bed. Do you like soup? I just made a fresh pot. I bet you're hungry. Let's get you into bed, and I'll bring you up a bowl. You need a good night's rest. Tomorrow, I'll make some fresh donuts for breakfast." She chattered all the way into the house. Molly followed obediently.

Tyler and Diane watched the scene with gratitude. Rebecca had everything under control. The healing process had begun.

CHAPTER 32

Tyler and Diane visited Molly the next morning. She looked better after a good night's rest, and some of Rebecca's homemade soup. Rebecca had her propped up on pillows in the same bed Tyler had used during his stay. Tyler missed the sounds of the farm animals and the company of his Mennonite friends. Molly would benefit from her experience with the Weavers as much as he had. Her eyes still expressed pain from the attack, but she looked pleased to see her visitors.

"Good morning," Tyler smiled. "How's the patient?"

"I'm feeling better," she replied.

"What did I tell you? A stay with the Weavers, and Rebecca's homemade soup can work miracles."

"They're nice people."

"The best. Can I get you anything?"

"No, I'm fine."

Diane stepped forward. "I called your mother. I told her you were doing well and being cared for. I promised you'd call home soon."

Molly's eyes registered a look of distress. "Did you tell her everything?"

"No. She only knows you were beaten, and not too seriously injured. I gave the same story to the newspapers. They've made this big news since you were Heather's roommate."

"Oh, great, my life is ruined."

"I'm not trying to worry you, but you need to know what's going on," Diane responded. "It's going to be tough for a while, but no one knows you're here right now. We'll help you get through the days ahead."

"I wish he'd just killed me. I can't live like this."

Tyler jumped like he'd been shot. "Don't say that. You have everything to live for. We're going to catch the bastard."

Diane restrained him with her hand. "It's normal to feel that way, but it will pass. You have to realize three things. First, this is not your fault. Second, you're a victim of a criminal act. Third, you're still alive and have lots of reasons to keep on living."

"Sounds real easy," Molly muttered.

"It's not, but try to focus on the future and the people who love you. Tyler tells me you have a unique talent. There's no reason not to continue your work."

"I can't go back there."

"Give it time. Don't make any decisions while you're still upset."

"I really need you, Molly. You know that. We've got the spring production coming up," Tyler pleaded.

"Why don't you talk about that later?" Diane suggested. "I'd like to ask you some more questions. Are you up to it?"

Molly covered her eyes with her arm. "I told you all I could."

"I know, but you're feeling better now. You might remember some important details."

Molly related the awful events. She vaguely described the rape, but recalled the rapist's parting threats in vivid detail. Diane asked her to remember his physical characteristics. Was he muscular? Was his skin hairy or smooth? What about the sound of his voice? Did he smell like alcohol or cigarette smoke? Could she guess his approximate age? She asked Molly to recall the smallest details. Molly considered everything.

"I'm sure he was white and in his twenties. He had fairly smooth skin and no beard. He smelled like cigarette smoke, and seemed in good physical condition. I thought he had a southern accent, but he whispered most of the time. I'm not sure. I can't remember anything else."

Diane patted her leg and assured her the description was helpful. After that, she asked Tyler to leave the room. She needed to ask more intimate questions. Once they were alone, she had Molly describe every aspect of the rape in graphic detail. Reluctantly, Molly recalled the horrifying experience from beginning to end.

"That's enough," Diane promised. "I'm sorry I had to ask those questions, but I need to form a profile of the suspect. We collected samples of his pubic hair and semen from you in the hospital. They'll tell us a lot. We already know he's a fairly young, dark-haired Caucasian. We'll match those samples to any suspects we round up. I know we'll catch him."

"I never want to see him again," Molly declared.

"Don't worry about that. Get some rest. Tyler and I will check on you soon."

"You really like him, don't you?"

Diane hesitated. "Yeah, I really do. You're special to him, too. I think we're both pretty lucky. We'll be back to check on you."

She left the room and closed the bedroom door. Diane found Tyler drinking coffee with the Weavers in the kitchen. They looked up as she entered.

"How is she?" Tyler asked.

"Confused, scared, angry – all the normal reactions. She'll get through it."

Rebecca poured her a cup of coffee. "Poor thing. How could anyone hurt an innocent young girl?"

"This was a planned attack. The man wanted to scare her. Molly must've been making someone real nervous."

"I can't understand the evil in some men," George remarked.

"We're going to find this sinner," Tyler pledged. "He needs to start feeling punishment right away."

They drank their coffee and discussed Molly's recovery. The Weavers offered to care for her as long as necessary. She could stay on the farm until she felt ready to return to the college. They welcomed her company and the opportunity to do their Christian duty.

"Ever since Tyler landed on our doorstep, we've been busy doing the Lord's work. I sure hope He doesn't keep us this busy for too much longer," George chuckled.

"You both have been wonderful. I can't thank you enough."

"Our pleasure. Now, why don't you show this lovely young lady around the farm? You need a break before you go back to town. We'll take care of things in here."

Tyler thanked them again, and left the kitchen with Diane. He guided her toward the barn. Diane took his arm.

"You really love it here, don't you?"

"I've never been in a more peaceful place. I leave refreshed after every visit."

"I can tell," she smiled. "I enjoy sharing this with you."

They walked through the barn holding hands, and strolled among the chickens. The air smelled sweet with the scent of hay and grain. The Weavers' dog followed on their heels. Tyler and Diane paused several times before leaving their sanctuary. They both wanted to hold onto the moment forever. Reluctantly, the time came to say goodbye, and they drove away from the farm.

******

Ben Grubb kept busy all morning while Tyler and Diane visited Molly. He pored over incident reports searching for evidence of past assaults on female students. He could not recall anything serious, but hoped to find something. Eventually, he came upon one complaint worth further investigation. He had not handled the case, but vaguely remembered the facts. Someone had mauled a drunken co-ed three months ago at a frat party. The culprit had not been a member of the fraternity. No one claimed to know him. Ben decided to drive to the fraternity house.

Initially, the brotherhood did not respond to the campus cop's questions. None of them claimed to recall the party, or the attack on the co-ed. Fraternity houses foster a tradition of self-preservation. Any brother who breaks the code of secrecy could expect severe discipline. Ben anticipated this corporate amnesia. He attempted tact and diplomacy at first, but soon became frustrated by the lack of cooperation. He called all the students into one room and hammered them with an emotional barrage of words.

"All right, enough bullshit! I'm investigating the murder of a female student, and the beating of another. We're under attack here. I need your help before someone else gets killed. I don't have time for games. If you don't help me, I'll close this dump down. I'll put your sorry asses out on the street. I need to know, right now, who molested that girl here three months ago. It could be the same asshole that attacked the student in her room. Tell me now, or you could be responsible for someone else getting hurt or killed."

He looked around the room. He had their attention. These were mostly good kids from good families. He saw concern on some of their faces. Eventually, one of them spoke up.

"I saw it. I saw the whole thing."

No one raised an objection to his confession.

"Tell me what happened," Ben replied.

"He used to hang around here. We let him stay because he brought food and beer. We couldn't let him pledge, because he wasn't a full-time student."

"Did he take any classes?"

"I guess so. I think he went nights."

"What's his name?"

"I don't know. We called him 'Demon'."

"Does anyone know his name?"

"Yeah. Damon...Damon Willis," offered another voice.

"Tell me what happened."

"It wasn't a big deal. The girl got drunk and fell on the

floor. Demon jumped on her and began rubbing her body. She started screaming and ran out of the house. We got rid of him after that."

"What does he look like?"

"He's pretty tall with short dark hair. I guess he has a medium build and brown eyes. He's got scars on his face – like he had acne as a kid. Most women wouldn't go near him."

"When's the last time you saw him?"

"Not since we kicked him out three months ago."

"Has anyone else seen him since then?"

No one answered.

"Okay, thanks for your help. This could be the guy. I want you to call me if he turns up."

They all promised to cooperate. After he returned to his office, Ben searched the files for a student named Damon Willis. He found nothing, but the registrar confirmed Damon Willis had taken night classes in computer science and business. He never completed the class work and had dropped out. He listed his home address as an apartment in Stonewater. Ben called Damon's landlord, and discovered he had moved out a month ago. Everything pointed to the possibility he had left the area, and probably the state.

Ben's phone rang. The caller identified himself as one of the fraternity brothers. He refused to give his name.

"I've got more information on Demon. I didn't want to say anything at the house."

"Go ahead."

"He had lots of money and threw it around like crazy. I think he made it from selling drugs."

"How do you know?"

"He carried *roofies* in his pocket, and offered to slip them into the punch at one of our parties. He said it was an easy way to get laid. We wouldn't let him do it."

"Did he have anything else besides *roofies*?

"Not that I saw."

"Can you tell me anything else?"

"He bragged about having lots of women. I didn't believe him. No girl in her right mind would go out with him."

"Did he ever talk about hurting or abusing women?"

"I never heard him say anything like that. He made it seem like they wanted him."

"Thanks for the information. You've been a big help. Call me if you think of anything else."

Ben considered the evidence. All his instincts pointed to Damon Willis as a prime suspect. The elusive stranger lived in the shadows and displayed a total disregard for the feelings of women. If he had not been responsible for Molly's rape, someone with the same profile had. He wrote down detailed notes to share with Deputy O'Malley. They needed to find this phantom before he struck again.

CHAPTER 33

The professor was grateful semester break had arrived. Exams were finished and most students had departed for Christmas vacation. Classrooms and dormitories sat empty, while their occupants enjoyed freedom from academic obligations. He hoped the vacation period would ease tensions and curtail the investigation. Law officials seemed satisfied to have captured Heather's killers and the newspapers had reduced their coverage. The case had turned into old news. Tyler and the campus cop were the only ones still promoting a conspiracy theory. Fortunately, Dean Henderson had promised to put a stop to their crusade.

Damon Willis posed the greatest threat to the professor's security. His stupid assault on Molly had turned attention back toward the college. The professor had expected Damon to commit the act off-campus. The idiot's bad judgment placed them both in jeopardy. If captured, Damon would confess to everything. Unlike Carl and Tiny, he lacked the stamina to survive an interrogation. The newspapers treated the crime like a random act of violence, but they knew Molly was Heather's former roommate. The coincidence generated new questions and called for more student protection.

Damon called the day after his assault on Molly. "I did it – just like you wanted. She's so scared, she won't cause any more trouble."

The professor suppressed his anger and replied calmly, "Thank you. You really earned your money."

"So, when's payday?"

"Today. I'll meet you in one hour at the usual place."

"Great. I'll be there."

The professor drove to the park at the appointed time. Damon stood next to the bench stomping his feet and blowing on his hands. He looked up as his mentor came into view. The professor grimaced as he approached his smiling accomplice. He hated the sight of the gloating man waiting for confirmation of his success. Damon wanted the money, but needed praise more. He steeled himself to perform the distasteful task.

"Did you bring it?" Damon blurted out.

"It's in the car. I don't want to give it to you here."

"Why not?"

"Someone might be watching. I need to get you out of town. I'll drive you to the bus station in Staunton. A bus leaves for Florida in two hours."

"I'm not so sure I want to go back to Florida. What's the rush?"

The professor fought for self-control. "Listen, the police are looking for you all over the state. They won't quit until they put you behind bars. You need to get out of town fast. They might already have your fingerprints."

"No way," Damon smirked. "I wore gloves."

"What about hair? Fabric? You could have left a hundred clues without realizing it."

"I was careful."

"Trust me, it won't take long for them to put the pieces together. You need to change your name and go into hiding."

"I don't want to go back to Florida."

"Then don't. Take the money and start your life all over. How about California?"

"Yeah, maybe."

"Good. You can find a great job on the West Coast. You might even decide to move to Mexico for a while. You'd be safer in Mexico."

"I'll think about it."

"Think about it in the car. The sooner you get out of Stonewater the better."

Damon obediently followed his employer to the car. They stopped at the motel to pick up his clothes, before heading north. The professor avoided the interstate, and took an alternate route on a county road. He explained that road construction might slow them down. Damon accepted the explanation and launched into a full account of his attack on Molly. The professor suffered through the details and offered appropriate praise on cue. He hid his revulsion as Damon basked in the approval. Fortunately, they encountered few cars on the rural back road. Ten miles out of Stonewater, the professor jerked his foot up and down on the accelerator. He slammed his fist down on the steering wheel as he guided the car off the road. "Damn, something's gone wrong with the engine."

He popped the hood latch and stepped out of the car. Damon followed him around to the front. The professor opened the car hood and peered inside.

"I don't see anything. Do you?"

"No," Damon replied.

"Wait here. I've got a flashlight in the back."

Damon continued to stare at the engine. The professor looked up and down the road. Satisfied, he reached inside the trunk and pulled out the flashlight. He also picked up a tire iron. After closing the trunk, he returned to Damon with the tire iron behind his back. He turned on the flashlight, and aimed the beam under the hood.

"That's better. Look in there and tell me if you see anything."

He backed off as Damon searched for the problem. The professor slowly lifted the tire iron and slammed it down on the young man's head. The force of the blow sent Damon's face smashing into the engine block, and the hood collapsed on his back. He never saw it coming.

The professor jumped out of the way. Damon's body dangled from the front of the vehicle. The professor, once again, looked up and down the road for signs of traffic. He saw nothing. He dragged the body deep into the underbrush. He checked for a pulse and found none. One blow had been sufficient. Damon's dented skull and gushing blood from the wound confirmed the fatal injury. Damon Willis no longer served as a threat to anyone.

The professor returned to his car and picked up the tire iron. He wiped it clean, and noted the blood on his engine with disgust. He would have to wash it down later. He removed what he could, and dropped the bloody rag into a plastic bag for disposal later. The impact of the act had little effect on him. Damon needed to die. His first experience with murder had turned into a messy affair, but the result justified the inconvenience. He had neutralized another threat and his peace of mind was worth the price. After one last look around the area, he got into his car and headed back to Stonewater.

******

It took three days for someone to discover Damon's body. Two boys stumbled upon it in the woods. They rode their bicycles full-speed to the nearest farmhouse and called the sheriff. The story quickly spread throughout Stonewater, and a reporter from the *Stonewater Times* rushed to the site. A second murder in two months defied comprehension, especially since the last murder in the area had occurred over fifteen years ago.

The sheriff's department had good reason to suspect Damon's involvement in the Molly Cross case. His age was right, and he fit the profile. The coroner validated these suspicions after completing the autopsy. The pubic hair matched, and a blood sample confirmed the identification. Damon had raped Molly. But who had killed Damon?

Diane observed the autopsy and discussed the findings with the pathologist. Damon had died from a single blow to the head. His face suffered trauma on impact after falling. Oil residue on his face probably came from a vehicle. Bruises on his back had not contributed to death. Deputies determined the murder site from bloodstains on the road. A blood trail led from the road to the location of the body. They found no other physical evidence. The frozen ground negated the possibility of tire tracks and investigators did not find a murder weapon. Someone had committed murder on an open road without being seen.

The sheriff's department began to search Damon's background for prior arrests and places of residence. He had at least one local enemy, and there may have been others. Ben Grubb assisted the investigation by supplying Damon's student records, information about the fraternity connection, and the name of his landlord. The investigators focused on the fraternity incident and tracked down those brothers on vacation.

Tyler and Diane discussed how to break the news to Molly. They needed to tell her, before she read about it in the newspapers, or heard about it on the radio. Diane cautioned Tyler that the shock could cause a setback. The news of more violence might deepen her depression. On the other hand, she might experience a release from fear. Tyler insisted Molly had the strength to endure this new development. They called the Weavers and prepared them for the visit.

Molly looked upbeat when they arrived. They found her dressed and chatting with the Weavers at the kitchen table. Her color had returned, and Tyler noticed some of the old sparkle in her eyes. George and Rebecca had worked another miracle.

Molly smiled at them. "People are going to talk if you two keep hanging out together."

Tyler wrapped his arm around her and tousled her curly hair. "It's too late. I think the secret's already out."

She returned his hug, and Rebecca poured coffee for them.

"Have you called your mother?" Diane inquired.

"Yesterday. She wants me to come home. I promised to

visit, but I'm not up to it yet."

"She's going to stay with us a while longer," George announced. "I like the idea of having two women around. She's already offered to help me with chores in the barn."

"What about Christmas? Aren't you going home?" Diane asked.

"It's no big deal at our house. I'll go later."

"Why don't the three of us have Christmas at my place?" Tyler glanced at Diane.

"That's fine, but you're going to have Christmas dinner with us," Rebecca insisted.

"Don't argue," George warned. "Rebecca has a fearsome ability of getting her way."

"You stop that." She flicked him with a dishtowel.

Tyler looked at Molly and Diane for signs of approval. "We'd love to," he agreed.

"I'm glad that's all settled. You saved me from a terrible fate," George winked.

They all laughed, and Rebecca responded with the appropriate amount of indignation. Diane waited for the right moment, before changing the mood.

"We've got something to tell you, Molly."

"What is it?"

She placed her hands on Molly's shoulders. "We found the man who attacked you. He's dead. Someone murdered him three days ago."

Diane watched for a reaction. Molly dropped her head in her hands and shook her head. "How did it happen?"

"We don't know for sure. Some boys found him in the woods with his skull crushed."

Molly looked up with pleading eyes. "When is this nightmare going to stop?"

"I don't know, but you're safe here with the Weavers. We'll find out who did it."

Molly got up from the table. "I'm going for a walk. I need to be alone."

Tyler started to protest, but George restrained him. "You go do that. I always do my best thinking in the barn. We'll be here if you need us."

She grabbed her coat and ran out the door.

"Don't worry about her," George advised. "Leave her alone and she'll work things out."

Tyler watched her run towards the barn. "You're right, but she has a lot to forget."

George moved behind Tyler, and put his hand on his shoulder. "She'll heal, but she can still use our prayers."

Tyler nodded, and returned to the table. The four of them discussed plans for Christmas. Tyler's eyes kept straying in the direction of the barn.

"Stop worrying about her," George advised. "You two go on home. Come back and visit her tomorrow."

Tyler helped Diane put on her coat. They discussed Molly's reaction during the return to Stonewater. Diane felt Molly had taken the news well. She also complimented Tyler on his plans for Christmas.

"I knew I wanted to spend Christmas with you. It just seemed right to include Molly," he said.

"It sounds perfect. This is going to be a special holiday."

She snuggled against him and kissed his cheek. He put his arm around her. Like Molly, Tyler wondered when the nightmare would stop. Damon's murder had added another twist to the mystery. Someone had killed for revenge or protection. Heather and Damon's deaths were linked by a common denominator. That missing link could kill again.

CHAPTER 34

Dean Henderson's secretary called Tyler five days before Christmas. She apologized for disturbing his vacation, but the dean needed to see him on an urgent matter. Would he be available to make the appointment? The tone of the request sounded ominous, but he agreed. He doubted the old man intended to spread Christmas cheer. He felt a sense of melancholy as he prepared for the encounter.

He stopped by Ben Grubb's office before the appointment. Ben was at his desk attempting to wrap a Christmas present. The effort of the enormous task had taken a toll on his sense of humor. He cursed while trying to fold the paper over one end of the package.

"I'm no good at this crap. Do you know how to do it?"

"I'll do my best," Tyler smiled.

He untangled the wrinkled paper and tried to make sense out of the mess. After several attempts, he produced a close facsimile of a wrapped Christmas present.

"You know, this is one of the life skills they never teach you in school. I put it right up there with learning how to write checks and pay taxes."

"You got that right. I go through this every Christmas."

"Well, you've got a whole year to worry, before you have to wrap another one."

"No way. Next year, I'll just call you to do it for me."

"Next year, you should have the store wrap it for you." Tyler settled back. "Any news on the Willis guy?"

"Nope. The sheriff is still conducting a background check. So far, they've got no prior arrests or convictions on the bad boy. He lived like a gypsy. No military service record, and no long-term employment anywhere. There's no telling what brought him to Stonewater."

"It doesn't make sense. You said he threw lots of money around, but he didn't have a steady job. Where'd he get it?"

"Probably selling drugs. He just never got caught."

"Why did he get killed?"

"Who knows? You should ask Deputy Diane that question. She's closer to the investigation than I am."

"She doesn't tell me too much, and I don't ask."

"She tells you enough, but you can pretend to be dumb if you want."

"I've learned more about the case from you. You're the one who traced Damon to the fraternity house. I think you missed your calling, Ben."

"Nah, I like the quiet life. Seven more years, and I'll collect my retirement pension."

"I'll start building you a rocking chair. I should have it done by the time you retire."

"Smart ass. Build one for yourself."

They slipped back into discussing the murder. Ben believed an acquaintance had driven Damon into the country and crushed his skull. He guessed a man had committed the violent act. Women tended to favor more subtle methods of murder.

Tyler agreed with his assessment and got up to leave.

"I don't want to keep Dean Henderson waiting. He wants to see me at two o'clock."

"No shit? He called me for a three o'clock meeting. Looks like we're stepping on his toes."

"I have no idea, but I'll try to let you know what happens. He may want to fire me again."

"That doesn't sound too good. I might not make that pension, after all. He must be spooked about something."

"Maybe he just needs some professional advice. No need to expect the worst."

Tyler smiled, and waved goodbye.

Dean Henderson's secretary nodded as he entered the office. "The dean would like you to go right in."

The words caught him off balance. Normal procedure required a wait of at least fifteen minutes. He searched her face for any clue, but she dropped her eyes. The signs did not look promising. He straightened his back and entered the dean's inner sanctum.

"Come in, Mr. Richmond. Please take a seat."

The dean got up from behind his desk with some effort. The pallor of his skin caught Tyler by surprise. The old man had never looked worse. Deep circles lined his eyes, and his face had taken on a yellowish tinge. He moved like someone in acute pain. He felt a pang of sympathy for the old boy, and almost jumped to his feet to assist him into a chair. He let the moment pass.

"Thank you for coming in. I apologize for interrupting your vacation."

"That's no problem. I'm sure you have a good reason for requesting this meeting."

"I do. First of all, I would like to extend my sympathy for the attack on Ms. Cross. I understand she is one of your students."

"She is. I'll make sure she's told about your concern."

"Thank you. It's a terrible thing to have one of our students assaulted on campus. We are fully committed to keeping the college environment safe for everyone."

"I'm sure you do your best."

"These are extremely difficult times. I need your assistance to stabilize the situation."

A grandfather's clock ticked relentlessly in the corner of the room. The dean sniffed and dabbed at his nose with a linen handkerchief. Sounds of children playing outdoors filtered through the window. A telephone rang in another office. The dean replaced the handkerchief in his pants pocket and waited for a reply.

"What can I do?" Tyler inquired.

The dean fixed his watery eyes on the young instructor. "It's over. The man who attacked Ms. Cross is dead. The men who killed Ms. Andrews are in jail. I want you to acknowledge these facts, and help us return the college to normal."

Tyler swallowed hard. The old man wanted him to roll over and take part in the cover-up.

"You can't believe that. Someone else is behind all this. Whoever it is, probably works right here."

"Nonsense. Your games of intrigue are contributing to the unrest."

"Don't you understand? There are witnesses who will testify that Heather Andrews and others like her were lured to a bogus college dinner party. One female student recently left the college, and lives in constant fear. There are others like her. These students all worked at the 'Fantasy Lounge'. Before she died, Heather admitted she was being blackmailed. Molly Cross was not attacked at random. Someone wanted to scare her and keep her quiet. This is not nonsense. These are facts."

The dean's face turned purple. "How dare you! You've twisted everything around to suit your purposes. There's not one ounce of truth in anything you say."

"I'm not saying these things. I'm repeating the facts from eyewitnesses. Stonewater College still has a big problem. It won't go away just because you want it to."

"You're the problem," the dean hissed. "You've been a source of agitation since you arrived."

"I'm not responsible for murder, blackmail, and attacks on innocent women. I'm only interested in finding out who's behind all this. You should be interested in the same thing."

The dean looked ready to have a heart attack. "You impertinent...don't presume to tell me my job. I'm going to petition the trustees to have you dismissed immediately."

Tyler shook his head. "On what grounds? We've been down this road before. All I'm doing is cooperating with the authorities. I've done nothing to bring discredit to the college."

The dean pulled himself out of his chair, and pointed a shaking finger in Tyler's direction. "You've done more damage to this college than anyone in history. Your lies and scare-tactics have almost ruined this fine institution. No one will want to enroll here in the future."

"They won't, until you get rid of the cancer at the core. It's time to find the real villain and clean house. Denying he, or they, exist won't solve the problem."

The dean's body slumped, and he steadied himself on his desk. "Get out of here. This time, I hope you disappear forever."

Tyler got to his feet. "It's too late for threats. I'm not going anywhere – not until this is over. I didn't want to get involved in the beginning. I was afraid I'd lose my job. I love teaching and wanted to build my life here. Now, it seems more important to end the fear. I hope I'll be able to stay after the case is solved. If not, I'll leave knowing I did the best I could." He left the office without waiting for a response.

Tyler bumped into Dr. Jack Lucas on his way out of the administration building. The economics professor seemed determined to engage him in conversation. Tyler had made it a point to avoid the man ever since their confrontation at Barry's party. He could not tolerate this unsavory character, and his lack of moral responsibility.

"Tyler, hold on for a minute."

"What's up, Jack?"

"I just wanted to tell you how much I appreciate everything you're doing."

"What do you mean?"

"You know, the way you tried to help Heather. The papers said you assisted with the investigation."

"I didn't do very much."

"You're too modest. I heard about your troubles with the dean. News travels fast around campus."

"Your information is right about that."

"I wouldn't want to be in your position, but I admire your

efforts. Heather was one of my students. I'm glad they caught her killers."

Tyler regarded him curiously. "I didn't know Heather was in your class."

"She sure was – a beautiful girl. It's hard to forget the real pretty ones."

He ignored the comment. "What kind of student was she?"

"Very bright. Top-notch grades in the beginning, but her work started to slip towards the end of the semester."

"Did you ask her about it?"

"I sure did. She gave me a vague reply about personal problems. She never did get her act together."

"Do you know Molly Cross?"

"No, but I read about her in the paper. She's one of your students, isn't she?"

"Yes. She's still recovering from the beating."

"I'm sorry to hear that."

Tyler started to leave and turned back to Jack. "Tell me something. Did you ever hear about the 'Fantasy Lounge' before Heather's murder?"

"No. I didn't know the place existed. I can't imagine a beautiful college girl working in a place like that. Why do you think she did it?"

"I don't know. We may never find out."

"That's too bad. This whole thing's been a terrible nightmare for everyone at the college."

"It hasn't been too easy on her family, either."

"Of course, I didn't mean to omit them."

"That's all right. The investigation is making me touchy."

"I understand. Have a Merry Christmas."

"Yeah, you too."

Tyler walked down the steps and away from the administration building. He stopped by Ben's office before driving off the college grounds. He told him about the meeting with the dean, and the threat of being fired again.

"Looks like you got what you expected," Ben said.

"I don't know what he wants with you."

"Probably the same thing. The old man is trying to get back in control. I could be next on his hit parade."

"Good luck."

"No sweat," Ben shrugged. "I've been in worse spots. I'll call you later."

Tyler returned to his apartment. The session with the dean left him puzzled. For some reason, he felt more pity than anger for the old man. The dean had lost his grip on reality and sickness had ravaged his body.

Jack Lucas was another mystery. Something about the economics professor seemed off-center. Tyler considered the information about Heather being in Lucas' class. The revelation raised new suspicions about Jack's extracurricular activities.

He drank a beer and collapsed on his bed. Tomorrow would bring more challenges.

CHAPTER 35

The professor shivered has he walked down the steps of the County Hospital. Christmas was two days away and the temperature had dropped below freezing. The weather report called for several inches of snow. He turned up his collar, and dreamed of living in a warmer climate.

Doctors had admitted Dean Henderson yesterday, after he suffered an attack of bleeding ulcers. The professor was the only one to visit him. This fact pleased him and reinforced his determination to gain the dean's favor. The sick old man could not continue in the saddle much longer, and a successor would have to take his place. The professor considered himself the most likely candidate. A recommendation from Dean Henderson would secure the nomination.

The dean looked terrible. The pain was evident on his face. He attempted to minimize his condition, but the act fell short. The once vibrant college administrator looked decrepit propped up on pillows.

"I appreciate you coming to see me," the old man said.

The professor smiled and took hold of the dean's hand – the one without the drip tubes. "It's my pleasure. I'm just anxious to see you get healthy."

"No one gets well in a hospital. I asked them to give me some pills and send me home, but they're obsessed with tests. I'm certain they're holding me here for scientific study."

"Well, I'm sure they consider you an important subject," the professor teased.

"They treat me like a laboratory rat." The dean licked his parched lips and pointed to the bedside table. "Pass me some of those ice cubes. They won't let me drink fluids, and my mouth gets dry." The professor handed him the ice in a plastic cup. "Thank you."

"You're welcome. Can I get you anything else?"

"No. Just tell me what's happening at the college."

They spoke for an hour about the on-going investigation. The professor promoted the theory of a conspiracy, headed by Tyler Richmond. The mention of Tyler's name brought back the fire into the dean's eyes. The professor saw the hate and used it. He blamed Tyler for all the problems at the college, and suggested the drama instructor had introduced Heather to the 'Fantasy Lounge'. The dean accepted the possibility and praised him for his insight. They both agreed Stonewater College could not return to normal until Tyler Richmond left town. The dean was pleased to have a sympathetic ally. He promised his subordinate a position on the powerful College Planning Committee. The professor feigned gratitude, but had set his sights on a higher prize. The old man took his hand and thanked him for the visit. The professor smiled, and left the patient behind to endure his misery alone.

The future looked promising. Past setbacks were inconsequential. No one remained as a threat, except Tyler Richmond. Fortunately, Tyler had nowhere to go with the investigation. All the witnesses were dead or too scared to talk. Fear served as a great equalizer. The professor had learned how to shatter and manipulate the human spirit. It gave him great satisfaction to exert total control over beautiful young women, and fend off challenges from his adversaries. He lived in the shadows and enjoyed the power of anonymity. No one could touch him.

He drove toward the campus. The sights and sounds of the season assaulted him from all directions. Store windows twinkled with colored lights. Carols blared from the radio. Last minute shoppers scurried along Stonewater's narrow sidewalks. A Salvation Army volunteer jingled his little bell without conviction. Ridiculous. The scene made him laugh. These fools had no idea they were pawns of the Christmas conspiracy. Like sheep, they followed the siren's call of the season and emptied their wallets at the behest of the retailers. Everyone needs illusions to survive the harshness of reality, he surmised. Temporary escapes from the routine made life more bearable for the weak. He had profited from this knowledge. The 'Fantasy Lounge' existed because it fed on this weakness. Customers parted with their money in the obscure hope of achieving fulfillment. Pretty faces, smiles, naked flesh, caresses, and vague promises satisfied most of their needs. On the other hand, those men who engaged in unauthorized contact with their fantasy women risked a confrontation with Tiny.

He turned his car toward the main entrance of the college. The campus looked deserted, except for an occasional student or tourist gazing at the Civil War statues. He felt all-powerful as he surveyed his domain. I am invisible, he thought. No one can see me, but I'll soon be the most influential force at the college. Soon, my authority will be complete. No one ever challenged Dean Henderson and survived to tell the tale. No one except Tyler Richmond and his days were numbered. The professor smiled as he recalled the dean's words from one of his speeches to the faculty.

"Discipline and order must be maintained at all costs. Without these controls, chaos will reign, and chaos is not conducive to learning. Without learning, Stonewater College can not exist."

I will establish a new order, the professor vowed. I will encourage new teaching methods and maintain an open forum for ideas. Stonewater College will gain the reputation as a progressive institution of higher learning. The days of demanding traditional standards will end. He felt pleased with his cleverness and prospects for a bright future. He smiled and drove away from the campus.

******

Tyler learned about the dean's hospitalization from Ben. The campus cop called him at home.

"They rushed him to the Emergency Room after he called 911. The old boy is in rough shape from his ulcers. They got him stabilized, but he might need surgery."

"I thought he looked bad during our meeting."

"Pressure chewed him up inside. The way he was going, something had to bring him down."

"Do you think he'll be back?"

"Who knows? He's a tough old bird, and he won't resign unless he has to."

"You're right. He'll be back. Did he threaten to fire you?"

"Nah, he just tried to shake me up. Luckily, he wasted all his energy on you. By the time I got there, he was a physical wreck."

"I'm glad I wore him down for you. You don't need to share in the fun. I keep losing track of my employment status."

"You do make life interesting, Tyler."

"Tyler? What happened to Doc?"

"I just promoted you. You're more amusing than the other tassel heads."

"Thanks, Ben. You're not too bad for a flat foot."

"I'm deeply flattered. You need to ask Deputy Diane to teach you our secret handshake."

"I can hardly wait. Thanks for calling, and Merry Christmas."

"Yeah, you, too. Stay out of trouble."

Tyler considered the news about Dean Henderson. He doubted the sick old man had followed through with his threat to fire him. President Colson had almost guaranteed his continued employment until the end of the school year. The dean had no grounds to challenge that decision. Tyler breathed easier and concentrated on his Christmas plans. He could think of nothing better than spending the holiday with his friends and the woman he loved.

Tyler and Diane joined Molly and the Weavers at the farm on Christmas day. Tyler carried an armload of presents into the house. He and Diane had spent the previous day in the Staunton Mall. They had collaborated like a pair of thieves before purchasing each gift. The experience left them breathless and laughing. Tyler could not remember enjoying a more perfect day in his entire life. The only present not in his arms, was the one for Diane tucked in his coat pocket.

Rebecca had gone out of her way to decorate her home. A large Christmas tree twinkled with colored lights in the living room. Delicious smells emanated from the kitchen. The dining room table was set with her finest china. Both of the Weavers glowed with anticipation. Molly smiled watching all the preparations.

"We don't usually make such a fuss at Christmas," George explained. "Good Mennonites don't favor such displays, but we always had a tree when the children lived at home."

Rebecca elbowed him in the back. "Big, tough German using the children as an excuse to celebrate Christmas. He couldn't wait to bring home the tree every year, and start singing Christmas carols. Now, all of you get out of my kitchen. I've got work to do."

"Is there anything I can do to help?" Diane offered.

"All right, you stay. The rest of you git."

Christmas dinner was a masterpiece: roast turkey, dressing, mashed potatoes, squash, corn, fruit salads, freshly made bread and pies. Rebecca blushed from all the compliments. Everyone agreed the holiday feast could not have been better. Later, they gathered around the tree to open presents. Molly ripped into her gifts with unrestrained enthusiasm. Tyler gave her a handbook on acting. Diane presented her with a soft sweater. George gave her a pair of work overalls so she could help around the farm. Molly giggled as she held up the baggy denims. Tyler opened his gift from George and Rebecca, a book titled *The History of the Shenandoah Valley.*

"If you plan on living here, you need to know about the history," George explained.

"Thank you," he replied. "I can't think of a better place

to call home." He squeezed Diane's hand and she returned the pressure.

After all the presents had been opened, Tyler reached into his pocket for Diane's gift. She unwrapped the small box and withdrew a gold link bracelet. She placed it on her wrist and gave him a hug. Next, he opened his present from her and discovered a gold pocket watch. The back of the watch bore the inscription: *To my favorite detective – Love, Diane.* He smiled and wrapped his arms around her.

"Oh, go on and kiss her," George encouraged him. "We're all friends here."

Tyler followed George's advice. Diane responded without hesitation. They all laughed and drank spiced cider into the early evening. Tyler announced he had never celebrated a more enjoyable Christmas. Molly agreed and thanked the Weavers for their love and caring. She advised everyone that she planned to drive home the next day. She felt obliged to spend the rest of the college vacation with her family.

"Of course, dear," Rebecca replied. "You can stay with us anytime, but family comes first. Your parents need you."

"I know. I wasn't ready before." She turned to Tyler. "I'll be back after New Years. I'm not going to quit."

Tyler reached for her hand. "I never thought you would. We've got lots of work to do."

"I'll be ready," she promised.

He squeezed her hand. The party ended a short while later. Tyler and Diane thanked the Weavers for a wonderful time. Tyler hugged Molly and cautioned her to drive carefully. She agreed to call him after she returned to Stonewater.

George pulled Tyler aside. "That's a very special lady you've got. I wish you all the happiness in the world."

"Thanks. I hope we find what you and Rebecca have together."

"I hope you do, too. Come back soon and see us."

Tyler shook George's hand and promised to return after the holidays. Molly and the Weavers waved as they drove away from the farm. During the drive to Stonewater, Diane snuggled against Tyler and placed her hand on his knee.

"I really love the bracelet."

"I really love the pocket watch. I've always wanted to own one. Now, I need a vest with a watch pocket."

"I'll help you pick one."

He swallowed. "I hate to take you home so early. Would you like a glass of wine at my place? After all, it is Christmas."

"I'd love a glass of wine at your place."

They held hands as they walked to his apartment. He helped her remove her coat.

"I'll go get the wine," he said.

Tyler returned from the kitchen and handed her a glass. "Here's to a wonderful Christmas."

They both drank and Diane gave her toast. "Here's to the man I love."

He blinked in surprise. "I don't want you to leave tonight."

"I don't plan on leaving."

She glided into his arms and they kissed. She began to unbutton his shirt. He helped her out of her blouse. In a few moments, they were both naked. The sight of her unclad body took his breath away. He held her warm flesh against his.

She whispered in his ear. "Merry Christmas, darling. Now, take me to bed."

He swept her into his arms and carried her into the bedroom.

CHAPTER 36

"I feel like we've reached a dead end," Tyler fumed.

He paced around the apartment in boxer shorts, while Diane poured him a cup of coffee. It was the day after Christmas. She wore one of his old tee shirts.

"Relax, it just looks that way. Every case has hidden opportunities. We'll find one soon enough." She moved behind him and wrapped her arms around his chest.

"Do we have to talk about business? Our relationship has just started to get interesting."

He turned and looked into her soft green eyes. "I'm sorry. You're the most important thing in my life. I just can't let go of the investigation. It feels like we're real close, but the villain is still out there."

"Don't worry, we'll find him. I still have a few more ideas, but not right this minute." She stretched up to him on her tiptoes, and kissed him on the mouth.

"Are you sure?" he replied in amazement.

"Of course I am," she teased. "We waited too long to get to this point."

She grabbed his hand, and pulled him into the bedroom. They fell heavily onto the bed laughing.

Later, he stroked her hair and kissed the soft nape of her neck.

"What ideas?" he whispered.

"Oh, no," she groaned. "He only wants my mind."

"I want everything." He threw a leg over her and tickled her ribs.

"Stop...Not fair...Stop," she pleaded.

"All right, but give me the goods," he replied, in a gruff stage voice.

She caught her breath and turned toward him. "The key is Amy Flanders. She knows who we're looking for."

"Yeah, but she won't talk. We've already tried. You said she's being blackmailed."

"Yes, but she wants a way out. She'll never be free, until we put the bad guy behind bars."

"She's too scared to tell us anything."

"The blackmailer is counting on that. That's why he's left her alone. We've got to find a way to make him nervous. Nervous criminals make mistakes."

"He might come after her if you make him too nervous. This could be the same guy who killed the Willis guy."

"I think he is. Everything is beginning to tie in together. We have most parts of the puzzle except for the main piece. We'll protect Amy."

Tyler pulled her against him, and whispered in her ear. "Okay, what's the plan?"

"It's a police secret. I'm not sure I can trust you."

"I have ways to make you talk." He bit down lightly on her ear.

"Careful," she warned. "I can change your gender with one flick of my wrist."

"That would be the end of a beautiful relationship."

"Don't worry. I said I could, but I won't. We need to keep you in one piece." She patted him.

"That's a relief. So, what's the plan?"

"I'm not sure. I need to go talk to her."

"Can I go with you?"

"No, not this time. I want to try a woman-to-woman ap-proach. You'd bring back the guilt of her past. Also, she might confide in me without any witnesses present."

"What if she doesn't talk?"

"Then, I've got to make her scared – scared enough to

235

run. If we're lucky, she'll run straight to the main man."

"She might run in the opposite direction."

"That's true, but we'll be watching. I've already arranged with the Winchester police to help us with surveillance."

Tyler touched her face. "I'm impressed. No wonder I love you so much." He kissed her tenderly.

"Thanks for the vote of confidence." She ran her fingers through his hair. "If this doesn't work, we'll go after some of the other girls. One of them is bound to crack."

"When are you going?"

"Tomorrow. I'll call you after I get back."

"What can I do to?"

"Nothing. You have to keep a low profile. We might need to use you as a witness later."

"I hope you catch this guy."

"I'll do my best. I caught you, didn't I?"

"You sure did."

She pulled him down to her. "Just hold me. I want to stay like this all morning."

"What about breakfast?"

"Later..."

Diane left for Winchester at 9 a.m. the next morning. Traffic moved slowly on Interstate # 81, as families headed home after Christmas. She passed mini-vans full of children playing with new toys and parents struggling to maintain control. The memory of Christmas with Tyler and the Weavers made her smile. No other man had ever filled her with such total happiness. Her future with the college instructor seemed full of promise.

She turned her attention back to the task at hand. She hated putting pressure on the young ex-student. Amy had gone through pure hell at the 'Fantasy Lounge' and she still lived in fear of being exposed. Diane could only guess how much Amy had been exploited. She suspected that many of the waitresses had been coerced into prostitution. The scam used by Carl Russo was hardly unique. Unfortunately, Amy would have to endure more pain before the nightmare ended. Diane disliked this part of her job.

She parked her car and walked to the front door of the Flander's house. A woman who looked like an older version of Amy answered the doorbell. She smiled and greeted her visitor.

"May I help you?"

Diane had prepared for this contingency. "Yes, thank you. I need to see Amy. Are you Mrs. Flanders?"

"Yes, I am. Why do you need to see Amy?"

"I'm Diane Rogers from the dean's office at Stonewater College. We do follow-ups on our students who leave the college. I need to ask Amy some questions, and I have some forms for her to complete. May I speak with her, please?"

Mrs. Flanders regarded her curiously. "We've just finished celebrating Christmas. Isn't it a bit unusual to do this during the holidays?"

Diane smiled. "I have two reasons for the visit. First, the dean is concerned about the circumstances surrounding her withdrawal. Second, we'd like her to return for the second semester. I need to see her now, or it'll be too late to confirm her enrollment."

Mrs. Flanders sighed. "We'd like nothing better. The poor girl has been miserable since she left. Please come in. I'll go get her for you."

Diane waited in the hallway while the woman told her daughter about their visitor. She heard muffled voices coming from the rear of the house. Amy sounded reluctant to meet someone from the college. In the end, Mrs. Flanders prevailed. Amy arrived a few minutes later. She expressed shock at seeing Diane.

"What are you doing here?"

"We need to talk," Diane replied. "Do you want to do it here or go somewhere private?"

"Not here. Why did you have to come?"

"I'll explain everything. Why don't you tell your mother you're going out with me for a while? I told her I'm from the college."

"You're going to ruin my life," she whispered, hoarsely.

"No, I'm going to give you back your life. Go tell your mother we'll be back in an hour."

Diane overheard her talking with her mother. "I'll be back soon." She could not hear the mother's response, but Amy reacted loudly. "Because you make me too nervous. I need to talk to her alone." She returned a minute later.

"Let's go."

Amy walked straight to Diane's car and jumped into the front seat. Diane started the engine, and pulled away from the curb.

"Where can we go for some privacy?"

"There's a coffee shop downtown. It should be almost deserted today." She gave Diane directions.

The coffee shop looked like a relic from the 1950's: vinyl, stainless steel, plastic, old soda pop advertising, and wall mirrors. An ancient jukebox played a scratched rendition of Bing Crosby's *White Christmas*. The oldest relic in the place stood slouched behind the counter. She regarded Diane and Amy indifferently as they moved toward a rear booth. The old waitress grabbed her pad and shuffled over to take their order. She seemed perturbed the two women had chosen to seat themselves in a distant corner.

"All right, what can I get for you?"

They both requested coffee and a danish.

"I can remember that. I don't need to write it down." She stuffed the pad into her apron and huffed her way back to the counter.

"Charming," Diane remarked. "A classic example of southern hospitality."

"Don't mind her. She's a fixture around here, but she bakes the best pastry in the city."

"I can hardly wait."

"You'll love it, I promise."

Amy tensed as they waited for the coffee to arrive. Diane attempted to put her at ease, but the young woman looked ready to jump out of her skin.

"I won't take up much of your time," Diane assured her.

"Why did you have to come back?"

"You didn't call me, so I had no choice. Besides, there have been some new developments."

She reacted suspiciously to the information. "What developments?"

The crusty crone delivered their order. She slid a danish and a mug of steaming coffee in front of them both. The hot danish dripped with white icing and melting butter. Diane took a bite and savored the flavors of cinnamon, sugar, and buttery pastry. The warm confection melted luxuriously in her mouth.

"What new developments?" Amy repeated.

Diane added cream to her coffee. She stirred the hot beverage before taking a cautious sip. The coffee tasted delicious. She sat the mug down and told Amy about the attack on Molly, and gave her the details of Damon's murder.

"I don't understand. What's that got to do with me?"

She reached into her purse and withdrew a photograph. "Have you ever seen him before?"

"No." Her face gave no indication of recognition.

"That's Damon Willis, the murder victim. He's the one who attacked Molly Cross."

"I still don't understand. I don't know him or Molly Cross."

"Damon made a habit of hanging around frat houses and we believe he attacked other women. Molly Cross was Heather Andrews' roommate. You knew Heather."

Amy nodded. "Not very well. I didn't know her real name."

"This whole thing's coming together. Damon Willis had ties to the college. Molly and Heather were roommates. Damon targeted Molly to scare her away from the investigation. We believe Damon had ties to Heather, and that he worked for someone in authority. All the signs point to someone at the college. We know Damon wasn't the head man, but we suspect he was killed by the head man." Diane stared into Amy's frightened eyes. "You know who that is."

Amy lowered her head and stared into her coffee cup. She had not touched her danish.

"Why don't you tell me who he is? You could save us all a great deal of time."

"I can't," she sniffed. "He doesn't exist."

"Oh, yes he does. We already have a list of suspects. We're getting closer every day. It won't be long before he's behind bars, and the entire truth comes out in the open."

Amy looked ready to fall apart. "You're wrong."

"No, I'm not." She reached for the young woman's hand. "Tell me who he is. It's the only way to stop the nightmare."

"I can't...I don't know."

Diane squeezed her hand. "He's hurt you and you're afraid. I understand that, but you have to trust me. I can help you."

"You can't help me. Nobody can."

"Tell me why you're afraid."

"I'm not afraid. I just want to be left alone."

"He made you work at the 'Fantasy Lounge', didn't he? You didn't want to work there."

Amy refused to respond, but her eyes revealed the truth.

"He threatened to kill you, or he used some other threat to set you up with Carl Russo. Is that how it happened?"

"Please stop."

"I can't. There's a killer loose. Tell me his name, and I'll try to keep you out of it."

Amy hesitated. "I can't. There's nothing to tell."

Diane sighed. "All right. You're making a big mistake. If we don't stop him, he might kill someone else." She stopped short of suggesting Amy might be the next victim.

"I've already made some big mistakes. I'm not going to make a worse mess of my life and embarrass my family."

"Come on, I'll take you home."

She paid the bill and thanked the old woman for the delicious pastry. The owner nodded without smiling. They returned to Amy's home in silence. Diane stopped the car and placed her hand on Amy's shoulder.

"We're coming after him at any moment. We have other witnesses. Once we catch him, you'll have to identify him. You can't stay out of it. If you don't cooperate, we can force you to testify under oath."

"May I go?"

"Yes."

Amy jumped from the car, and ran to her front door. Diane waited for her to disappear inside before starting her car. She hated adding to Amy's distress. Unfortunately, she had no other choice. Now, she needed to wait for the girl to make the next move. With any luck, Amy would make contact with the killer. Diane would be watching.

CHAPTER 37

Three days after Christmas, the first major snowfall of the season blanketed the valley in pristine splendor. Once the storm passed over the mountains, the early morning sun danced across the surface and illuminated the crystals of snow. The sunlight ignited a twinkling display along the whole expanse of white. The reflection played havoc on unprotected eyes, but the breathtaking spectacle compensated for the temporary discomfort.

Tyler enjoyed the scene from his kitchen window as he washed the breakfast dishes. Diane had left for work an hour earlier, and he used this quiet time to restore order to his apartment. The scent of her still lingered on his sheets and towels. The image of her beautiful face still radiated from his pillow. He had to force himself to concentrate on his chores. She had half-heartedly threatened to call in sick to spend the day with him, but the snowstorm added an extra burden to the Sheriff's Department. In the end, he helped her shovel a pathway to her car. She waved goodbye as she pulled out of the parking lot.

Diane had shared little information with him about her visit with Amy. She seemed disturbed by her lack of success. Tyler also detected a hint of guilt in her tone during her sketchy description of the encounter. She admitted pushing too hard, but stopped short of giving him specific details. He stopped asking questions and took her in his arms.

Tyler waited for the snowplow to clear the streets before venturing out of his apartment. He cleaned off his car and warmed the engine. He recalled snowy days in New York

242

when the city-that-never-sleeps had stopped functioning for hours. This experience seemed less confining, but he was eager to explore the terrain. The snow crunched under his tires as he pulled onto the street. The BMW seemed completely at ease with the slippery conditions and moved steadily on course.

Tyler smiled as he observed small children playing in the snow while their parents shoveled sidewalks and driveways. For the first time in his life, the idea of owning a home and starting a family seemed appealing. The valley had already claimed his heart. He could think of no other place with as much to offer. His future lived in Stonewater, but his career at the college was in jeopardy. Even if they solved the Andrews case, Dean Henderson remained an adversary. He needed a miracle to secure a permanent position on the faculty.

He turned onto the campus and felt relieved to see the streets clear of snow. The maintenance crew must have worked all night plowing and shoveling. Pride would not allow the college to close because of natural or manmade conditions. The institution had survived storms for over a hundred years and would certainly prevail again. He parked in front of the Campus Police Office, and found Ben working at a computer terminal. The campus cop pushed away from the screen when he spotted his visitor.

"Well, look who's here. I thought you'd still be busy unwrapping all your presents."

"You don't quit, do you? Christmas is over."

"That's true, but some gifts keep on giving and giving…"

"Why are you so interested in my Christmas? Tell me about yours."

"Mine never change, but I bet yours was peace on earth. Where is the beautiful deputy today?"

"She's working. What are you up to?"

"You must be real lonesome to show up here."

Tyler settled into a chair next to Ben.

"Not at all. I thought you needed my advice on the case."

"If you've got some answers, hot shot, I'll take them. I

called four girls on our list and none of them would talk to me. They got uptight and hung up the phone."

"What did you say to them?"

"I introduced myself, and said I was working on the Andrews murder case. None of them admitted knowing Heather, and as soon as I mentioned the 'Fantasy Lounge' – they hung up."

"Why didn't you go visit them?"

"Are you nuts? I'd be fired for harassing ex-students."

"Oh, I forgot about your pension."

"Listen, wise ass, it's not only the pension. I have no jurisdiction off campus. If these girls won't talk to me here, or let me call them on the phone – that's as far as I go."

"How far away are they?"

"Three of them live out of state, but one girl lives in Harrisonburg."

"I could go up there. I might recognize her."

"Why? You're already in deep shit. Let the cops handle it."

"That's the smart thing to do, I know. I just can't watch from the sidelines. Diane's frustrated because she can't get cooperation from our key witness. We keep going in circles. No one's talking."

Ben nodded. "I know it seems like a dead end, but all we need is another good break – one more piece of information, and this thing could break wide open."

"I know, Diane told me the same thing. It's just tough being patient." He paused, as he remembered something. "What do you know about Dr. Jack Lucas?"

"Not much, why?"

"He got drunk at a party one night, and referred to our female students as 'objects of pleasure'."

"Scumbag," Ben snorted. "I've heard rumors about him."

"How can he get away with it?"

"As far as I know, no one's complained and he hasn't broken any laws. The college does take exception to fraternization between faculty and students, but our students are above the age of consent and have the freedom to choose their own partners."

"What if he's using influence or threats to get what he wants? I just found out Heather was one of his students."

"Then, we've got a crime, but it still takes someone to complain. Every crime needs a victim and enough evidence to get a conviction."

"This guy's not right. I need to ask Molly if Heather ever talked about him."

"I'll check him out, too. It could have been the booze talking, but he's not the only one who's crossed over the line. I know a dozen others suspected of the same thing."

Tyler expressed surprise. "That many? I had no idea."

"That's only the ones I know about. A couple of those only target homosexuals, and I know of two female faculty members who make themselves available to students after hours."

"Unbelievable."

"It's only a conservative guess. Imagine what the numbers are at larger universities. Some of our kids are victims of too much higher education."

"I saw the same kind of thing in New York. Young people are easily flattered by the attention of those in authority."

"Yeah, or they need an easy way to get good grades."

"No wonder Dean Henderson's so nervous about scandal."

"The old boy's been dodging bullets for years, but Heather's murder was too big a bullet for him to handle."

Tyler got out of his chair. "Call me if you find anything on Lucas."

"Sure, but I don't think I'll find much. He's too smart to leave a trail. Let me know if anything develops on your end."

The sun had climbed high in the sky, warming the earth. The snow turned heavy and mushy underfoot. Tyler sloshed down the sidewalk to his car and stomped his feet before getting inside. Sand and dirty salt pellets still clung to his boots and soiled the carpet. He cursed the mess and turned toward home. He found a message on his answering machine from Molly.

She answered on the first ring with an energetic, "Hello."

"Hi, Molly. What's up? I'm returning your call."

"Oh, God. I'm going crazy here. I can't wait to get back."

"What's wrong?"

"My mother. She keeps asking questions, and treats me like an invalid."

"I'm sure she's just worried about you."

"I could understand that, but it's almost like she's embarrassed by what happened. She's afraid to look me in the eyes."

"It's been a shock for her, too. Give it time. She'll come around."

"You don't know how she thinks. She holds onto emotional turmoil for as long as possible."

"Hang in there. I'm sure she needs your help to get through this."

"I'd rather be back on the farm."

"I know, me too. Give it a few more days and call me back. Maybe we can work something out."

"Okay, thanks."

"Tell me something. Did Heather ever say anything about Dr. Jack Lucas? She was in his class."

Molly paused. "Not much. I don't think she liked him. She thought he was trying to put some moves on her."

"Was she afraid of him?"

"I don't think so. She had lots of practice fighting off advances from men."

"How about her other teachers? Did anyone else come on to her?"

"Not that I know of – just a bunch of college guys. Tell me, what's going on?"

"I'm not sure. I heard some rumors and I'm just checking them out."

"Any luck?"

"No. We've reached a dead end. I'm just trying to keep busy."

"How's Diane?"

"She's great. Listen, call me back in a few days if things don't get any better, okay?"

"All right," she replied, and hung up.

Tyler thought about his conversation with Ben as he unpacked cartons of Chinese food and iced down a bottle of white wine. He wanted to have dinner waiting when Diane returned to the apartment. He knew she would feel tired after a long day of writing snow-related accident reports.

Ben's assessment of faculty and student sexual encounters left him unsettled. Conventional morality aside, he could not condone using grades or influence to solicit sexual favors. Even worse, it seemed that someone in authority had resorted to terror and murder to protect his personal agenda. The corruption had to stop before it claimed more victims.

Diane arrived after 7 p.m. looking exhausted. He met her at the door with a kiss and a glass of wine. She brightened when she saw the candlelit table set for dinner.

"What a man. Not many women get this kind of treatment."

"Only the very special ones." He helped her remove her coat and seated her at the table. "Tonight, the menu features gourmet cuisine imported from a local Chinese take-out."

"My favorite," she declared.

They both laughed, as they tasted the various dishes. Diane sampled a little of everything. Tyler watched her with pleasure.

"I could really get used to this."

"What, watching me eat?"

"No, sharing our meals together."

"We have been for almost a week."

"That's a start. I'm thinking about a more permanent arrangement."

She put down her fork. "There's not enough room for both of us here. My apartment isn't much bigger."

"Then, we need to find a place big enough for both of us. How about a house? I'm tired of apartments."

"Do you think you'll stay in Stonewater?"

"I hope so, but if I lose my job I'll need to find another teaching position."

She reached across the table and took his hand. "If it

makes any difference, I'll go with you. I can always find another job in law enforcement."

Tyler swallowed hard. "Of course it does. I want to spend the rest of my life with you. I just hate the thought of you giving up your job."

"No problem. Love means sacrifice, right?"

"Even if it means heading back to New York City?"

She shook her head. "Well, maybe not New York."

"Don't worry – not a chance."

They made plans for the future while cleaning up the dinner dishes. Later, they settled down on the couch to finish off the bottle of wine. Diane fell asleep in his arms.

He held her that way for a while, before whispering, "Let's go to bed." She allowed him lead her into the bedroom and out of her clothes. She collapsed naked on the bed. He stripped off his clothes, snuggled against her warm body and stroked her hair. She fell asleep immediately. The telephone rang just before midnight.

CHAPTER 38

Tyler banged his hand on the bedside table as he groped for the receiver. The voice on the other end sounded deep and official.

"Deputy O'Malley, please."

He passed the phone to Diane, as she rubbed sleep from her eyes. "I'll be right there." She jumped out of bed and began grabbing her clothes. "Sorry, I've got to go."

"What's up?"

"She's moving. Amy is heading this way. We just got a call from the Winchester police."

"Can I do anything? Do you want some coffee?"

"No time, thanks. We've got to pick her up at the county line."

Tyler marveled at her ability to shake off the effects of sleep. "I hope this works."

"Me, too." She finished dressing and embraced him. "Sorry, I had to leave your telephone number with the desk sergeant. They need to contact me around the clock."

"That's okay. I guess our secret's out anyway."

"It sure is. We're the talk of the whole Sheriff's Department."

"Is that a problem for you?"

"Nothing I can't handle."

"Good. I love you, Deputy O'Malley. Now, go catch that bad guy."

"I love you too, Doc. I'll let you know what happens."

"Oh, no," Tyler groaned. "You've been hanging around Ben Grubb too long." He shook his head in mock frustration. "Be careful," he added.

"I will." She gave him a parting kiss and rushed out the door.

Tyler paced around the apartment. It felt awkward to sit on the sidelines after being so involved in the investigation. He knew the sheriff needed to close this chapter without him, but the urge to participate would not go away. He decided to call Ben. The campus cop was not on duty at the office, so he called him at home.

Ben answered on the second ring with a sleepy, "Hello."

"Ben, something's happening."

"What is it?"

Tyler told him about the development with Amy.

"You're right. This could be something."

"I'm going nuts here."

"Sit tight, stud. I'm heading for the office to catch the action on the police scanner. If I hear anything, I'll give you a call."

"Great, you want me to wait, too."

"That's it. You need to keep out of the way."

"Can I meet you at the office?"

"Nope, stay put. I'll call you right away if anything develops."

"I guess I'll stick around here."

"Good boy. I'll be in touch."

Tyler collapsed in the chair after the conversation ended. He could not think of anyone else to call. Minutes ticked by before he shuffled into the kitchen to make coffee. He would probably be awake for a while. It seemed useless to go back to bed and wait for Diane or Ben to call.

He returned to the living room with a hot mug of coffee and peered through the balcony window. Snow remained piled high around the parking lot, but all the spaces were clear. Streetlights illuminated the parked cars below. Most of the residents had gone to bed hours earlier.

He looked at his watch. 12:20 a.m. Diane had left fifteen minutes ago. It would take her thirty minutes to reach the county line. No sounds interfered with the night – no barking dogs, no traffic sounds – nothing. The quiet felt unnatural. The calm contrasted with his nervous excitement. He wanted to break the tranquillity by yelling, but settled for another cup of coffee. The minutes ticked by, and his restlessness increased. He took a long drink from the steaming mug and settled back into his lounge chair.

So much had happened during the last four months. He thought back to his arrival in Stonewater, meeting Dean Henderson, and his involvement with Molly Cross. Molly's loyalty and determination had unleashed this horror. Heather's death was a tragic and unnecessary loss. Her innocent life ended as a result of evil and greed. Nothing could ever replace her spirit and warmth. The criminal justice system only had the power to punish the wicked. The righteous were always left behind with a life sentence to mourn their dead.

His telephone rang and broke the silence. He looked at the clock. 1:15 a.m. Ben's voice boomed over the line.

"I just got into the office and turned on the police scanner. Amy has exited off the interstate and is heading into town. Diane's hot on her tail."

"Damn, she's going to meet the mystery man."

"It looks that way. Diane's already called in back up, but she's warning everyone to keep a distance. She doesn't want to spook the girl."

"Is there anything else?"

"That's it. I'll call back when she reaches the target."

Tyler's heart pounded in his chest. He remembered Barry's advice about not confronting someone with a mental condition. Amy's life hung in the balance, and only Diane had the power to prevent disaster. He returned to the kitchen to refill his mug. His lack of involvement in the chase heightened his frustration. Every sound began to catch his attention. He noticed the hum of his refrigerator, the ticking clock, water running through the pipes, heat coming out of the vents, and the slam of a car door in the parking lot. All his senses screamed for information, but he forced himself to accept the waiting.

The shrill ring of the phone made him spill his coffee. Ben's voice exploded in his ear.

"She's there. She's at your place – Dogwood Apartments. I'm on my way!"

Tyler rushed to the window and scanned the parking lot. Nothing seemed out of place. No one moved. She's here. Where did she go? Where's Diane? He partially opened the balcony door and listened through the crack– nothing. He considered stepping outside. He had promised not to interfere. Diane must be out there. Where? He recalled hearing a car door slam minutes ago – Amy? She must be in one of the apartments. Which one?

His mind raced to process all the questions barraging his brain. Suddenly, a gunshot shattered the silence. Tyler jumped and slammed the balcony door. The shot sounded close. He raced out of his apartment and down the stairs. He stopped running when he reached the sidewalk. Car doors slammed, lights started flashing, and he heard voices yelling from the street. A single figure rushed toward him. The man was hunched over, moving with an awkward gait. Tyler strained to identify the runner, but could only see the top of his head. More footsteps thundered toward him from the parking lot. His body froze as the form lurched into the light. The fugitive stopped, and stared up at him with wild-eyed desperation.

"Barry!"

"Get out of my way!" Zucker screamed, and pushed him aside.

His hand left an imprint of blood on Tyler's shirt. Barry stumbled for the woods behind the apartments.

Without thinking, Tyler took off after his colleague. Streetlights provided enough illumination to silhouette Barry's frantic efforts to escape capture. Tyler's heart pounded as he plowed through the snow and struggled to keep his footing. Barry slipped out of view as he entered the woods, but the sounds of his panting were audible. Twigs snapped, and bushes rustled as Tyler closed the gap between them. Visibility decreased to almost nothing. The blackness and unseen dangers in the underbrush slowed his progress, but determination drove him forward. Scratches and punctures from tree branches went unnoticed. He had to stop Barry from getting away.

The crashing noise ahead stopped. Tyler paused and strained his eyes for signs of movement. He observed nothing. He heard nothing. He crept forward, listening for the slightest hint of activity. Barry must have collapsed from his wounds, or was catching his breath. Suddenly, Tyler remembered the gunshot. Could Barry have a gun? He did not recall seeing one, but the possibility caused him to falter. He tiptoed ahead. His lungs ached from the cold and tension of the chase. He advanced toward a large oak tree, steadying himself against the trunk with his hand.

Without warning, someone grabbed his pants leg. The motion made him lose his balance. Tyler looked down and saw Barry sitting against the base of the tree. He pulled his leg free of the injured man's grasp and stepped backwards.

Barry's head slumped against his heaving chest. "The bitch shot me."

"I'll go get help," Tyler offered.

"No. Get away from me. It can't end like this."

"You need a doctor."

"No!" Barry gasped. "Still trying to be a hero."

Tyler attempted to help the injured psychology professor to his feet.

"Let go of me, asshole!"

Barry swung at his head. The blow glanced off Tyler's temple. The sound of voices interrupted the exchange. Beams of light searched the underbrush.

"Does he have a gun?" a male voice yelled.

Tyler looked into the face of Deputy Harris. "I don't think so." He touched the blood on Barry's shirt. "He's bleeding."

"Step back. We'll take care of him."

Deputy Harris took control. He pushed the prisoner against the tree, and pulled both arms behind his back. The other deputy held Barry fast while Harris slapped on handcuffs. Once they had him immobilized, they started dragging the wounded man back toward the parking lot. Barry screamed in pain.

Tyler suppressed an urge to follow them, and ran towards Barry's apartment instead. The front door was wide open. He stopped at the threshold, and saw Diane kneeling on the floor consoling Amy. He noticed bloodstains and a handgun on the carpet.

"He's gone. It's over," Diane assured her.

"I didn't mean to shoot him," she sobbed. "I just wanted the photographs."

"It's all right. He can't hurt you."

"I called. He said not to bother him again. I grabbed my father's gun and drove here. He laughed at me. He said if I shot him, my life would be destroyed. He tried to grab the gun."

"He could have killed you."

"I know. I just had to *do* something. I couldn't take it anymore."

"It's done. We'll catch him. He can't run far."

Tyler felt a hand on his shoulder. He turned and saw Ben Grubb standing behind him. Ben motioned him away from the apartment.

"Don't get too close. This is a crime scene."

Tyler stared at him in bewilderment. "It's Barry. Barry Zucker. He's a friend of mine."

Ben shook his head. "You never know."

They heard shouting from the parking lot. "We've got him. Get an ambulance here, fast!"

Deputy Harris rushed up to Barry's apartment and shouted to Diane.

"We found him. He's bleeding real bad. An ambulance is on the way."

"Thanks, I'll be out in a minute. I need to seal off this apartment." She spoke softly to Amy. "We need to go. We'll take you to the sheriff's office to make a statement. Don't worry. Everything will be all right."

Amy followed her outside.

Diane patted Tyler's arm as she passed him on the sidewalk. "I'll be home in a while."

He nodded. "I'll be waiting."

The ambulance arrived with lights flashing and stopped in the middle of the parking lot. The EMTs lifted Barry onto a stretcher and applied compresses to the wound in his side. Tyler observed the activity with disbelief. Barry grimaced in agony and looked up at him.

"What's the matter? You look surprised."

"I am," he replied, hoarsely. "Why did you do it?"

"Because it was so easy." Barry clenched his teeth. "You should try it."

The emergency team lifted the stretcher into the back of the ambulance. Tyler watched as they closed the doors and drove away.

He responded to Barry's invitation under his breath. "I wouldn't think of it."

"It's been a rough night," Ben sighed.

"I can't believe it. He doesn't show any remorse."

"His kind only feels remorse about being caught. He had to be stopped. He couldn't stop himself."

"It doesn't make sense."

"It's late, and we're both real tired. Let's try to figure everything out tomorrow."

"You're right. Goodnight, Ben."

"Goodnight, Tyler."

Eventually, the deputies left the parking lot. Quiet returned to Dogwood Apartments, but the residents remained shaken by the episode. Tyler walked back to his apartment without speaking to anyone. He felt confused, betrayed, and angry. He recalled Rebecca's wise words about recovery.

'Physical wounds heal rather quickly, but it takes the human spirit a while longer.'

CHAPTER 39

Diane returned to Tyler's apartment after 7 a.m. He met her at the door with a long kiss of welcome. She looked exhausted and happy.

"Thanks," she smiled. "I needed that."

"You did a great job, deputy. How's Barry?"

"He'll live. Amy's bullet hit him in the ribs."

"What's going to happen to her?"

"She'll probably face charges for assault with a weapon, but any good lawyer can get her off. No jury will convict her after what she's been through."

"What's next?"

"Zucker took blackmail photographs of all the girls. We need to find those, and tie him into the Willis murder. After that, the legal process kicks in."

"No more questions," Tyler promised. "We both need sleep. We'll have lots of time to discuss this later."

"Years," she yawned.

He picked her up and carried her into the bedroom. They fell asleep in each other's arms.

The Sheriff's Department found the photographs two days later in a security lock box. Barry had placed each set in a separate manila envelope. The lurid detail of the photographs shocked the investigators. They tagged each set with a number and scheduled interviews with the victims. The case against Barry grew stronger, but the suspect refused to cooperate.

Tyler Richmond formally proposed marriage to Diane O'Malley on New Year's Eve at the Stonewater Inn. She smiled and accepted his proposal. He poured them both a glass of champagne and offered a toast.

"Here's to love and an uncertain future in Stonewater."

"There's nothing uncertain about our future together," she countered. "All the other stuff will work itself out."

Tyler kissed her and sealed the bargain. They celebrated their engagement with the Weavers the next day. George and Rebecca fussed over them. George offered Tyler congratulations and advice. Rebecca presented Diane with a handmade quilt. They settled on a May wedding date. Diane thrilled Molly by inviting her to be in the wedding party. Tyler shocked Ben Grubb by requesting his service as best man. Ben grumbled about wearing a tuxedo, until Tyler promised him an informal ceremony. The days ahead looked full of promise, except for the dark specter of Dean Henderson.

The dean's secretary called two days into the New Year. The dean wanted to speak with Mr. Richmond that afternoon. Could he make the appointment? Tyler found it hard to believe Henderson had recovered so quickly, but agreed. Diane kissed him for luck and courage. He squared his shoulders and departed for the showdown.

Much to his surprise, the dean's secretary smiled when he entered the outer office.

"Good afternoon, Mr. Richmond. The dean would like you to go right in."

He thanked her, and opened the door. Tyler was astonished to find the walls empty and the room full of cardboard boxes. Dean Henderson sat hunched over his desk, pouring through a stack of papers. He studied each document with deliberate precision. The dean looked thin and his skin projected an unhealthy pallor. He spoke to Tyler without raising his head, and gestured for him to take a seat.

"Well, Mr. Richmond, it looks like you survived your ordeal."

Tyler settled into the chair "Thank you. I hope you're feeling better."

The dean waved off the concern as if responding to a minor annoyance. "I'm still alive." He glanced up at Tyler. "I see this fact is not entirely pleasing to you."

Tyler started to protest.

The dean held up his hand. "Don't bother to deny it. We're not here to discuss my health. I have some news for you."

Tyler waited for the ax to fall. The dean pushed away from his desk, but kept his seat.

"It seems the president and the board of trustees appreciate your participation in the arrest of Professor Zucker. You should be pleased."

"I'm not pleased with the way it ended. Barry Zucker was my friend."

Dean Henderson formed a tent with his fingers and gave Tyler an icy stare. "Dr. Zucker contributed great things to this college. I am deeply disappointed by his involvement in this episode."

Tyler nodded without replying.

The dean cleared his throat. "All right, back to your situation. You are well aware of my opinion of you. Nothing has changed. I still regard you as unfit for our faculty. However, our president and the trustees do not share in this assessment. They feel you deserve a reward. What do you think?"

"I'm sorry I don't have your support."

The dean shook his head. "Very clever, but that doesn't matter. I have been directed to offer you the gratitude of Stonewater College. In addition, you will be elevated to the rank of assistant professor, with a three-year contract. Are you pleased with your reward?"

Tyler's heart jumped. "Thank you. I realize this must be difficult for you."

"You have no idea. Forty years in education and I'm forced to end my career like this." He gestured around the room at the boxes.

"I'm sure you have many great accomplishments to your credit."

"Don't patronize me. I can find nothing to ease the pain of my departure.

It should be obvious. I have been forced into retirement. This is *my* reward. You continue on in glory, and I return to the hospital for more treatments. The scales of justice are out of balance."

"I hope you feel better soon."

"Don't bother. Go away, Mr. Richmond. Leave me. I'm sure you'll have a successful relationship with my successor."

Tyler stood up and moved toward the desk. "Thank you for passing on the message. I do hope your medical condition improves soon."

The dean turned his attention to the papers on his desk. "Goodbye, Mr. Richmond."

Tyler took one last look at Dean Henderson, and walked out of the room. Three more years in Stonewater. He and Diane had a future. They celebrated by going house hunting.

CHAPTER 40

The first day of the second semester dawned brightly. Tyler whistled as he leaped up the steps of the Performing Arts Building. Not much looked different. Hugh Newsome still sat hunched over his desk. Tyler's office looked the same, but his collection of drama books had grown. He noticed a pink envelope on his desk addressed to 'Mr. Richmond'. He tore open the envelope and removed the note inside.

Dear Tyler,
I heard the good news. Congratulations! There's only one thing. I still need that money to buy dance supplies.
Fondly,
Ms. Edna